The BBC Television series TYCOON stars Diane Cilento, Norman Rodway and Edward Hardwicke. Other regular parts are played by Jean Kent, Christopher Gable, Denise Buckley, Deborah Fallender, Sue Nicholls and Hugh Ross.

TYCOON

Scott Marshall

BASED ON THE BBC TELEVISION SERIES
CREATED AND PRODUCED BY JOHN SICHEL

Hamlyn Paperbacks

TYCOON

ISBN 0 600 38790 9

First published by Hamlyn Paperbacks 1978
Copyright © 1978 by Scott Marshall and John Sichel
This novelization is based on scripts written by
Luanshya Greer, John Kershaw, Simon Masters,
Nick McCarty, Roger Parkes, Paul Wheeler and
John Wiles. (Story editor for the series: Paul
Wheeler.)

Hamlyn Paperbacks are published by
The Hamlyn Publishing Group Ltd,
Astronaut House,
Feltham,
Middlesex, England

Made and printed in Great Britain by
Hazell Watson & Viney Ltd, Aylesbury, Bucks

1

Charles Clark knew they were going to smash into that line of parked cars. He had only just missed that car coming the other way, but he over-corrected. On the wet surface there was no chance.

The screech of metal scraping against metal seemed to go on for ever. Charles's head crunched against the driver's side-window. He felt a biting pain where his leg had smashed into the door handle.

For a moment, the silence was complete – except for a gentle hiss coming from under the bonnet. Then the sound of voices came, urgent and getting closer.

Charles managed to push himself upright and look at Sarah Vyner. He could see she was shaken. A little frightened. A smear of blood on her chin. The euphoria of winning over three thousand pounds at the tables had gone.

It was meant to be a business supper for Lady Diana Clark and the two men: Philip Wilkins, the family solicitor, Donald Sanders, the new emperor of the Clark empire.

The dining-room had featured in several magazines – the entire ceiling was covered in light green silk, hung from the centre so that the folds gave the impression that the diners were inside a magnificent sheikh's tent. Sydney had always referred to it as the Rudolph Valentino room; 'At least it will make our Arab friends feel at home,' he would say.

The two men had been delighted with Diana's surprise – a bottle of 1961 Château Latour.

As they sipped their final glass appreciatively, Wilkins explained the duties of an executor to Diana. She should certainly keep all papers, deeds, documents. Send them over to his office.

'All being well, I see no reason why we shouldn't apply for probate by the end of the year.' He paused for a minute as he held up his linen napkin just underneath the rim of the glass, tilting it and gently swirling the wine so he could admire the colour.

'Diana,' he went on, 'this television programme on Sydney's life – just how much control do you have over the content?'

'None,' Diana shrugged. 'Why?'

Lady Clark Mark One – Wilkins apologised for using the office shorthand for Sydney's first wife, Mary – had been on to him. She wanted him to be sure that there was no mention of her on the programme. 'Yes, I realise *you* can do nothing but mention it to the producer. But at least I can say I've tried ...' He asked Diana how Jane and Charles were coping? He suspected they were as resilient as their father. And how was she getting on? Was she all right for her immediate cash needs?

Diana laughed. Sydney always kept a great deal of ready cash. She was fine for the moment.

Wilkins smiled and finished the last of his wine. 'That's the mark of a self-made man. They never forget what it was like to have nothing in their pocket but fluff.'

The three of them said nothing for a moment, each with their own particular memories. In a far part of the house a telephone rang.

Diana looked up. 'My crying's done. I keep occupied; I try not to think how unfair his death seemed at the time. I loved him totally. I'll always cherish his memory – but I'm not going to grieve. He wouldn't want me to ...'

Just then Ellen walked into the room, her face tense.

'There's been an accident ...'

'Charles!' Diana exclaimed. 'What happened? Where

6

is he?' She nearly said 'Is he dead', but the words would not come out.

Ellen told her he had been taken to hospital, but it didn't sound too bad.

Charles certainly didn't look seriously injured. There was a bandage round his head, some bruising on his cheek. One arm was resting on top of the bed, bandaged as well. But his eyes were open and alert. He tried a smile at the three solemn figures looking down at him.

'Good Lord, Diana, all these people! Why didn't you sell tickets?'

They all relaxed as Charles told them what had happened; the car was a write-off of course. Sanders glanced at his watch and said he'd better be off.

'Diana, I wonder if we might have a chat sometime tomorrow about the television programme. Liz is a bit concerned about the fact it's going out live.'

'Why does that worry her?'

Sanders buttoned his coat. 'She says if anything goes wrong, twenty million people will see it ... Charles, do what you're told. Here ... did you win tonight, by the way?'

'As a matter of fact, Donald, I did.'

'Makes a change. 'Bye.'

Wilkins looked shrewdly at the patient. 'Charles, was there anyone with you tonight, in the car I mean?'

Charles hesitated, then agreed that there was. She hadn't been hurt, a bump or two maybe. She had made her own way home.

'Is she,' Wilkins persisted, 'the kind of person who's going to sue you – for dangerous driving?'

Charles gave a laugh, a painful one. He assured them both that she wouldn't. But he was reluctant to answer Diana's question about her identity; he finally managed to screw together his courage.

'Sarah Vyner, actually.' His eyes swivelled from one to

the other. 'Diana, I swear to you, there's absolutely nothing going on. I simply gave her a lift. . .'

The door burst open then and in strode the commanding figure of Mary Clark. She nodded brusquely at Diana and Wilkins. A few quick questions showed her Charles wasn't badly hurt. It was time to look for other targets.

'I must remember to thank Ellen properly for letting me know my son was in hospital.'

Diana fumbled for an apology; she had only just realised Mary hadn't been informed.

Charles cut in, 'Mother, you look wonderful. Is this your fur for visiting hospital, or were you just sitting around like that when Ellen called?'

The decoy attempt worked; Mary turned her attention back to Charles. When she made ready to leave she addressed the room and asked if Jane had been told.

'I'll see she knows, as soon as I get home,' Diana replied.

'Oh, don't go to all that trouble, my dear. I'm sure Ellen will take care of it.'

Diana thought of Mary again the next day as she watched Liz Walters speaking into her telephone. She had come to accept that the three women closest to Sydney would always resent her – first wife, daughter and, of course, Liz Walters. She must be, what? Thirty-one, thirty-two? Personal assistant to Sydney for ten years, ever since she had come down from Girton.

At last Liz finished her conversation.

'Donald tells me you're rather worried about the programme going out live,' Diana said. Donald Sanders was standing by the window. He suggested to Liz that it was a perfectly justifiable homage to the man. And a nice piece of free publicity for Clark Enterprises.

Liz sighed, as if she was used to being the clear-thinking one in the organisation. 'Clark Enterprises needs publicity like Ireland needs rain ... Look, Ian Shaw is doing it. He's made his name by staging television confrontations.'

'Liz,' Sanders crossed to her desk, 'this is an hour on the

8

life of Sir Sydney Clark. Where's the confrontation in that?'

'Ian Shaw could stage-manage a punch-up with the Pope.' She shook her head at the accusation that she was being uncharacteristically alarmist. 'I hope so. At least I'm not appearing, so it's you two who'll have to carry the can if anything goes wrong.'

The talk switched to Charles, how he was and when he was coming out of the hospital. Diana was amazed to hear that the wrecked car had belonged to Clark Holdings. It was explained as one of Sydney's indulgences.

'Well, it isn't going to be one of mine – please transfer the car, and anything else Charles might charge up, over to his private account.'

'His private overdraft, I think you mean,' Liz remarked drily.

Diana felt that if Charles was old enough to crash a car, he was old enough to pay for it. He was twenty-seven, after all. Sanders nodded and agreed.

Diana lightened her tone. 'I hope this doesn't come under the heading of interfering with company affairs?'

She was assured that it was not. In fact Liz rather welcomed the idea.

Diana realised she hadn't left enough time to get to the House of Commons, where she was to meet Sarah Vyner, but thought she'd find a taxi easily enough. It took ages before one dropped a fare right beside her. By the time she reached the dark-panelled dining-room Sarah had finished her first drink and ordered a second. As Diana sat down, Sarah leant across the table and asked in a heavy whisper if Diana had ever seen so many men plotting at the same time. Diana glanced around. She had to laugh – practically everyone seemed to be whispering conspiratorially together.

'Probably concocting cover stories for their wives while ...' Sarah stopped, and made a rueful face. 'Lord, who's in the glasshouse throwing stones. I spoke to Charles this morning. He said he'd told you everything.'

'There's hardly anything, Sarah,' Diana teased. 'Charles was quick to say that much.'

Sarah arched an eyebrow, 'I'm not sure I don't feel a teensy bit insulted by his hot denial . . . but I must admit – and don't you dare tell anyone else – if it gets out I'm ruined. The truth is, darling, he's absolutely right.'

Diana grinned at her. 'It's not my affair.'

'I wish you would pick another word, dear.'

They settled down to one of their typical, jokey lunches. But there was a particular point why Sarah had suggested they get together at such short notice: with an election in the wind her dear MP husband wouldn't want to see an item in the gossip columns about his wife cruising around the gambling clubs with smart young men. Diana was just saying she wasn't likely to tell anything, when Sarah looked up with a startled expression.

'My God, I haven't even told you . . .' Tom Vyner had reached their table and bent down to give Diana a kiss on the cheek.

He sat down and asked his wife how her chin was. 'Can you imagine anything more ridiculous?' He asked Diana.

Diana felt confused: 'Ridiculous?'

As Tom fussed over ordering some more drinks, Sarah shot Diana a trapped look. 'Tom means how I missed my chair in the restaurant last night, and hit my chin on the table.'

'Oh, yes . . . yes, of course.'

'Diana darling, do tell Tom that when we have supper together we only drink a half bottle of Sancerre. He's worried his 2,300 majority in that retired gentlefolk constituency of his will melt away because his wife was falling down drunk last night. After all, you were there.'

Diana made a face at Sarah as Tom waved to someone across the room. 'Sarah was perfectly sober, Tom . . . perfectly.'

'I see,' said Tom, giving them his attention again. He raised his glass to Diana. 'A toast – to loyal friends,' he suggested, with not a single trace of suspicion.

Sarah was able to look calm and relaxed.

Charles was sitting up in his hospital bed, drink and cigarette in hand, watching the television. It wouldn't be long till the programme on his father started.

The door banged open and Jane looked through. 'Is this intensive care? Daddy's programme hasn't started yet, has it?'

Charles welcomed her, commented on her lack of presents for him and asked her how she was getting on at college.

'As if you care.'

'I like to keep in touch with the younger generation. What about that group you just joined, what was it called – "Violence for Peace" or something?'

'I didn't come all this way to be insulted,' Jane replied primly.

'Oh? Where do you normally go?'

Again the door crashed open and a young man of Charles's age looked in.

'Sorry . . . am I intruding?'

'Well, well, it's the scourge of Fleet Street,' Charles greeted him. He laughed as Jane gave a cold 'How-do-you-do'. 'Your reputation, it appears, precedes you.'

'Parker's Pen!' Jane snorted. 'We all have to scratch a living the best way we can, I suppose.' She looked at Robin Parker suspiciously. 'And may I ask just what brings you here?'

Parker patted Charles on the head. 'This poor boy and I opened for the First Eleven at school, we stood together against the worst the enemy could hurl at us. It's my duty to see how the old thing's getting on.'

Charles told them to shut up – the programme was about to start. The three of them turned their attention to the television set, Parker helping himself to a drink from the bottle by Charles's bed.

The familiar theme music swelled up as the camera tracked in on the figure in silhouette. The lights came up to reveal Ian Shaw sitting in front of a giant photograph of Sir Sydney Clark.

Parker glanced at the brother and sister, they were watching with great intensity. He turned his attention back to the television.

Shaw was giving the introduction – reminding people of how Sir Sydney Clark had died just six weeks before at the tragically early age of fifty-eight. Not only one of the great businessmen but also a great philanthropist. Like Lord Nuffield, or Andrew Carnegie in America, he believed the only justification in making money was to use it for the benefit of society.

The programme then showed clips of film of Sir Sydney opening buildings, including the £5 million Clark College at Cambridge. He was shown leaving Buckingham Palace after receiving his knighthood. Reference was made to his famous 1974 speech at the United Nations General Assembly, when he spoke of the duties and responsibilities of private individuals towards the underprivileged members of their respective societies.

'The speech restored an acceptable face to capitalism at a time when that system was under heavy attack.'

At last the camera pulled back as Shaw introduced his studio guests: four financial journalists, Donald Sanders and Lady Diana Clark.

Diana was one of the first to be asked about Sir Sydney: what quality did she admire most.

Diana spoke firmly, and sincerely. 'He was a very genuine man. I cannot think of one occasion in which he was devious, insincere or dishonest. It was this quality, more than any other, that made me fall in love with him.' She paused and smiled ... 'Although he did have many others.'

Sanders was very nervous; unlike Diana he wasn't used to appearing on television. He too agreed that Sir Sydney's most attractive attribute was his honest approach to everything.

'He played with a straight bat,' Sanders ended rather lamely. Diana glanced at him sympathetically.

Shaw then turned to the panel of financial journalists. Two of them took turns to launch into amusing little anecdotes about Sir Sydney. They went down very well; everybody laughed except one of the journalists, who looked rather morose and ill at ease. The camera swung on to him.

'Jonathan Browning, of the *Post* . . .?' Shaw said enquiringly.

Browning coughed several times. 'I'm afraid I'm not much good at telling anecdotes. Besides which, I really don't have one . . . But there is one point I'd like to make.' He took a breath and started to speak with much more confidence. 'I have always admired Sydney Clark, and what he's done over the last thirty years, so I don't want to diminish him by taking part in a false eulogy.'

'Would you just like to clarify what you mean by that?' Shaw asked. You must be delighted with this turn-up, Diana thought, as she waited to hear what more Browning would say.

'I'll tell you what I find cringe-making – it's this making Sydney Clark out to be an almost impossible human being . . . I mean this paragon of virtue that seems to be emerging here tonight, it's just too good to be true.'

Another one of the journalists raised his eyes to the high studio ceiling. 'Dear old Jonathan, stirring it up again.'

Browning glared at him. 'I'm just concerned that people watching this programme should gain a fair idea of what the real Sydney Clark was like.'

'Do you know what he was really like,' Shaw asked. Browning shook his head. 'Then what is your point?'

Browning took a folded sheet of paper out of his inside pocket and held it in his hand. 'We've heard a great deal tonight about how impeccable his business affairs were. Well, that simply isn't true.'

The stage was his now, and he paused while everyone stared at him. His eye caught and held Diana's for a moment.

He held up the paper. 'This is a list of half a dozen enterprises undertaken by Clark's various companies, where there is a considerable doubt about the legality of the negotiations.'

A chorus of voices demanded he give some instances.

'I am not about to go into details . . .'

'I very much doubt that you have any,' someone called out.

Browning ignored this. 'I would simply like to make it clear that Sydney Clark was as tough and as ruthless as any other man of his ability and power . . .'

Again there were half a dozen questions fired at him. Shaw shushed them up. 'Please, one at a time. Mr Browning, what do you mean by that?'

'I mean,' Browning continued, 'that he would use whatever influence he could bring to bear in order to achieve his objectives . . . whether he was making money or giving it away.'

'So you admit that he was occasionally charitable.'

'The only part of what has been said tonight with which I disagree is that Clark never cut corners, broke the rules or behaved unethically in his professional life. This list . . . contains precise examples of cases where he did.'

Browning still adamantly refused to give any of the details on his list, not even when someone accused him of using the same trick as Senator McCarthy. Inevitably, the programme's time ran out. Sanders took Diana's arm and hurried her out of the building to where Tommy Meadows and the car were waiting. Tommy had been watching the show from the viewers' gallery. 'God,' he muttered as he opened the door for Diana and Sanders to get in, 'I'd like to fill that Browning in . . .'

Before they drove off, they saw Browning and Ian Shaw come out in deep, earnest conversation. Both men glanced

14

up at the same time, and appeared somewhat shamefaced when they saw Diana.

'I see,' grimaced Sanders. 'Liz was right all along.'

Jane was furious – more so that Charles appeared to be taking it so calmly, simply pouring himself another drink. Parker obviously wouldn't care less, she felt. But he surprised her by explaining quite gently why he thought the whole thing was a put-up job.

His theory was that Browning told Ian Shaw he had something on the late Sir Sydney Clark. So Shaw set up a live programme purporting to honour the dead man – a recorded one is no good; you can be forced to edit it, or be stopped with an injunction. But with the programme live – wham! A good old barney and headlines in the morning papers.

'You see, Jane, not all the conniving underhand swine work on gossip columns.'

Jane thought about this for a moment – it made sense. Charles offered her a drink.

'Your answer to everything – how can you sit there so calm when Daddy's been so slandered? . . . so exploited!' She slammed out of the room.

Robin Parker looked at Charles, 'I like women who slam doors.'

'You don't like it, Robin. You're just used to it.' He asked Parker why he had come by.

'What are old friends for?'

'In your case, my old mate, they're for selling down the river.'

Robin Parker had a very thick hide – he needed one. Sticks and stones, he shrugged. Anyhow, Charles once ran him out when he was on ninety-nine, so he reckoned he was owed one.

'Not this one – or the sticks and stones will start flying.'

Parker put on a puzzled face. What story was there in a simple prang? Unless, of course, he was with someone he shouldn't have been? He put down his glass and stood up.

'Take care of yourself, Charles. Like the doctor said to the sick courtesan: a few days on your feet and we'll soon have you back in bed again.'

After Parker left, Charles stared at the door for a few moments – somehow the little gossipmonger knew about Sarah Vyner being with him.

Jonathan Browning was delighted; the reaction to the programme had gone just as he hoped. Nice stories in the papers, one call already from a publisher asking about the possibility of a book on the great man. He looked up as his editor strolled into his office.

Gerry Speares was the original Fleet Street whiz-kid, just thirty-two when he had become the editor of the *Post*. But Browning liked him – he was a damned good professional. Quite a politician too – sometimes that aspect led to quite fierce arguments between them. But neither man was bothered by them. Speares came to Browning's side of the desk and looked down at his collection of clippings about the television programme.

'Who said the days of instant stardom are dead?' He patted Browning on the shoulder. 'I like the idea of a TV personality in charge of our financial pages.' Speares started walking around the room, peering at the bits and pieces of paper pinned to the two large notice-boards. He told Browning that their dearly beloved chairman had seen the programme. The chairman wondered if there might be a book in it?

Browning feigned surprise. 'A book?'

'Yes, you remember. They were quite common pre-television. They had pages and a kind of hard cover. They keep a specimen in the British Museum.'

Speares had come to offer time and money, whatever was necessary to do it. But they'd want some good stuff: Saint or Sinner – the Man Behind the Image – that sort of thing.

Browning raised his hand and rubbed his thumb with his index finger. 'Whatever I need?'

'As much as it takes.'

'What's the catch?'

'There's no catch – our usual deal. The paper takes eighty per cent of the royalties.' Browning gave an uproarious counterfeit laugh. 'What are you getting hysterical about?' Speares asked, with a grin.

Browning gestured to the telephone. 'I've just been talking to a real publisher, he was talking about a lot better than twenty per cent of the royalties.'

Speares was unperturbed. He asked what sort of advance they were offering? A couple of thousand? All right if he wanted to write the book sitting in a library – but Clark had interests from Tierra del Fuego to New Zealand. He grinned at the reflective Browning. 'I'll give you time to think about it. I'll be in my office . . . Let's say thirty minutes.'

Sanders had been slightly dreading the inevitable appearance of Liz Walters the next morning – she wouldn't actually say 'I told you so', but then she wouldn't have to. When she did finally drop by his office it was with the news that three of the Clark subsidiaries had already telephoned wondering what head office was going to do about the television programme.

He gave an embarrassed smile. 'Well, as the man replied when the blackmailer showed him the incriminating photos, "I'll take twelve of the large and half a dozen of the small".'

Liz stared at him: 'I wish I could see the funny side of this.'

Sanders could feel his temper going. 'All right, you tell me what to do.'

But, as Liz well knew, there was no simple answer. She walked over to the window and watched the people scurrying along the street below. 'What do you think he had on that list?'

Sanders slumped in his chair; getting angry with Liz

was certainly no solution. He ran his hand over the top of his head. 'I'm hoping it was merely his laundry.'

Jonathan Browning wasn't the only person to be offered the chance of having a book published about Sir Sydney Clark. Diana was approached by Marjorie Reynolds, an old journalist friend of hers who was now a senior editor with Baker and Stoddard.

Marjorie's news was the gossip that Browning was being given a year off by his newspaper, all expenses paid, to write a book. They seemed to think they'd get their money back – they'd probably take eighty per cent of the royalties. A first print of fifty thousand hardback, then around a hundred and twenty thousand paperback, plus the serialisation rights. Sydney was a world figure; they were bound to have a bestseller.

Marjorie tried to persuade Diana to do her own book about Sydney. She had been a fine writer in her time. She could do it. The alternative was to let Browning have his say unchallenged, until his book was out . . . unless she decided to horsewhip him on the stairs of his club, of course.

Diana indicated she'd think about it. However, Marjorie should remember that the only things she'd written in the last few years were dinner-party menus.

Tommy Meadows drove Charles home from the hospital the following day. Ellen watched concernedly as Charles limped past her into the sitting-room. She did her best to provide a cheery welcome.

'Now, keep him away from the scotch, Tommy.'

Charles paused; he looked at her haughtily. 'May I remind you, woman, you are the housekeeper here, not my nanny.'

'May I remind you, you are a guest. So watch it.'

Then she and Tommy made a great fuss of helping the wounded soldier to his armchair. Charles's jokes had them both laughing so much they missed the first rings of the telephone.

Ellen answered it – she handed it to Charles. 'It's for you. A Mister Robin Parker.'

Diana was expecting just a tête-à-tête lunch with Donald Sanders, so she was surprised to find both Mary Clark and Liz Walters in his office. The two women were smiling rather benignly at her. Diana felt something was up.

'You didn't tell me this was to be a party, Donald.'

Sanders smiled and asked if she'd like a drink. As he went over to pour out her usual dry vermouth, Mary Clark commented on how well she looked the other night on the television. She was so photogenic, Mary envied her.

Diana knew something was up now; no one was ever paid a compliment by the first Lady Clark. She asked Mary what she thought of the programme itself.

Mary flicked an imaginary piece of lint from her skirt. 'Very interesting,' she replied. 'Mind you the only television I usually watch is Blue Peter.'

Sanders returned with Diana's drink. 'I hear there's a remote chance that you might become an author shortly.' The tone was a little too casual.

Diana looked at him carefully; it was obviously the idea of the book that had brought the three of them together like this. She decided to play along with them. She suggested that 'remote' was probably the right word.

'The girl from Baker and Stoddard, ah . . .' He flicked his fingers.

'Marjorie Reynolds,' Liz Walters filled in for him.

'Yes. Marjorie Reynolds. Well, she called to ask if we had any objection in principle to someone writing a biography, an authorised biography, of Sydney.' He helped himself to another drink. 'When I asked her "authorised" by whom, she said by us. I agreed that we'd think about it in principle; she said that you'd already been approached in principle.'

'And what did I say . . . in principle?'

'She said, in principle, you were considering the idea.'

Diana told them that was quite true: she was thinking

19

about it – but she hadn't made up her mind yet. It needed careful thought. She asked if they approved of the idea of an authorised biography? Sanders said he was sure he was speaking for them all: yes, they did approve – provided it was she who wrote it.

Mary spoke up. 'I agree with Donald, I think you would be excellent.'

'I'm flattered.' Diana felt even more suspicious.

Sanders topped-up Diana's glass. 'There's no question of flattery, my dear. After all, you were an absolutely first-rate journalist at one time.'

Liz echoed him.

'Everybody seems to be agreeing so nicely . . .'

'I'm sure,' Sanders said affably, 'that all of us would be only too happy to chip in with the odd memory, a few reminiscences. Anything to help.'

The other two women nodded their agreement.

Diana glanced at Mary. 'But you were reluctant to have your name mentioned on the television programme.'

'Ah, but as you recall you had no control over that. A book is much different, isn't it?'

Sanders asked if Mary and Liz would like to join them for lunch. They both said no. Mary had a dental appointment at 2:00, Liz, some people in her office.

'I think you're just the person for the job,' she said to Diana in parting.

'I seem to be the only person for the job, according to you.'

'What do you mean?' The normal sharpness had crept back into Liz's voice.

'The only authorised person,' Diana continued, 'that you'll allow. Isn't that what you said.'

Sanders cut in smoothly. 'Take your time deciding. No hurry. No immediate hurry, that is.'

Diana looked at him shrewdly. 'Is the exercise to beat Jonathan Browning to publication day?'

'The exercise, Diana, is to tell the truth.'

Late that afternoon Diana stretched out on her bed. Accepting that she did do the book, where should she start? Charles's helpful suggestion was that she start at the beginning. But which beginning? Hers with Sydney – or Sydney's own?

She wondered about the approach Marjorie Reynolds had suggested when she last spoke to her – a sort of personal memory: 'Life with a Millionaire Husband'. Browning's book would be something else, of course.

Diana had taken a little portable tape-recorder from the library, it was on the bed beside her. She pushed the 'record' button down and tried a possible opening paragraph. 'I first met Sydney Clark . . .' She tried it in several different ways, but felt it sounded just awful.

The telephone rang, Diana picked it up with a sigh of relief – a welcome distraction. It was Sarah Vyner, somewhat disturbed by an enquiring telephone call she'd just had from Robin Parker, asking about the car crash, about her involvement with Charles. Of course she had said he was just giving her a lift home, the accident was just one of those things.

'Oh God, Diana,' she groaned, 'can't you just see the column: "While the world grieved at the sad demise of the much-loved millionaire Sir Sydney Clark, and wept at his moving television obituary, guess who was squiring MP Tom Vyner's wife in and out of the gambling dens and ultimately into a hushed-up car smash? None other than his footloose and fancy-free son Charles, no stranger to these pages" . . . What am I going to do?'

'When is it coming out?'

'Any day, I should think – while the TV programme is still fresh in people's minds. Diana, I'm sorry. I made you part of the lie I told Tom, about banging my chin on the table. You know what he'll think . . . I'll be hung for a sheep, when I'm only a lamb.'

Diana wasn't sure how she could help. She'd try and have a word with Wilkins – Charles too. At least he had been at school with Parker; that might mean something.

Wilkins was coming round about five, with some papers. Charles was just watching the racing on television; she'd see him straight away.

But Wilkins wasn't very helpful – it depended on the wording he explained. She must remember that Parker was an expert at avoiding law suits. It was part of his professional qualifications. They could try and have a word with Parker's editor, but he knew what he'd say – the Clarks are a public family, they're fair game.

'Charles, any chance of the old school tie. . . ?'

'Only for strangulation. He'd sell his grandmother to a Turk if it meant a single column inch.'

Wilkins agreed he'd try, for what little use it would be. As he was about to go Charles asked if he could give him a lift into the West End.

Charles limped along to the car. Wilkins asked him where he wanted to go.

'Anywhere. It doesn't matter. I thought we might just have a chat about things.'

For the next three days Diana scanned Parker's column, but there was no sign of the item. She was puzzled. Surely Sarah was right: he would use it while people were still talking about that television programme.

Just as she put down the paper on the third day of checking, Sarah Vyner herself telephoned. 'Thanks, darling. I rang that Parker chap. I couldn't stand it anymore. He said he'd decided not to print anything after all.'

'But . . . I—'

'Look, love, I must dash. I'll remember this. I owe you a favour – a big one.'

' 'Bye.'

Diana put the telephone down thoughtfully. Her well-honed journalist's instinct told her something had happened. She made herself a cup of instant coffee and thought it out logically as she sipped it. She soon felt she had the answer and rang Wilkins's office. He was delighted to bring their meeting forward. He'd be with her within the hour.

When Wilkins did arrive he started straight in on the latest details on the will, opening his briefcase and pulling out several files.

'Never mind all that,' Diana said, 'how much did you pay . . . to buy off Robin Parker?'

Wilkins was stunned, as Diana meant him to be. She looked at him steadily.

'It wasn't the Vyners. It wasn't Donald Sanders, or Liz. They knew nothing about it. That leaves you or Charles. I know Charles has that money he won the night of the crash . . . I thought at first it had to be him. Then I remembered he asked you for a lift the other night, when he knew I told him to use Tommy and the Rolls. That's not an opportunity he'd let by lightly – so it had to be because he wanted to talk to you. If he was going to square Parker himself he wouldn't have to . . . I want to know how much you paid to stop the story, and where the money came from.'

Wilkins stared at Diana for some while, with a mixture of a new respect and admiration. He considered his position carefully.

Finally, he told her. 'Two thousand.'

'Now it didn't come out of your pocket, or the firm's. I want to know who provided it.'

Wilkins hesitated, then: 'I can't tell you, Diana. I'm sorry.'

Diana stood up. 'So am I, Philip. How long has your firm looked after the Clark family?' Wilkins shrugged uncomfortably. Diana went on. 'Actually, I've checked. Twenty years. We must represent a sizeable income to you.'

Wilkins stammered incoherently. Diana showed the determination she had developed during her years as a journalist.

'If you don't answer my question, be prepared to explain

to your senior partner how you singlehandedly lost the Clark estate as a client.'

Wilkins was utterly convinced she wasn't bluffing so he explained that Sydney had a sort of emergency fund. Something that a lot of large companies did.

'You mean a slush fund.'

'Really, Diana, that's such an emotive term . . .'

He had paid Parker at his own discretion. He felt it wouldn't have done the Clark name any good – just two months after Sydney had died. And Sydney and Vyner had been good friends too.

Diana sat down again. She told him she wasn't thinking of criticising him; he had acted for the good of the family and for that she was very grateful.

Wilkins relaxed. 'Parker wasn't going to hold out for what was little more than a couple of sentences. Charles spoke to him. Two thousand settled the entire thing.'

Diana thanked him again – but she felt that Jane and Charles ought to live their own lives from now on, like anyone else. She wanted this special account closed. In fact, as it was set up purely to assist the personal affairs of the family, it'd better be turned over to her.

There was a long pause. Wilkins realised that Diana was perfectly aware he hadn't told her everything. He reluctantly explained that it wasn't just for family matters – it was for the businesses too. It was a fact of commercial life that buyers, sometimes, had to be bought. Sydney had to operate like that from time to time; he was no different from anyone else at that level.

Diana sighed. Wasn't Sydney supposed to be different from the ordinary tycoon . . . because he didn't bend the rules?

'Diana, Sydney was an honourable man. Sure he bought business from time to time. But look what he did with his money. He gave a major share of it away.'

Diana closed her eyes for a moment, she had to admit she wasn't greatly surprised. She realised bribery was an everyday fact of international business life.

'Philip, just how much is in this . . . special account?'

'Oh, I've no idea.'

Diana arched an eyebrow. 'You've just written a cheque for two thousand. Don't you keep your stubs? Aren't you meant to be one of the best solicitors money can buy?'

Wilkins grimaced; there was no way out. 'When Sydney died, the balance stood at three hundred and eighty-four thousand, six hundred and forty-two pounds.'

Diana showed no reaction, but she was astounded. She stood up and held her hand out. Wilkins recognised the dismissal; there was now a definite change in their relationship. She smiled quite warmly at him.

'Thank you, Philip. By the way, I'm having a dinner party on Friday. Can you come?'

Wilkins was relieved, and delighted. Of course, he'd come.

Diana's other guests were Jane and Charles, Mary Clark, Liz Walters and Donald Sanders. After everyone had arrived, Diana announced that she had decided to do the book. There was a chorus of congratulations. Sanders offered a toast to the new author.

'I know I speak for everyone here, Diana: if you want any help, any help at all, don't hesitate to come and ask.'

'Why, thank you, Donald, I'm awfully glad you said that. Because first thing on Monday morning I'd like to come down to the office and start going through every single file.'

The moment froze; the bonhomie suddenly stopped.

'If it's not convenient,' Diana went on, 'I can always make it the day after.'

Donald almost choked on his drink; he said Monday would be fine.

Liz spoke, 'I wonder if you have any idea what you're letting yourself in for?'

Mary cleared her throat. 'Ah, I thought the book, your book, was meant to be personal – well, more of a reminiscence.' The others all turned towards Diana.

'I thought it might be too,' she said, 'but then I've learned a few things lately, enough to show me I knew very little of the man I married. I'd like to know more. I'd actually like to know everything. If it's possible.'

Sanders face had hardened. 'And publish everything?' The question was clipped, all warmth gone from his voice.

2

Sir Sydney Clark ... As the taxi squelched its way across London I tried to wrack my brains to come up with whatever I could remember about him from newspapers and magazines over the years.

I knew he was meant to be one of the twelve wealthiest men in the country, that he had made this wealth himself in the thirty years since the war. I had often seen photographs of him with various women; he had been divorced for years, several children. He knew a lot of people in show business. I remembered I had seen him a few times at Variety Club award lunches: a broad-shouldered, powerful-looking man, seeming a bit hearty from a distance – laughing a lot, slapping people on the shoulder ... that sort of thing.

Normally I would have prepared myself fairly fully before doing an interview, though I wasn't doing many then. The administrative work of being the *City Girl* editor took most of my time, as it had since the magazine was started six years before.

Earlier that day I had been sitting in my office waiting for a call I had placed to come through. It had been pouring with rain then, too, and I had been kicking myself for not wearing one of my trouser-suits, when Laura came in, bursting with excitement. As she was like that even when she brought in the tea I didn't expect the crisis to be too serious.

Jo Davenport, our senior reporter, had just rung in while I had been on my previous call. Her little boy had cut his head; it needed stitches so she felt she ought to go to the hospital with him.

This gave us an immediate administrative problem to sort out.

After we had won the serialisation rights of a new 'How to be Successful' book we planned to have ten interviews with 'successful people' in the weeks preceding the first extract. Jo was meant to see two people that afternoon: the actor George Vidler, and Sir Sydney Clark.

I could see Laura was on the verge of suggesting herself; there was no one else available and it might take several hours of phoning to get a freelance to take over; it would be too late for the appointments. Vidler had been easy to arrange, but Clark hadn't, I recalled.

Jo had told me she had been blocked all the way by his personal assistant. She had only got the appointment through her father knowing Clark from his club and running into him there one day. Clark had claimed he had known nothing of the interview request and was only too willing to agree. It was nice to have contacts in high places I told Jo – her father was a leading tax barrister.

Laura was just too inexperienced. I'd have to do it myself. I felt like getting away from the office and the telephones for a few hours.

'Laura, you know those notes we prepared on vasectomies, I wonder if you could run up something that might do for my editorial in the January 8th issue.'

She beamed with delight. I told her then that I'd better do the interviews myself – it kept the hand in.

'Besides, George Vidler is far too dishy for the likes of Jo.'

The actor had been rather beautiful, but a little unreal. Perfectly charming, with a deliberate self-deprecating sense of humour. But I got the feeling he never answered any question as himself. Each answer was coming from the part he was playing; the one dictated by his public image.

But, to give him his due, he had chilled a lovely bottle

of white wine, so it was all quite painless. He had even taken the trouble to call a radio cab after we had finished, so I was very grateful to him.

I noticed we were passing near the street where we had had our first flat, Brian and I, all those years ago. As always, I felt a wave of guilt and sympathy. Perhaps we had been just fifteen years too early. Would he have had the same pride thing today – about me working to support us both while he spent all his time on his novel? I'd not heard from him for ages. He was happily married now, two children – he was teaching near Birmingham. The last time he rang was with the news that a publisher had accepted a children's book he had written. His wife had done the illustrations. It had done well, too – won a prize and was on a lot of Christmas recommendation lists.

He had sent me a delightful little note after *City Girl* had suggested it as the ideal present for that ten-year-old brother or sister. His wife had drawn one of the book's characters in the margin. I got a sudden mental impression of all four of them sitting around a roaring fire, drinking hot chocolate . . . a happy family together. I felt lonely and a little sorry for myself.

I did feel tired, but it was more than a lack of sleep. It was deep-rooted; the spirit was weary. I seemed to have to make an effort to keep up with everyone else's enthusiasms. Sometimes, I knew, I was pretending. Good story, great lay-out, I'd say – but they were empty words.

I was thinking that at least I should try to have a vacation and sort out my thinking a bit. A change should do me good. I owed it to the people who worked with me to consider my position; perhaps I should even think of leaving the magazine, not for good maybe – six months or so. Find a country cottage to rent, far away from everything; take a couple of boxes of books with me.

Finally we were passing the Connaught Hotel and rounding the corner into Berkeley Square. The cab pulled up in front of a building. When I asked how much I owed, the driver gave me a cheery grin and told me that it had already been taken care of; it was on account. Why, thank you, George Vidler, I thought – I can see why you're successful.

The building was one of those elegant town houses just around the corner from the J. Walter Thompson advertising agency. A small brass plaque simply said CLARK HOLDINGS LTD. I liked that: it was simple, to the point. I pushed open the heavy oak door and went up to the smartly-dressed middle-aged woman at the reception desk and mentioned the appointment. A moment later a young woman, late twenties, maybe thirty, and very attractive, come out of some inner sanctum.

'Miss Davenport? I'm Liz Walters, Sir Sydney's personal assistant.'

I had just given the magazine's name at the desk.

'No, I'm Diana Morris actually. Jo Davenport couldn't make it. Her child, you see, well he cut his head and . . .'

The young lady's aura of self-confidence was intimidating me. I really was in a vulnerable frame of mind. I thought to myself that I should try and bring her down in my mind. Arrogant cow . . . yes, that's more like it. I mustn't sound so apologetic.

'I'm sorry,' I said. 'I hope I haven't inconvenienced you.'

'Of course not. Please come this way. Sir Sydney can give you fifteen minutes before his next meeting.'

I quickly followed her, babbling on about this new American book on how to be successful, how lucky we were to get the serialisation rights, how very good it was of Sir Sydney to see me . . .

Ms Liz Walters hardly seemed to be listening.

'Go right in please, Miss Morris,' she said, opening the polished dark wood door.

The large office had three girls typing happily away – busy little bees. But the atmosphere was almost quiet, serene rather, and clearly very efficient.

'Sir Sydney: Miss Diana Morris, the editor of *City Girl*.'

As she flipped up the intercom switch a dull click sounded and the inner office door peeked open. I never said I was the editor, I realised, as I followed her into the room. I bet you're good at your job all right.

'Thank you, Miss Walters.' I squeezed past her in the doorway. 'I'm so pleased to hear you're a reader.'

That's one for me, I smiled to myself.

The office was large and airy, more like a sitting-room than anything, with a large coffee-table in the centre, surrounded by long sofas on three sides. The table was piled with files, arranged in neat groups; there seemed to be copies of all the daily newspapers, with the odd story circled in red ink. Someone probably does that for him, I thought, to save him the trouble of ploughing through all the rubbish. Probably Liz Walters.

I noticed that the walls of the room had low banks of framed photographs and other things, almost too low it seemed to me, until I sat down and saw that they were at eye-level when you sank deep into the soft sofas. Many of the pictures seemed to be of Sir Sydney with various celebrities. From where I was sitting I could recognise one of him with Lyndon Johnson, another of him leading a race-horse; everyone was smiling – even Lester Piggott, sitting on the horse with his knees nearly touching his chin. Sir Sydney's horse, I was sure, and it had obviously just won a big race.

'I know – what an ego, you're thinking.'

The voice was amused, a good voice – English but classless. His eyes were warm and friendly. He knew he had charm, but it was effortless, unlike the poor actor earlier that afternoon. The difference, I supposed, between believing you needed the publicity and not caring about it at all.

'And you're right too. Why else did I agree to give your magazine an interview?'

'But you have much to be proud of, Sir Sydney. That's why I'm here.'

'Ah, you want the secret of my success, don't you?'

'Well, that is the idea. This new book—'

'How much did the serialisation cost?' he suddenly interjected, his eyes brightening like a hunter seeing his target.

'Now that's a secret, Sir Sydney. I wouldn't want our competitors to be amazed at how much we out-bid them by.'

'But that's it,' he leaned forward with a laugh.

'That's what?'

'The secret of my success – confidence. Confidence in myself, my judgements. If I had been you I would brag about the price, say how cheaply I had got the serialisation, and I would have made the others think so too.'

I laughed. This is better, I'm going to enjoy this, I said to myself.

And so it went – he kept surprising me with the way his mind worked, he almost seemed to be interviewing me rather than me him. He made me laugh. Then there was the satisfaction of the intercom buzzing twice, reminding him of the people waiting in the meeting.

'Tell them to start without me. I'll be five minutes – I'm having much too much fun,' he said and winked at me.

I could feel the slight blush on my face.

When I got to the main reception desk, the middle-aged lady was just putting down her phone. She turned to me with a smile.

'Sir Sydney's car will be at the door in one minute, to take you back to your office. It's still pouring, you know. You'll never get a taxi.'

I didn't feel surprised when he rang two days later to invite me to join a party of friends he was taking to Newbury races on the Saturday. We all travelled first-class on the train, as it saved getting caught in the race traffic.

There were at least fifteen people and we must have got through a crate of champagne in the members' bar. Sydney, as I was now calling him, insisted on marking our cards. He laughed with everyone else when his only winner was 8–13 on, and tipped by every paper as well.

'If I was always right, I'd be so boring,' he said to me.

'But this is just fun. I bet your city tips do better.'

'Oh that's different,' he smiled. 'There's a world of difference between gambling on the stock-market and gambling on horses. The horse punter picks his horse for its quality, its chances over the others. The real stock-market punter couldn't care less about the share's individual quality; he bets on how he thinks others, the herd, will react.'

'Well, I don't understand high finance. I never could and I never will.'

'Don't worry, I'll teach you,' he responded. 'There's no one better.'

'Self-confidence – the secret of success?'

'That's right. There you are: you're learning already.'

On the train back to London, Sydney announced his surprise – he had a block of seats for *A Chorus Line*, and when one couple protested that they had seen it already, Sydney told them they had to come or they wouldn't get the special dinner he had ordered at the Savoy. It was nearly three in the morning when the car dropped me at my block of flats. I was amazed to hear Sydney say he was flying to New York first thing in the morning and would be back in a week.

'But how much sleep will you get?' I asked.

'Enough, enough. I'll ring you when I get back. Shall we have dinner, just the two of us. I like quiet evenings too.'

He put his hands on my shoulders and lightly brushed my cheeks with his lips. He waited outside the lobby door as I nodded to the night porter and stepped into the lift, then he waved and grinned. I could see my reflection in the aluminium of the lift doors as I was whispered up to my floor, still grinning in reply.

I knew what was happening, and I was happy. I felt alive again, and I could still feel myself smiling as I drifted into a dreamless sleep.

Surprisingly, the week spun by; I worked well and quickly. I felt my old confidence again and enjoyed the problems.

'Diana, how are you?' His voice was, well, sexy. 'I'm still in New York, but I'm flying in on Tuesday morning. How about dinner Tuesday night?'

3

It was a bright sunny morning – the world was beautiful,
birds singing. Tommy Meadows whistled contentedly to
himself as he polished the bonnet of the already gleaming
Rolls, enjoying the warmth of the sun on his back. Inside
the house Ellen went through her usual morning routine
of gathering the post and newspapers and glancing
through them while sipping a cup of coffee in the kitchen, waiting for Lady Clark to ring down for breakfast.
The tranquillity of the morning was broken by the harsh
ringing of the telephone.

'Ellen, it's Jane. Let me speak to Lady Clark, please.'
Her voice was firm, but urgent.

'But she's still asleep.'

'Then wake her up,' Jane insisted.

'I can't do that—'

'Ellen, you must! Now, please.' Ellen had no chance
against the authority in Jane's voice, the natural legacy of
money and position.

'Ellen, take the *Post* up with you.'

Raising her eyebrows, Ellen laid down the phone and
went into the hall to pick up the *Post* before climbing the
circular staircase to Diana's room.

Diana was asleep in the king-size double bed. The room
itself was a *House and Garden* delight. It had been de-
signed by Diana and Sydney together. An oil painting of
Sir Sydney smiled from one wall; it was a good likeness
and Sydney had told everyone it was a masterpiece. 'It will
be in the Tate Gallery long after I'm gone and forgotten,' he was fond of telling the guests, who could never

resist his enthusiastic invitation to show them the house. These memories were flooding through Diana's mind as, half asleep, she rolled over at Ellen's knock.

'What's the time?' she asked sleepily as Ellen entered the room.

'Nine o'clock, madam.'

'Nine?' Diana asked, somewhat sharply, having left Ellen a note late last night she didn't want breakfast until she rang down.

'I'm sorry to wake you, but Miss Jane's on the phone. She said it was urgent.'

'Urgent?' Diana repeated as she sat up rubbing the sleep out of her eyes and trying to bring her mind into focus. She picked up the extension next to the bed.

'Jane?'

'Has Ellen got the *Post* with her?' Jane said crisply.

Diana saw Ellen had the newspaper.

'Turn to page seven,' Jane's voice insisted.

Diana frowned at Jane's peremptory tone and wondered what on earth the mystery was all about.

'Column three, halfway down.'

Diana's finger traced down the paper and jerked to a stop as the headline leaped out at her: ALLEGATIONS AGAINST MP AND LATE TYCOON.

'Sorry if I've spoiled your breakfast, Diana. 'Bye.' The phone clicked down.

'No, wait,' Diana implored, still confused, but the connection had been broken.

Sitting up straight, with all traces of sleep gone, Diana read on, noticing the byline: Jonathan Browning. She felt shocked at what she read, and angry at the implications being made. Made only because Sydney was safely in his grave.

She threw off the duvet and swung out of bed. In one movement she pulled her nightgown over her head and turned on the shower spray, oblivious to the stunning figure revealed in the bathroom's mirrored walls.

As soon as she was dressed and made up, Diana's first

thought was to ring Donald Sanders, ignoring the breakfast Ellen had set on the alcove in the kitchen.

'Donald . . . you've seen it . . . all right, would you ask Liz to come along . . . yes . . . thank you.'

For the first time the lush comfort of one of Sydney's favourite restaurants had no effect on her. Her drink was untouched, the menu ignored, as she watched Donald Sanders intently. The man was as smooth and urbane, as smug, damn him, as always. Liz Walters looked smug too, of course.

'Allegations, that's all it says,' he oiled on to troubled waters.

'That's all?' Diana said sharply. She wasn't going to be put down, patronised by this man.

'Allegations are meat and drink to the lawyers,' he went on slowly, enunciating carefully as if he was speaking to a child or someone who didn't know English very well. 'They end up with apologies and large settlements paid to a deserving charity of our choice.'

'Don't patronise me, Donald. I was a journalist for fifteen years and I can think of quite a few cases where allegations weren't dismissed as easily as you seem to think.'

Sanders claimed that these would be. Diana remarked that he seemed very confident; there was a drop of acid. Then she turned to Liz.

'What about you?'

'What about me?' There was a hint of a challenge.

Diana asked her to define her reactions when she read the paper; did she choke on her roughage? Liz Walters probably ate her way through a bag of fine-ground bran every week, she thought to herself.

'No,' Liz answered, and remained quiet.

Diana looked from one to the other. 'I'm delighted to know the company is in the hands of non-hysterics.'

Sanders told her that there was no need to be hysterical and went on to explain the background, as Diana only remembered that there had been something about an enquiry – it was long before she had met Sydney. The company had gone into land development in quite a big way in Malta, mostly holiday homes. Sydney got a good offer for the whole lot and took it. About a month later Mintoff came down heavily on British involvement on the island; land and house values came down drastically. Tom Vyner had been a junior minister, closely involved with Malta, and some people tried to stir things up with a rumour that he had tipped Sydney off about what might happen; privileged information leaked to private speculators and so on. The press got on to it so there had to be an enquiry. Both Vyner and Sydney were completely exonerated and that was the end of it; the file, as it were, was closed.

'Jonathan Browning seems to think he has a reason to reopen it,' Diana pointed out.

Publicity for his book, Sanders suggested.

Liz shot a barb at Diana: 'Writing books about Sydney Clark seems to be this year's fashion . . .'

Diana pushed on – Browning's paper had a legal department; they wouldn't have let the article be published unless they were happy Browning could substantiate what he was suggesting. She asked Sanders if he, the company, was going to sue. He agreed that it was probable. Tom Vyner?

'Why not ask him?' Liz Walters answered for Sanders. 'You know them, I believe.'

Diana knew Sarah, but had only met Tom a few times. Surely Liz would know him better?

'He and Sydney were friends at one time. I mean in your day, Liz. Before mine.'

Liz coloured. Diana felt she had the advantage – for a change. Liz claimed she had had nothing to do with the Malta deal really.

'Oh, I understood you were involved with everything that went on in the company,' Diana went on smoothly.

Sanders raised his eyebrows as he watched the two women and smiled to himself. It was a time to be diplomatic.

'Yes, they were friends,' he interjected.

'A well-placed friend . . .' Diana observed.

'There's no law against having friends in the Government.'

'No, but such things are meat and drink to a journalist,' Diana said in a good imitation of Sanders's deliberate style.

Sanders acknowledged the reference to his own phrase with a nod. He announced that all this talk about food and drink was making him hungry, it was time to order.

Tommy Meadows and the Rolls had been waiting outside the restaurant. Diana slid across the back seat and closed her eyes for a moment. She felt so tired. God, how she missed Sydney. An image flashed through her mind of a troika racing across the frozen steppes with a pack of howling wolves getting closer and closer. They're after you, my darling, she thought. I feel this is just the start.

Tommy looked at her in his driving mirror, she suddenly looked older. 'Tired, madam?' he enquired gently.

'I shouldn't drink at lunch,' she sighed.

Instead of going home, she instructed Tommy to take her to an East End address. Wonder why, he thought as he piloted the big car through the crowded narrow streets of the City of London.

Eventually the car glided to a halt alongside some wasteland with a small group of winos sipping from cider bottles around a fire. A begrimed sign indicated the road Diana had asked for: Langton Road E15.

'Are you sure you got the right address?' Tommy enquired.

'Look for number eighteen', Diana answered as she took her camera out of its leather bag.

One side of the street had its houses boarded up; on the other the houses had been demolished already. The odd numbers were on the houses still standing. Tommy pointed this out to Diana, and was told to stop so she could get out.

For a moment Diana stared at the desolate scene, while

Tommy kept an anxious eye on the group of children gathered around the car. Diana found herself looking into the expressionless eyes of the small group of winos. She gave an involuntary shudder.

'I don't think we should hang around here long,' Tommy urged.

Diana turned to him. 'My husband was born at number eighteen.'

'Sir Sydney? Here?' There was wonder in his voice.

Diana explained she had hoped to take a picture of the house for the book, but – pity. Tommy yelled at one of the children, bolder than the others, who attempted to crawl into the Rolls. As they drove off, Diana found herself watching the human derelicts staring after the car.

Jonathan Browning entered the editor's office. On Speares's desk he could see the *Post* opened at his article. His journalist's antennae twitched; there was trouble coming all right.'

'I can prove every word,' he grinned at Speares. 'Our legal department OK'd it you know.'

'You came across this story while researching your book?'

'Not my book,' Browning emphasised. 'The paper is paying for it . . . and copping eighty per cent of the royalties for the privilege.'

Speares tapped the paper. 'This isn't just advance publicity for your book?'

'Honest to God, Gerry, no. I've got fresh evidence. It's kosher and it'll stand up'.

Gerry Speares got up from his desk and paced the room slowly – there was something sticking in his craw.

'Out with it, Gerry.'

'You know', Speares said after a pause, 'the widow is also putting together a book.'

'A snow job!' Browning relaxed into his chair. 'Bound to be. "My Life with a Wonderful Guy".'

'Maybe he was,' Speares voice dripped irony. He leaned forward.

'You know, Jonathan, the whole thing is beginning to smell like a witch-hunt.'

Browning straightened in his chair and glared at Speares.

'This paper has hunted its fair share of witches. And burned them. And danced round the fire too. Property speculators, slum landlords, MPs on the take. Weren't they witch-hunts? It's the standard protest of crooks under fire. It was Nixon's complaint, remember? Find Martin Bormann and I'll lay odds he'd say the same.'

'Clark equals Bormann?' Speares's tone was hard.

Browning relaxed again and took a breath.

'A couple of months ago, Gerry, you agreed to finance a book on Sydney Clark. You and the chairman thought it was the best thing since the Gutenberg Bible. What's changed?'

There was a pause. Speares looked at Browning directly.

'We're pulling out.'

'Why?' Browning asked.

'Look, Jonathan—'

'I'm looking . . .' Browning's voice was flat.

Speares poured himself a glass of water from the jug on the desk.

'Over the years,' he explained, 'we've taken a stand on chequebook journalism, invasion of privacy and so on. Now, how is it going to look if the *Post* allows time and money to one of its senior reporters to write a book that incorporates everything we've piously denounced.'

The two men continued to argue, with Speares sounding less and less sure of his ground, which was very much out of character. Finally—

'You've been got at,' Browning accused. 'Who is it? The chairman?'

He went on to suggest how it must have happened: a quiet approach in some London club. His scorn was evident as Speares tried to explain further.

41

The feeling at the *Post* was that the public might see it as a desecration of the grave – Clark was an institution, everybody's favourite capitalist. So what if he might have made a million under the table; he gave away ten above it.

Speares got up from his desk and walked to the window. He looked out – there was nothing more to say.

'It's scrubbed, Jonathan. Finito.' he paused. 'But what you do in your spare time, of course, is your own affair.'

The message was clear: Speares was signalling that he personally didn't disapprove of the book. Browning gave him a withering glance and left the office; Speares had hated the interview and returned to his chair gloomily. He picked up his phone, asked for an outside line, then dialled his call.

'This is Gerry Speares. It's done.'

He slammed down the phone – it was an impotent gesture.

Diana was tired from the effort of sorting through Sydney's papers, and there were boxes more in the attic, so she didn't handle Jane very well. She liked her, but the girl was stubborn and used to getting her own way. She obviously felt that Diana should be raising cohorts of lawyers to attack the defamers of her father's memory; she accused her of thinking there was some substance to the allegations.

'I suppose it's all grist to the mill,' Jane went on.

'What grist? And which mill?'

'Your book on Daddy. A chapter on shady deals down the corridor of power is bound to give it a lift. Saleswise, like they say.'

Diana sighed. 'Jane, I'm tired, and so are you. Let's quit while we're both behind, shall we?'

It was a relief when the doorbell rang and Charles arrived. Seeing her amusing stepson always made her feel good. After a typical exchange of insults with her brother, Jane flounced out. Diana explained what Jane had been saying. Maybe she was right in fact.

'That's not likely. Jane is incredibly wrong as a rule.'

Diana was shaken by Charles's opinion that she had better be sure of her ground before making the writs fly about the place.

'Charles, he wasn't a crook.'

'He was a fantastically successful businessman. Sometimes it's hard to see the distinction. Maybe he did lean on Tom Vyner for some inside information.'

Charles commented on the piles of papers around the room. He thumbed through some of them and came across a number in German. They seemed to have something to do with a motor-cycle factory in a place called Neuss, wherever that was. Diana wondered if there were English translations in the same box.

'There won't be. I mean, he was virtually bilingual—' Charles saw her surprise '– didn't you know that?'

Diana knew he spoke some German, certainly; he used to go there a lot before they were married. They had gone together once or twice afterwards, with some American business people, but just English had been used. Charles commented drily that she was back where she started, wondering how well she really did know the old fellow.

Diana felt perplexed and unsure as they walked to the door, Charles told her she looked a little tired. If she was really serious about the book she'd better start getting up earlier and give up boozy three-hour lunches; besides Sanders always liquors people up when he's trying a fast one – it's something the old man taught him.

Diana walked back into the living-room, not so elegant-looking now with all the boxes, all the paper. It looked a formidable task; she knew well enough that there was some truth in what Charles had advised. By the time Tommy Meadows had got the last of the boxes and an enormous trunk down from the attic Diana began to think she would need some sort of research assistant, it was all such a jumble. The first thing she found inside the trunk was a cup inscribed to Sydney as 1949 Hampstead Badminton

Champion. Badminton! Diana had never thought of Sydney playing any sports in that sense.

It was a relief when Ellen took an interest and it wasn't long before they had a sheet spread out on the floor and most of the things from inside the trunk were spread out in an orderly fashion. Ellen had got out an old ledger from somewhere and busily catalogued the items in chronological order. Yet another surprise on this day of surprises was that Ellen actually had a librarian's degree.

Ellen admitted that she had done odd jobs for Sir Sydney, sorting order from chaos – in the days when they still had files, and computers hadn't taken over. She didn't seem too keen to talk about the details. Diana commented that she would have to hone up her journalistic skills; they had grown a little dull. She had used to be very good at getting things out of people.

Ellen looked at her shrewdly. 'People will talk if you use the right approach.'

'Are you trying to tell me something, Ellen?'

Ellen was tactful – she suggested to Diana that the trip down to the East End in the Rolls was, perhaps, a little ostentatious.

'That's the second ticking-off I've had today,' Diana smiled.

She pulled a photograph out of the trunk and looked at it closely. She felt a thrill of excitement as she realised it was an old school photograph. The caption said 'Stanley Road Grammar School – 1934'. This might be it: a real lead to the unknown young Sydney.

Taking Ellen's words to heart, Diana turned up at what was now Stanley Comprehensive in her Mini, wearing ordinary practical clothes. A crusty master showed her to the record-room where, coughing through the dust, she was able to find the roll-calls for 1933/34. She found form 5B and the name 'S. F. Clark' and quickly jotted down the names of the other boys in the form.

It took some hours of working through the list and the phone directory before Diana struck gold. A Mr J. R. Staffman agreed he had been at the Stanley Road Grammar with a Sydney Clark. Diana was exultant and Mr Staffman agreed to meet her next day.

Arriving early at the rendezvous, Diana didn't take in the blind man at first until he paused beside her.

'I am John Staffman', he stated.

They talked easily, sitting on a bench in the small park. Staffman explained how he had been blinded during the war; but that might prove useful to Diana as a sightless person tended to develop his memory much more than someone distracted by everyday sighted life. He remembered Sydney's house and street well as he lived just round the corner.

'God, it was a horrible area! The blitz got rid of most of it. The only thing Hitler did I approved of.'

'You said on the phone you knew Sydney after you left school,' Diana pressed.

Staffman told her how they had knocked about a bit. Times were difficult; it was hard enough to get enough money for the rent and a few beers. But Sydney was different. He would work harder than anyone to get money together, in order to travel. He always used to go to Germany. His mother was German and so Sydney spoke the language well.

Diana pointed out that he was going to Germany at the time Hitler had come to power, when so many people were trying to get out of the country.

Staffman told her that Sydney had loved Germany and was able to stay with his uncles there; his mother, of course, had died soon after they all left school.

'When was the last time you saw him?' Diana asked.

'Well now, that was the mystery.'

'Mystery?'

'I've often wondered what happened,' Staffman went on, 'It was 1938. The end of the summer. There were some jobs coming up picking hops in Kent. We'd done it before. Suddenly Syd was gone. His father said he'd taken his bike and set off yet again for Germany.'

Diana then found out that Staffman had never seen Sydney again. He had heard on the radio about the East End-born millionaire Sir Sydney Clark dying and he had wondered if it was the same person. Now he knew. As for what happened to Sydney during the war years, he just didn't know.

'Let me know if you ever do find out what happened.'

'Yes, I will,' Diana said kindly.

'Good day. And good luck.'

I'll need it, Mr Staffman, Diana thought. You may have answered one question, but you've posed a dozen others.

Liz Walters was coolly formal as she buzzed through to Donald Sanders that Lady Clark was here to see him. During the short wait she pulled out a file from a nearby cabinet and handed it to Diana.

'I suppose you had better have this now.'

'What is it?'

'It's the accounts file on Sir Sydney's father.'

Diana was staggered. She'd had no idea that Sydney's father was still alive. She felt that Liz Walters was enjoying her discomfort. The file proved to be some letters and some Direct Debit payments made out to the Sunnybrook Nursing Home, where Sydney's father now lived.

Diana was still bemused when she was greeted by a very affable Sanders with a kiss on the cheek and the triumphant announcement:

'Diana, good news. Browning's book has been given the chop.'

He gleefully turned aside Diana's questions about how it had happened, whether he had had anything to do with it, with the explanation that the *Post* got cold feet because Vyner had issued a writ against the paper. 'So Jonathan "Scoop" Browning is back where he belongs – chasing ambulances. I thought you'd like to know.'

Diana remained silent, thoughtful, then 'Donald,' she said, changing the subject, 'did you know that Sydney's father was still alive.'

Sanders explained to Diana that he did and went on to tell her that though Sydney and his father had fallen out years before, Sydney had been paying the major portion of the nursing home bills from the beginning. With the help of the nursing staff the old man thought he had been paying them himself.

Diana still felt shocked.

'But Jane and Charles don't even know he exists! Their own grandfather!'

'All families have a skeleton somewhere, Diana,' Sanders comforted. 'I had an aunt who thought she was Anastasia. Spoke fluent Russian. Sometimes I think she really was.'

The heavy humour didn't go down well and Sanders went on to suggest that he would look after the arrangements from now on, if she liked. But Diana said she'd take care of it all herself. As they walked to the office door Diana told him she had been going through Sydney's papers.

'Ah yes, your famous book. Found any buried bodies yet?'

Diana ignored the question. 'In 1945, a month after the war ended, Sydney formed his first British company.'

'Really?' Sanders said with a hand on the door.

'Do you know what the starting capital was?'

'Surprise me.' Sanders took his hand off the door and he watched Diana carefully.

'Fifty thousand pounds.'

'A lot of money in those days.'

Diana looked at Sanders directly and he could feel her determination.

'Now where does a young Englishman make fifty thousand pounds? In wartime.'

'No idea,' Sanders was casual.

'Germany perhaps?' There was a pause before Sanders replied, dropping his bantering manner.

'Why do you say that?'

'Because that's where he was,' Diana answered.

'Germany? During the War? That's impossible!' Sanders retorted.

'My husband did a great number of impossible things, Donald. You ought to know that.'

Diana left Sanders looking really worried for the first time. His normal bland smile was gone now.

That night Diana stayed awake for a long time. The novel she had promised herself she would start reading in order to take her mind off things was unopened on the bedside table. She found herself staring at Sydney's portrait, wondering yet again about her decision to do the book. The two years they had had together had been the best of her life. They had travelled to places she had never dreamed of; he had introduced her to things and people new and exciting to her. Was it wise, she wondered, to try and unravel the man behind the man she knew? What purpose would it serve? Sydney had tried to teach her not to be a slave to what she thought she should do, but to do what she wanted to do – for that was where happiness lay.

It hadn't been easy: she had to struggle within herself and try to learn to behave in a way her whole training and instinct told her was selfish. She looked again at Sydney's painting and he seemed to be telling her yet again, 'Live the life you want. You're only here for a brief span of time. You could die tomorrow.' *He* had done so certainly.

He had, she realised, rarely talked about the past. 'Forget it,' he would say. 'Never look back with regret or guilt. It won't change anything, so why make yourself unhappy. Look back at the past only for lessons of what you won't do again. And don't worry about the future either – live for the present; that's what matters.'

He had always been persuasive and irresistible. The two men she had known best before Sydney – her father and former husband – had been weak men. She had told them what to do; she knew now that was just what she had not wanted. She had wanted the man to take charge, to look after and to cosset her. As Sydney had done. All those years of hard work – more so after her first marriage had gone wrong – leading to the top of her profession: editing her own magazine from the very first issue. It was funny. She had been accepted as the perfect example of the modern successful woman. Someone to turn to for advice and counsel, for understanding. But she had never understood the person she might have been expected to know best: herself.

Sydney had given her so much; apart from anything else she was now a wealthy woman. Those two years were special, so special. Would her memory of them be damaged by what she might find out?

Sydney smiled down at her from the bedroom wall. No, she thought, that was for us; nothing will change that. I can forgive you anything I think. What do I want to do? She turned off the light and stared across the shadows of the darkened bedroom. I want to know you, Sydney, I want to know everything there is to know about you.

And tomorrow I'll start with your father.

The Sunnybrook Nursing Home was set in a couple of acres of greenery, about an hour's drive from London. The people there had been reluctant to let her see the old man, and she had had to be very firm in order to get her way. As she followed the nurse along the corridor Diana believed she could see the back in front of her twitching with disapproval.

'You're the first visitor he's had in four years,' the nurse said. 'The only one.'

She stopped at a door and told Diana to wait for her there while she went into the room. Before the door closed, Diana could see the outline of an old man sitting in an easy chair by the window – he certainly looked robust enough. It seemed ages before the nurse came back and Diana suddenly felt nervous and apprehensive about the visit. What was she going to say? The old man didn't look round as Diana entered the room.

'Here's your visitor, Mr Clark,' the nurse said with

professional brightness. Before she left she held up her fingers to Diana and mouthed 'Five minutes'.

The room was bright and cheery, comfortable. But, except for a few books, Diana couldn't see any personal belongings. It was as if Mr Clark had just arrived. She pulled out a chair and sat down beside him.

'I'm Diana Clark. I was married to your son.'

'I have no son.'

'He died two months ago—'

'I never had no son,' he repeated even more emphatically.

Diana shifted her position and the old man turned his head to look at her for the first time, a quick sharp look. He then gazed back at the gardens outside.

Diana tried to answer his question about how she had found him, but it was hard going as he clearly didn't want to talk about Sydney and found it hard to admit that he even had a son.

'Did you also know you have two grandchildren?'

Diana felt a tinge of remorse as Mr Clark reacted. Of course he knew, she realised – he had just tried not to think about it, to forget them.

'I know,' he said softly, 'I read the papers.'

Diana pointed out that he had never met them.

'Don't you want to? Surely you must. They're your only descendants, Mr Clark. There must have been times when you've—'

''Course I have,' he said indignantly. 'What do you take me for? But how could I? With things being what they were between me and him.'

Diana tried to press him on why he had hated his son so – but he refused to tell her. He just said he was a wicked man. He did speak of revenge; he said that outliving Sydney mightn't be much but it was the only revenge he had.

Diana looked out at the gardens herself, wondering what to say next to this sad and bitter old man. She could see people strolling there, others sitting on benches reading or talking. Two men were busy in a large vegetable garden – for a moment Diana's mind wandered off to a childhood memory of picking fresh broad-beans for her mother.

Mr Clark's voice broke through her thoughts. 'What are they like? My grandkids.'

'Jane is beautiful and clever. She's at university,' Diana replied.

'What's she doing there?'

'She's studying Politics, Philosophy and Economics.'

'Politics?' he questioned.

'Yes. You have a radical in the family, Mr Clark.'

He seemed pleased and told her to tell Jane not to let the bastards grind her down. With a smile Diana assured him that that was certainly not likely to happen. He didn't like the sound of Charles and ignored Diana's suggestion that he shouldn't judge people before meeting them. Isn't it amazing, she thought, the way parents and grandparents have a favourite child or grandchild – there's really no logic to it.

'She sounds fine, though. Jane,' he said again.

Glancing at her watch, Diana could hear the footsteps of the nurse coming down the hall. She quickly tried to persuade him to allow her to bring Jane and Charles down to see him. At first he said no, but then agreed to think about it. As she left she could see that his eyes were watering and that he was fighting to keep control.

Diana found herself thinking about the old man as she stared at the blank piece of paper lodged in the typewriter – she was trying to plan some sort of work-schedule for the book's research by typing down a list of the questions she needed answered. There were certainly enough of these; she hardly knew where to start.

It was a relief when the internal telephone rang. Ellen said she'd better turn on the television right away – Panorama was just about to show an interview with Jonathan Browning.

Diana got to the study just in time to see a close-up shot

of Browning, focused on that wolfish grin. She could hear the interviewer's voice asking what reasons his paper had given for changing its mind about sponsoring the Sydney Clark book he was preparing.

Browning then tried to make out that it had been his decision, not the *Post*'s, that he thought it would work out better if he did the book independently – particularly as he had received a substantial offer from a major publisher.

Diana turned her head at the sound of the door opening. She motioned to Ellen to come and join her as the interviewer referred to Vyner and the Malta affair, asking if Browning hadn't just released the story to publicise his book and win a big publishing contract. If Vyner had released privileged information to Clark he must have been close to him, yet there seemed to be no evidence of expensive holidays, gifts, the usual perks cases like this threw up. What was the extent of their friendship?

'Mr Vyner owes his life to Sydney Clark.'

The interviewer looked as surprised as Diana and Ellen felt. It was common knowledge, he agreed, that Thomas Vyner had been born Thomas Vinsdorff in Germany. That his parents had been arrested and subsequently murdered by the Nazis in 1938, and the six-year-old boy smuggled out of Germany to family friends in England.

'What isn't common knowledge,' Browning answered, 'is that the young man who helped him escape, who brought him every inch of the way, was none other than Sydney Clark.'

Diana glanced at Ellen, who put up her hands in a 'I don't know' gesture.

Browning was asked if he could substantiate his statement. Browning guaranteed that he could and would – in his book. And he smiled. As the interviewer introduced the programme's next item Diana walked forward and turned off the set.

'He could speak German . . .' Ellen hesitated.

'And he was in Germany in 1938,' Diana informed her.

'Doing what?'

Diana nodded towards the television set, 'If you believe Browning... playing the Scarlet Pimpernel.'

Diana sat in Sanders's austere office. It had none of the warmth and charm of Sydney's with its collection of personal photographs. Neither she nor Sanders had spoken since the routine exchange of polite greetings a few minutes before. After Jonathan Browning's statement on television she had wondered what the next surprise would be. She hadn't had to wait long for it to arrive. The morning paper had another headline to punch out at her, this time: VYNER WITHDRAWS WRIT.

The intercom on the desk buzzed and Sanders told Liz Walters to show his visitor in. Thomas Vyner was a lugubrious-looking, erect man in his early forties.

'Donald,' he said, 'nice to see you again. Diana! Sarah sends her love.'

Liz Walters started to leave, but Sanders asked her to stay.

Vyner said how sad it was to be in the building again, and after a few more pleasantries agreed to have a scotch, a watery one.

Liz took the initiative. 'We ought to stress that it was Lady Clark who asked for this meeting.'

Vyner was all sharp attention. 'I see.'

Diana gathered herself. 'I've only one question to ask you. Why have you withdrawn your libel writ?'

Vyner was the smooth politician at first, but when Diana pressed him he told her that he had done so in order to keep a solemn promise he had made to Sydney. A promise he would not break even to tell her.

He realised that some would take his withdrawal of the writ as an admission, but he would have to accept that. The writ had been issued in the first place as a means of fighting the charge of leaking privileged information; but he had never imagined that Browning would come up with what he had on television last night. Any legal investigation would now probe into all that in great detail, and that he just couldn't allow.

Diana asked if the story might harm Sydney's memory. Vyner indicated that it might. Diana then pleaded with him that he was doing so by remaining silent.

'Keeping silent never achieved anything. Except maybe some silly points in a schoolboy's code of honour.'

The immediate silence was broken by the sound of the intercom buzzing. Ellen had managed to break through the embargo Sanders had put on all calls, with a message for Diana to call the nursing home. Mr Clark was very ill.

It was the same fierce nurse who had escorted Diana on her first visit. Once more, she was shaking her head and complaining, this time that Diana's visit had caused the old man to become ill. Finally Charles told her sharply she might well be reported for gross insubordination and slander, so she'd better shut up or it would be back to the bedpans – where she belonged.

As they entered the room the nurse managed to recover from her initial shock and pushed in behind them.

'I insist you leave this room immediately—'

Charles turned towards her. 'I suggest you leave this room by the time I count three or I shall take leave of my senses – and it'll be you in that bed, not Mr Clark.'

The school bully had been faced up to; the nurse fled.

Old Mr Clark was delighted; he had been dying to speak to the old cow like that since the day he had arrived. He looked at Jane and Charles with great pride. He told Jane she looked like her grandmother.

'But I thought all Germans were blond and blue-eyed,' Jane laughed.

'Ah, but she was Jewish.'

All three of the visitors were surprised. Charles shook his head.

'I was C of E, as English as cricket and zero growth when I came in – now I'm not only half-German, but I'm half-

Jewish as well. I'll probably find out next that I'm a third cousin of the czar ...'

They all chatted for a bit, then Diana asked Mr Clark if he had ever known of a small boy just before the war called Thomas Vinsdorff. The old man clearly did know, but changed the subject by turning to Jane and asking her what she was doing studying politics.

Diana had been able to get access to the *Post*'s library of back issues and spent several days going through newspaper accounts of what was happening in Germany before the war started. She was trying to get some understanding of the atmosphere of the period. She wondered if she'd run into Jonathan Browning, and eventually she did. She introduced herself; he said he recognised her. They looked at each other cautiously, then Diana asked if it was true that Thomas Vyner was one of many people Sydney had helped to escape from the Nazis— He was— Then she asked if many were Jews— It was pretty likely, wasn't it?

They walked to the exit as Diana continued talking, almost thinking out loud – Sydney's mother was Jewish, he was helping Jews get out of Germany, yet his father disowned him.

Browning seemed uncomfortable – yes, he did know the father was still alive.

Diana remarked that he seemed very well informed; he must have some well-placed informants.

She asked if Browning knew why Sydney's father disowned him?

Browning gave a cynical shrug. 'As the man said: it's dirty water, long passed under the bridge.'

'Sydney did it for money.' The tone of Diana's voice made it a statement, not a question.

Browning's silence spoke assent.

'He knew how to get them out of Germany,' Diana continued, 'but they had to pay him. He made a fortune out of them, didn't he? And his father found out. That's the truth, isn't it, Mr Browning?'

Browning didn't answer. It was starting to spit with rain. He pulled his coat collar up, nodded goodbye and walked off. Diana watched him for a moment – and then turned and walked in the other direction.

She paused in front of a travel agent's window – the window emblazoned with posters shouting the cheap new rates for flying to America: SEE NEW YORK, SEE CALIFORNIA. She stared at the pictures of happy, laughing people; the rain came on harder so she hurried on her way again.

4

I thought the sun was always shining in California, but no – the sky was grey. There were little spots of rain striking the windscreen of the giant limousine that had met us at the airport. It had been near-blizzard conditions in New York the day before we left; Kennedy Airport had actually been closed for the morning. 'At least we'll have sun in Los Angeles, you'll see,' Sydney had assured me. 'It'll be like a balmy spring day back in England.'

I glanced at him, quickly leafing through the report prepared for him by Al Girard, who sat on the other side. Al was an American lawyer; he specialised in mergers and acquisitions – his report was on a tiny Californian mining company called Lacoma. That was the reason for our visit.

I thought back to how quickly it had all happened, after Sydney had come back from that trip to New York I had seen him two or three times a week. Sometimes more.

That was, what – not more than two months ago. So much had happened since our affair had started, for one thing. The first time had felt so right. I had just let myself go in a way I'd never thought possible. It had been natural to let him take charge ... and for me to give. What would my feminist colleagues have thought! I must have laughed out loud because Sydney suddenly looked up and smiled at me.

'Happy,' he said.

I leant against him, put my head on his shoulder – I *was* happy.

Sydney continued to read the report, making little notes

in the margin with a small gold pencil, a small frown of concentration on his forehead.

The sky ahead looked pink in places, a late afternoon sun trying to come through.

'Come to California with me, next week,' he had said.

'I can't possibly. There's so much on.'

'A good executive can delegate. He knows he's not indispensable.' Sydney liked to tease me, and I loved it.

'Oh, but I'm not a good executive. I believe that I am indispensable. I like to feel needed you see ... even if I'm the only one who thinks so.'

Sydney often talked about his man-management philosophy, about how to handle people: the stick for one, the carrot for another. It was a matter of finding the control-point for each person. He found mine quickly enough. 'But you are needed – I need you. Please come with me.' He had taken each of my hands in his, and looked deeply at me. How could I have refused? I did stall for a few days, just so he wouldn't think he had won too easily.

Sydney looked out of the limousine window and remarked that we'd be at the hotel soon.

So here I was, travelling the world, a rich man's mistress. I don't care how long it lasts, I thought to myself; I'm just going to relax and enjoy it. I was going to live for now, for the present – just as Sydney had always advised. The limousine pulled up under the giant glass canopy linking the old block and the new block of the Beverly Wilshire hotel. The canopy was so high it looked like a cathedral roof in the sky. We were instantly surrounded by smiling attendants, opening the doors, helping me out, taking the luggage. Before I knew what was happening Sydney and I were in the lift rising to a high floor, to our suite in the old block. Sydney said he preferred that side, the old Spanish-Californian style of the rooms. It was magnificent. The desk in one corner had a folder of stationery, postcards, even a little travel sachet of needles, thread, buttons and things. There was a list of the hotel facilities, it seemed to go on for ever.

'Look at this,' I showed Sydney the restaurant list. 'The coffee shop is called the Cafe of the Pink Turtle!'

'We're in Hollywood. Anything's possible.' He came up to me, put his arms around me. 'Let's have a nap, dinner later.'

I nodded and pressed against him.

I was luxuriating in a hot bath when Sydney came in, carrying a tray with a wine bucket and two glasses. The unmistakable wired head of a bottle of champagne peeked over the top of the bucket.

As I got out of the bath and slipped into the voluminous velour bathrobe provided by the hotel, Sydney opened the champagne. He twisted off the wire, then held the cork with a towel while gently turning until there was a soft kiss sound of it popping. He poured the two glasses. He always made it look so easy.

'Where are we eating?' I asked – and I thought: Isn't it marvellous; I know he has arranged something. Poor Brian could never do anything without asking me first. Maybe that was the basic, irreparable fault in our marriage: he wanted a mother figure, I needed a father figure.

Sydney lifted his glass in a mock toast. 'Ma Maison,' he said.

I knew the food would be special. Sydney would go miles out of his way to eat at a particular restaurant. 'The French have it right,' he would say. 'Look at the Michelin Guide: a three-star restaurant is described as "worth the journey", a two-star one as "worth the detour".'

He told me it was a bistro-style place, unpretentious but "worth a detour". It was very popular with the movie crowd, lunch was hard to book as so many people went there every day, and had the same table every day. We'd probably see a few film stars.

I had quickly learned that Sydney loved meeting famous people; he was mad about films and saw one or two a week in his private cinema on the top floor of his house in London. As we waited for the lift I remarked how much I liked the little white ash-trays spread around the suite. They were quite elegant with the Beverly Wilshire gold crest stamped on them. I'd like a couple as souvenirs.

'Put some in your case,' he said. But when we got down to the lobby I walked over to the reception desk and asked the Chinese under-manager on duty if I could buy a few.

'Please take some,' he said – then he smiled. 'I can't remember anyone ever asking before.'

'Well, I might come back one day – you could look me up in your index file and find my card marked "this lady steals ashtrays"!'

Sydney looked at me very thoughtfully during all this, then suddenly hugged me and kissed me on the cheek.

It was a short ride to Ma Maison. The meal was fantastic – one of the best I'd ever had. I had cause to remember it very well indeed.

Sydney told me the restaurant was owned by a Frenchman, from a famous family of restaurant owners. The chef was Austrian; his name was Wolfgang Puck – brilliant with seafood. Wolfgang Puck! I'll never forget that name as long as I live, nor any detail of the meal.

We decided to have seafood right through. Sydney had mussels baked in their shells with parsleyed garlic butter; I had scallops in a wonderful hollandaise sauce served with sautéed strips of carrot, celery and green beans. Then we had spiny lobster, served with a bearnaise sauce and smelling deliciously of fresh basil. We drank two bottles of Mercurey. I love sweet white wine so Sydney insisted we had a half-bottle of Château d'Yquem with our strawberry tart.

I asked him why he was interested in the Lacoma Mining Company. Sydney enjoyed his business projects; he would talk about them with an infectious enthusiasm. He was great fun to listen to.

It had all started, he told me, when he had read several articles about the dangers of asbestos. He called in a bright young chemistry don from Oxford and offered him a private research grant to look for an alternative. The chemist had come up with vitreous rhyolitic tuff.

Commonly known as rhyolite, it had started as volcanic ash some eighteen million years ago and was now a white rock, with countless bubbles in it left by gases trapped when the ash cooled. It had been mined for years in Northern California and used as an insulating material. But it also had many of the properties of asbestos and that was Sydney's interest. American government regulations were tough; new ones coming in would force people to cut back on the use of asbestos. Sydney planned to take control of the Lacoma Company very quietly in anticipation of this – Lacoma controlled much of the area in which rhyolite could be found.

'What happens next?' I asked.

Sydney talked of buying bits and pieces of the company through nominees and so on – I couldn't quite follow him. But I did understand that he had to keep his name out of it, otherwise other people would become alerted: if Sydney Clark was interested there had to be a reason.

'But getting control of the company is only the start.' Sydney took his cigar-cutter from his key-chain and carefully snipped the end of the cigar a waiter had just brought him.

'The next step is to build it up: get the chemists working on just how it can replace asbestos in certain products, find out what else it might be capable of, and so on. Then comes the work of promoting it. It's what the film people out here call the "hype". We'll get people to know about it, talk about it. Other industrial chemists will start looking at it; we'll limit our sales to build up the price. Rhyolite goes for about £6 a ton now – we'll ask for £20 a ton. If people pay that price we'll charge £30, then £40, and so on.'

He stopped for a moment to examine the glowing end of the cigar to ensure it was burning properly.

The sheer power and dynamism of the man was enthralling, exciting – I felt very small for a moment, and thought desperately for an intelligent question.

'It's £6 a ton now . . .' I hesitated, Sydney nodded. 'How many tons are there meant to be?'

'Lacoma could have access to about 13 million tons.'

'My God, that's—' My mind worked desperately.

Sydney looked at me with a smile. 'That's about £75 million pounds' worth, and that's before my promotion people start work and the price goes up . . . but it'll take years and years to get it out of the ground.'

'Won't it cost a lot to buy the company?'

'Not much. A lot of that tonnage is on land where Lacoma has just an option to mine. Fairly inexpensive – the real money comes with funding it all; that's millions. I think we'll be putting together a syndicate with the French, and the Germans. It's a lot surer than North Sea oil was.'

We had finished our first cup of coffee and decided to have a drink with our second. Sydney suggested I had Cointreau over crushed ice. I agreed. I was always fascinated by the way it turned cloudy.

'Diana . . .' he paused.

'Yes?' I smiled at him.

'I love talking to you – did you know that?'

'I'm glad,' I said. 'You never talk about yourself, do you? You talk about things, about what you're doing, about other people, but you actually never talk about yourself.'

He laughed. 'I'm a mystery man. I work at it quite deliberately.'

'Part of your charm, I suppose.'

Sydney agreed, quite charmingly.

Then he stunned me.

'Diana – please marry me. No, don't say anything for a moment. I'd like to say a few things first, unravel a little of the mystery perhaps.'

He didn't have to worry. I'd never appreciated before what the word 'speechless' meant – but I certainly knew then.

Sydney talked about the fact that his marriage had really

been over for years before it was actually ended formally. It was well known that he had many women friends; he liked women and enjoyed their company. It was good for the health in any case. But what he felt for me was special; it was love, but it was friendship too.

He wouldn't be easy to live with: he travelled a lot, worked hard – he was over fifteen years older than I was. All very well when he was sixty and I was forty-five. But when I was sixty, he'd be seventy-five, and probably senile.

'Diana, I won't press you for an answer. You'd probably say no if I did. I want you to think about it while we're here – then tell me what you've decided when we get back to London. I want you to have time.'

'I don't need time.' I put my hand over his. 'My answer is yes.'

Sydney looked at me for a long moment.

'Diana, I . . .' He suddenly smiled broadly. 'How about some champagne?'

'I'd love some,' I said. 'Tell me, is this an impulse thing, after a very good dinner and lots to drink? Maybe you'll feel differently in the morning.'

He shook his head, then looked at his watch. 'I decided I'd ask you about four hours ago . . . back at the hotel, when you asked about those damned ash-trays.'

5

Jonathan Browning was working. To anyone watching it would look merely as if a pretty young girl was being dropped by her boy-friend outside her office, even if he did look old enough to be her father. Browning watched the girl bounce along into the building; I can still savour a nice bottom, he comforted himself. His eyes quickened as he recognised Donald Sanders climbing out of the chauffeur-driven car. Sanders greeted the girl affably and held her arm a little longer than necessary as he escorted her through the door in front of him.

Dirty sod! Browning thought.

He sighed as he reached behind his seat and switched off the tape-recorder sitting underneath a raincoat.

Later that day he managed to bluff his way past the receptionist and find his way to her office.

'How did you get in?' she exclaimed, looking up from the typewriter.

'Helena, Helena,' he whispered, and mimed a passionate suitor on bended knee.

Helena laughed. 'Look, I've got to get on with this, you know!'

'I wish you'd say yes,' he reminded her of their conversation in the car. 'You know you will in the end anyway.'

'How do you know?'

'People always do. A weekend in Nice ...' the banter continued until a chill came into the room with the appearance of Donald Sanders from the inner office.

Browning grinned at him, with a hint of challenge as he held the grin.

'Jonathan Browning, isn't it?' Sanders snapped. 'How the devil did you get in here? Nobody told me.'

Browning smiled at Helena and looked back at Sanders. 'I've got friends in high places.' Browning brushed past Sanders and walked into the other office, leaving a confused Helena the recipient of a baleful glare from Sanders as he followed Browning.

'Now just a minute!'

'I'd like you to tell me about Neuss,' Browning interrupted.

Sanders's next remark should have been an order for Browning to leave the room – the building – immediately. It wasn't. Browning knew his instinct had been right.

'Neuss? Never heard of it,' Sanders replied, with a hardly noticeable flicker of hesitation.

When Browning pointed out that it was on the list of Clark holdings, Sanders's memory seemed to return; at least he remembered something about making picks or the like. Even Browning's prompting with the word 'motorcycles' didn't elicit further information. Sydney had been secretive, Sanders explained; he really didn't know everything.

'You were together nearly twenty years,' Browning insisted. 'Senior partner in most things. Right?'

'But not all. My point exactly.'

Sanders listened to the list of Clark activities Browning was now enumerating. He reacted to the mention of a civil airline in Uganda.

'Now that might be something for you to look into. For your biography. It would be right up your street.'

Browning grinned knowingly. 'You weren't involved in that one, then?'

'Not until the later stages,' Sanders was being very affable now, 'I don't suppose it's spilling the beans to say that Sydney nearly came a cropper over that little adventure.'

Browning knew he was being steered in the wrong direction.

'It might just bear looking into.'

Sanders diligently wrote down a contact address in Kenya for Browning.

'Nothing come to mind about Neuss?' Browning tried again.

''Fraid not,' Sanders answered, feeling in control again. 'Where is it by the way?'

Browning stood up to go. 'Oh . . . somewhere in Germany.'

Helena was the real sufferer. When Browning dropped her outside the small block of flats where she lived, later that day, she sensed something had changed between them. She referred to Nice.

'I really would like to go with you.'

'Sorry, love – duty calls. Got to go away for a few weeks. Enjoy your new job.'

Helena was stunned. 'What new job?'

'You'll probably be moved tomorrow.' Browning engaged gear and roared off into the evening traffic.

Diana enjoyed driving the Rolls; she luxuriated in the thrum of power underneath her. It was good to get out of London; the country air was exhilarating. Then, as her memory of the map told her she was getting closer, gradually her mood changed into one of anxiety. Soon the turning came up. The sign was prominent on the open gate: Heron Place. The house was impressive, half-timbered. She was struck by the profusion of flowering shrubs, trees and bushes lining the driveway. It was almost too rich, a slightly cloying chocolate soufflé of a landscape. She reached the house and stopped the car, then glanced at her watch to check the time. There was someone moving in the rose garden, the sound of the car must have been heard.

It was a woman. She went on about her business for a few minutes. Diana knew the woman was aware she was being watched. Finally she turned, as if she felt the waiting had gone on long enough. The two women stared at each other for a moment. Diana was the first to make a move. When she was within speaking distance she tried to lighten the atmosphere.

'Dr Livingstone, I presume?'

Mary Clark ignored the levity. 'My, you are punctual, aren't you? Come along into the house.'

The living-room had French doors opening on to the large garden patio; it seemed an extension of the garden, with plants, bushes, creepers and flowers everywhere. There was a photograph of Sydney on a side-table, laughing, hair awry – it looked like a holiday snap. On one wall there was an oil painting of Sydney, far more critical than the one in Diana's bedroom at home. She didn't like it, though she could see a true reflection of Sydney in it, an aspect she did recognise. The thought crossed her mind that she could understand why Lady Churchill had destroyed the Sutherland painting. Mary Clark was prattling on about Sydney's interest in gardening, his pride in his Dorothy Wheatcroft roses, his thrill at developing a blue-streaked orchid, an Epistephium, which had been named after him.

During all this she prepared them both gins and tonics, arranged her newly-cut roses ... and then placed herself in an elegant garden chair. She was a woman totally in control of her environment – a large woman, with one of those busts that seemed to go on forever. She reminded Diana of a puffed-up pigeon.

'You're not writing this down,' she said, with some surprise.

Diana took a breath. 'Lady Clark ...'

'Mary, my dear. Call me Mary. I don't think we can sit here Lady Clarking each other, do you?'

Diana agreed. Perhaps, she thought to herself, it won't be so bad.

'Sydney always said – but then you knew what Sydney

67

always said. You were married to him for ... six months, a year?'

Diana corrected her and Mary commented on how time flies. She knows very well it was two years, Diana thought; I don't think she means to be friendly at all. Some more verbal fencing went on as the two women sized each other up. Diana asked her for help in finding out about Sydney's early life.

'I wouldn't know where to start.'

'That's my trouble also,' Diana tried the frank, sincere approach.

Through the exchange Sydney looked down from his portrait. It wasn't the man she knew, Diana felt, but – yet it *was* Sydney. It was an older Sydney, a man at the end of his physical powers – but the eyes were arresting. There seemed to be so much in them – shrewdness, pride, even arrogance. Mary commented on it, saying it was better than the one Diana had; she told Diana that Sydney had never liked it, but it was quite famous. One of the colour sketches for it was in the permanent collection at the Tate.

'I see you're looking at the eyes,' Mary went on. 'Something devious there I always thought.'

After reaching the safer ground of Jane and Charles for a while, Diana tried to turn the conversation back to the younger Sydney.

'But, my dear, I know nothing, nothing at all. It's no use coming to me.'

'I can't believe that,' Diana exclaimed, 'you were married to him for twenty years.'

Then Jane walked into the room.

Diana was completely taken back. Jane had told her she was going to friends in Devon. She herself had just passed this news on to Mary – and Mary hadn't said a word about Jane being here! Diana felt a deep dislike for Mary building up. Watch it! she instructed herself. Count to ten. Remember: you're a professional, here to do a job, learn what you can. There must be something you can pick up.

Later Jane managed to manoeuvre Diana into coming to look at the garden and the rest of the grounds. As soon as they were out of ear-shot of the house she apologised to Diana for lying about going to Devon; she just felt it would be easier. Diana understood; she didn't mind. Jane introduced her to the young girl from next-door who was busily grooming the horse Jane had just been riding. They all joked about the horse-craze so many girls went through. It's all sexual symbolism, Jane confided seriously. They watched the horse nuzzling at the girl's trouser pocket, looking for the inevitable apple, and Diana talked to Jane about her frustration with what she had learnt, or rather hadn't learnt, from Mary. Jane's theory was that Mary knew only what she wanted to know. Her image of Sydney just wasn't real. She guessed that Mary had told Diana Sydney was a great gardening man, mad on roses, Brazilian orchids. She challenged Diana to match that with the man she knew. Diana couldn't.

'Father wasn't any of the things she imagines,' Jane repeated. 'He was strong and noisy and ... vulgar. Charles always said it was part of his German background.'

Diana felt closer to Jane at this moment than she had ever thought possible. She had come to accept that Jane was jealous of her relationship with her father. But now – it was, perhaps, one small benefit from Sydney's death. As they strolled back to the house Diana probed Jane on what she knew about her German grandmother, and she brought the subject up with Mary after they had returned to the house and their drinks were replenished.

'She died years ago, some time in the early thirties, I think. He hardly knew her,' Mary explained.

As if demonstrating her point made in the garden about her mother's distorted view of her father, Jane made a heavy issue of reminding Mary that he had come from a humble background. This resulted in a typical mother-daughter spat which Diana wisely stayed out of. Eventually Jane strode from the room in high dudgeon.

Mary turned to Diana. 'Everybody knows that Sydney was a ... self-made man, whatever that ridiculous expression means.'

'What do you take it to mean?' Diana asked quickly.

'Well,' Mary answered, slightly on the defensive, 'only that he seized his opportunities if and when they occurred.'

Diana referred to Sydney's sizeable capital stake soon after the end of the war. Did Mary ever ask him how he got it?

'No.'

'Weren't you interested?' The gloves were off now.

'No.'

'So you never found out?'

'Did you?' Mary said softly. Her tone was one of saccharin sweetness.

The next time Diana had a chance of talking to Donald Sanders – over dinner in a restaurant – she asked him if he thought Mary was trying to hide something. Sanders thought not; he explained that he felt she really wasn't very interested. In any case the business was very complicated.

At that very moment the legal side alone could keep the High Courts in action until 1980: breach of contract cases, negligence cases, the committal of unlawful acts causing loss and injury – there were patent infringements, claims by offshore nominee companies, a charge of sanctions-busting in Rhodesia, a foreign landlord's suit.

Diana quailed at the thought.

'Could you help me sort it out?' she asked hesitantly.

'I suppose I could. If that's what you want.' Sanders was pleased. This was exactly what he wanted. After his scene with Browning he felt his best plan was to try and persuade Diana to think of him as an ally; then he had a chance of controlling what she got up to, of editing any information she would obtain. He felt pleased with himself. He sat back and sipped his wine appreciatively.

'One thing we can be glad of,' he smiled at Diana. 'I've got rid of Browning. Sent him off to Africa.'

Charles had suggested to Diana that her best source of information might be Liz Walters, who had been with his father since she left university about ten years previously. She knew where the bodies were hidden, he said; she probably knew more than Sanders or Mary.

Liz had been reluctant to talk to Diana when she rang her, but she had no real choice when Diana simply appeared at the office. Liz was perfectly polite, closing the file she was working on and asking the new girl to leave the office for a few minutes. Helena, she explained to Diana, had just been promoted to another department.

'I'm sorry, Diana,' she stated firmly, 'I really do know nothing.'

'But you were with him for years. He must have mentioned his parents sometime. Look, Donald has offered to take me through the business details, but I'm really stuck on the personal side.'

'Donald has!' Liz was not pleased with this development.

Diana explained how he had suggested this at dinner the night before. She went on to quiz Liz about Sydney's mother; she was German of course. But Liz denied knowing even this, which Diana patently did not believe. She'd really had enough of this lack of cooperation – from Mary first and now Liz. Standing up to go, she looked down at the well-groomed woman in front of her. She was very attractive she had to admit. The obvious possibility of her having had a relationship with Sydney crossed her mind yet again; she had always wondered. There certainly seemed to be no other man in Liz's life. She was convinced Liz was withholding evidence; her experience as a journalist had taught her how to read people's thoughts through what they did, how they held themselves, rather than what they said – what they called 'body language' nowadays. Liz was expressing herself all right: her body was taut; she incessantly twirled a silver pencil in her fingers; she was clearly willing Diana to leave.

'You were very close to him, weren't you?'

'Yes,' Liz said. There was a touch of defiance.

'He must have been very grateful to you for your loyalty.'

There was a long pause. The two women kept their eyes fixed on each other – each waiting for the other to speak next.

Finally Liz said quietly, 'That's as maybe. I have nothing to tell you.'

But she did have plenty to say to Donald Sanders. He was evasive at first. He may have said something, he supposed. The subject had cropped up over dinner. Diana had asked about the business background. He had been polite, but noncommittal.

Liz's tone was steely, relentless. 'You offered,' she said.

'Did I? That's not how I remembered it.' Sanders waved his hand vaguely and sat down at his desk, reaching for some papers as if the issue was closed and they had more important things to discuss. Liz pressed on. She reminded him that they had agreed to face the whole business of the book – and what Diana Clark would get on to – together. She pointed out to him that there were certain things in the office that she regarded as completely confidential, things that even he didn't know. Sanders was more than aware of that; there were some things he really didn't want to know.

Liz re-stated that when she had agreed to stay on with the organisation she had made it clear that her first, and last, loyalty was to Sydney. If there was any conflict, she would continue to serve him.

'I think you're over-dramatising this, my dear.' That's the trouble with women in business, he thought; their emotions get in the way. If the truth about some of the deals came out, even now, there would be serious trouble.

He tried to pacify her and quickly agreed that the

element of confidence had to be maintained. As a token of his goodwill, or so he intended it, he told her about Jonathan Browning coming in and how he had sent him packing.

Liz knew who she would bet on in a straight battle of wits between Sanders and Browning. Like so many businessmen, Sanders had a contempt for journalists; he would think he had out-smarted Browning. Liz doubted that. If Browning had come to get something out of Sanders he had probably succeeded.

Sanders described how he had found Browning in the outer office. The man had made friends with Helena and wormed some information out of her about the Neuss works – that's why he had kicked her upstairs. He was very smug during his exposition.

'What did you tell him?' Liz waited patiently.

'Nothing, of course. Denied everything. Naturally I had to lead him off the scent ...' Sanders paused, he realised he had trapped himself. 'So I ... told him some lies, about the past – nothing that could hurt Sydney now.'

Liz could make a good guess; Sanders first and Sanders last was this man's motto.

'The airline fraud?'

'Something like that.' Again a vague wave of the hand.

'You put Browning on to the African business!' Liz smacked her hands on the arms of her chair in exasperation.

'I had to give him something,' Sanders pleaded.

'Oh yes,' Liz went on. 'And it's just a coincidence that you weren't involved in Uganda whereas you are heavily involved in Neuss.' Sanders claimed that that hadn't been his thinking at all.

Liz got up to leave the room, she looked at Sanders scornfully. 'I think you've just committed suicide.'

She left a very worried man behind her. She had no hesitation about what to do next. She had warned Sanders and now she would be quite ruthless in teaching him a lesson.

T.—4

The phone rang thirteen or fourteen times and Liz was about to hang up when a breathless voice answered at the other end.

'Diana Clark here.'

'Lady Clark, this is Liz Walters. I have something for you. An address in Germany, in Düsseldorf. Your husband sent monthly cheques to a family there. I thought you might like to have it.'

Diana had always liked travelling by air – the rush and bustle of an international airport. Before she married Sydney there had always been that last-minute rush to buy cigarettes and drink at the duty-free shop. She inevitably chose the wrong queue, someone in front of her fiddling with their money, trying to work out the right currency rate, while the tannoy barked out its final boarding instructions. She couldn't make up her mind whether being rich was an advantage because you didn't have to worry about the money saved on duty-free goods, or a disadvantage because you no longer had the satisfaction of making the purchase, the distinctive plastic bag in your hand when you got home, the perfect reminder of the trip just completed.

The flight to Düsseldorf was smooth. Diana refused the lunch; she felt a little unsettled and tired from a sleepless night. The drink was probably a mistake, but she persevered and eventually finished it.

She felt a little dizzy as she walked through the airport and found a taxi at the rank outside – a touch of flu perhaps. The driver nodded when she showed him the address on a bit of paper, and it wasn't long before he stopped the car outside an anonymous-looking building. She found the right bell and pressed it. Thank God, Herr Keller could speak some English, at least enough to understand her when she telephoned from London the day before.

Herr Keller was very welcoming, a little gnome of a man – certainly over seventy but warm, vital and friendly.

74

His energy made Diana feel tired. The room looked very lived in, music sheets piled everywhere, several violins and a grand piano. The old man fussed her into a chair and presently he proudly brought out some coffee and an ominous-looking fruit cake.

'It is many years since I am in England, but *ich weiss* ... I know you are always having refreshments when you are making the visit.'

'You shouldn't have bothered,' Diana insisted.

They chatted for a bit. Herr Keller was full of compliments for the efficient Fräulein Walters; the money always came in on the exact day. The talk turned to Sydney; he had known him since he was a boy of ten. Sydney's grandparents, his mother's parents, lived for years in number twelve, and he had lived, for ever it seemed, here in number ten. He explained that the Webers were very poor and that Sydney's mother had gone to England to take up a job arranged through an employment agency. That was before the First World War – and so the grandparents hadn't seen Sydney until he was nearly ten years old; but subsequently he had come back many times. His father, though, had only come once, and hadn't seemed to like it in Germany very much.

It was a difficult time then. You virtually needed a wheelbarrow full of money to buy a loaf of bread. It was really no wonder that so many people had turned to Hitler – at least some hope was better than none. But Sydney had made many visits. His German became perfect and it was hard to remember that he was an English boy. Herr Keller remembered many sing-songs around the piano with Sydney bellowing out the German songs better than all the other boys. He seemed to look on Düsseldorf as his real home.

Herr Keller remembered that the grandparents had been very excited when they received a letter from Sydney saying he looked like getting a job with a shipping agent, where his use of German would come in useful – though they would probably send him to New York initially.

'When was that? Just before the Second War?' Diana felt that this might be the solution to those missing war years.

He was about to answer when he remembered a box of old photographs he had found for her. He quickly extracted one of Sydney as a boy, together with his mother. Another showed him with his arm around the shoulders of a boy in a uniform. The Hitler Youth, Herr Keller agreed. The boy was a sort of distant cousin of Sydney's.

Diana asked him further about this, as Sydney's mother had been Jewish. Why was the other boy in the Hitler Youth?

The connection was distant, the cousin's grandfather had married a Christian and, well, there were many such cases. It was painful to remember those times. There had been several occasions when Sydney's grandfather had been pushed around, even beaten up – broken teeth, once some ribs. There was one time when he had called the police because Herr Weber had not returned home when expected, but they had been scornful – they had more things to do than go looking for an old Jew.

Diana wondered why Sydney had kept coming back. Herr Keller explained that he had grown very fond of his grandparents. After the war he had sent them money every month. They died within a few months of each other. Somehow he had found out about the predicament he, Herr Keller, and his old mother were in, and he had sent them money too in gratitude for what they had done for his grandparents ... and now Miss Walters saw that the cheque still came in.

Diana felt her forehead. She was perspiring a bit – it probably was the flu. She wondered about the timing of Sydney's last visit to Germany, before the war. Herr Keller didn't understand.

'Well,' Diana went on, having jumped to a conclusion, 'he was in America during the war wasn't he? I mean, that shipping company must have sent him there.'

Herr Keller touched her hand. 'No, my child, you are

wrong. I said they were going to send him. I did not say they did send him. Surely you know he spent the war here ... with us.'

Whatever ailment was bothering Diana now came on very strongly and Herr Keller realised she was unwell. He insisted she lie down for a while and he settled her on the sofa with a blanket and several soft pillows. She soon fell asleep.

It was dark when she woke. One small light was on, and Herr Keller was in the process of turning on another as Diana sat up.

'So, you are better?' His voice was gentle.

'I'm sorry. I'm not often sick.'

'No, I'm sorry. I think it was maybe a shock what I tell you about Sydney. I think you know – why else does Fräulein Walters send you?' His voice was puzzled. He asked if she'd like to go to her hotel now or later – there was someone he had asked to come and see her. Diana said of course she would stay.

She hadn't long to wait. The man ushered in was cold-faced with rimless spectacles. Diana suddenly had the wild thought that Keller had called Central Casting and asked them to send over one male, Nazi type.

'Fischer, Gottlieb,' he identified himself – there was a hint of a click of the heels.

Herr Keller excused himself; he was due to give a music lesson to a neighbour's child. He would use the room next-door.

Fischer gestured to the photograph still lying on the table beside Diana.

'I am the cousin of Sydney. You have seen?'

'Yes,' Diana virtually whispered.

Fischer told her he understood that she wished to know about her late husband, what he had done during the war. Diana nodded. Fischer went on to describe how they had been friends since they were fourteen or fifteen. For a while Sydney had done many things with him, joined him and his friends on outdoor hikes and so on. But there came a time when he could no longer come along with them – not because he was part-Jewish, for very few knew that, but because he was an Englishman.

'Why did he keep coming back?' Diana asked.

Fischer shrugged. 'Because he was half-German and fascinated by what was going on here,' he suggested. 'Many times we argue—'

'Please tell me, why was he here during the war?'

'In 1938 and again in 1939 he is here for his holidays. We are walking in Bavaria and climbing. One day he falls and breaks his leg. He goes to hospital. When he comes out the war has arrived – the frontiers are closed.'

'He could still have escaped, couldn't he?'

Fischer nodded in agreement.

'But he chose to stay.'

'By now he is more than half German. Germany is his motherland.'

'How did he manage?' Diana asked, and then, 'Did he become a Nazi?'

'No, no – or, if he did, not in his heart. At first I hid him. He was my cousin. I was very fond of him.'

'It must have been very dangerous for you to do that.'

It was, at first, Fischer admitted. But he had friends and he was able to get Sydney some papers identifying him as Klaus Lorenz, clerk. There was quite an industry in counterfeit papers thriving at that time. Lots of people had reason to seek a new identity. Sydney had literally to live on his wits at times, in the black-market, doing favours, selling information.

'Not . . . people?' Diana didn't want to ask that question, but she had to. Fischer shrugged; he obviously felt it was unimportant. He explained that really he couldn't know. He was at the war after all: an officer in the 9th SS Panzer Division of the 2nd Panzer Corps. He did know that Sydney had become very adept at getting currency, jewels and such-like out of the country.

'People?' Diana pressed.

Fischer nodded.

'Jews?' Diana questioned further.

Again Fischer nodded. When Diana inquired if he had done it for money, Fischer was once more quite unconcerned. Money, possessions what did it matter? Think of the danger Sydney was facing. At least they had their lives! Of course he was part-Jewish, but she must remember that he was living on a knife's edge; every day he was at risk of discovery. His grandparents were put into a camp; through his contacts Sydney virtually kept them alive, and many of their friends.

It went on until 1944, when Sydney had to escape – through Spain, then to the United States. Later on he returned to London.

'A rich man, a very rich man,' Diana murmured.

Fischer went on to tell of how Sydney later returned to Germany and helped the Webers – and Fischer himself, he admitted. Sydney bought into his factory at Neuss and thus provided him with the capital necessary to rebuild after the war. 'It brought him many handsome profits.' The tone was self-satisfied.

'And you too no doubt,' Diana remarked.

Fischer smiled coldly. 'Why not? I am still a Nazi. My profits go to the political party I still support.'

There seemed little more to say; clearly the dislike was mutual and Fischer withdrew. Once again there was a hint of heels clicking.

The hotel was antiseptic, and over-warm, as she entered. Diana still felt weak from the touch of flu. She was surprised to find there had been several telephone calls from London; the person would call back. She was more surprised to hear a voice address her by name, offering to buy a drink.

'What are you doing here? It is Mr Browning, isn't it?'

'People are always saying that,' he smiled. 'It must be the way I blend into my surroundings.'

Diana blurted out that she had thought he was in

Africa. Browning laughed and again offered her a drink. Diana declined and was about to go on up to her room when she was halted by a sudden question.

'Did Gottlieb Fischer tell you much?'

'What do you know about him?' Diana was wary.

Browning explained he had visited him and that Fischer had mentioned he was going to see the Lady Clark that night. He commented that he thought the Neuss motorcycle works was a very shady place indeed.

'Profitable, yes, but undisclosed profits, if you take my meaning. No wonder friend Sanders wanted me in Africa. He's in it right up to his Old Etonian tie.'

Diana stated that she knew nothing about it.

Browning looked hard at her. 'Then you'd better get your lawyers on to it. Your husband made his money in some very off-beat ways, you know – some would say unethical.' He studied her more closely and asked if he could buy her a strong drink – she did look as if she needed it. Diana shook her head, and questioned him further about Fischer. But as Browning resumed his bantering manner with talk of Nazi war criminals escaping the net, Diana was called to the phone. The call was from Mary Clark, attempting to be forceful and domineering, which wasn't the best way to handle Diana at that moment of time. She seemed determined that Diana should abandon the book forthwith. Donald also thought she should drop it, Mary added. Finally able to get a word in, Diana flatly refused to discuss it at all. She was hurt to learn that Mary was calling her from her own home, where she was visiting Jane and Charles. She had discussed it with them, too, she implied.

Diana was unswayed, so Mary tried another approach.

'You'll regret this, you'll be very sorry indeed.'

'Is that a threat?' Diana exclaimed. Mary's answer didn't satisfy her. She felt on the point of tears. 'Oh, go to hell!' She handed the phone back to a startled-looking receptionist and turned away, trembling, not trusting herself to speak.

Browning approached and handed her the handbag she had left on the table.

She looked up at him and wondered how he came to be in the hotel anyway.

'Were you waiting for me tonight?'

Browning nodded yes, quite cheerfully.

'The Clarks always stay here when they're in Düsseldorf.'

Diana asked him how he knew that. Browning replied that it was obvious – by then they were stepping into the lift.

'Why is it obvious?' Diana asked.

'You mean you don't know?' he teased as he pressed the lift button. 'You *own* the place, don't you?'

6

We had been married in Las Vegas. In all his trips to the
States, Sydney had never been there before. He thought it
would be a 'fun thing' to do. We were in the city for two
nights and a day and managed to see four different shows.
Some of the performers Sydney knew from their visits to
London, so we'd always go round to see them afterwards.

Sydney taught me to play craps; it was great fun – your
money could ride for such a long time until you won or
lost. Every so often you got the chance to throw the dice
yourself, rolling them down the table to crash against the
high green-baize sides. The tall American men standing
around, some with Stetsons on their heads, would shout
encouragement at me to throw their chosen numbers.

'Come on, honey, be nice to me' ... 'Give me eight,
baby. I know you're as lucky as you're pretty.'

I won five hundred dollars. I had never won more than
five pounds before – that was on an office sweep when Red
Rum first won the Grand National. I had always backed
horses with 'Red' in their names. Sydney was delighted for
me. Later that night he had come up to our suite slightly
embarrassed. He had been to the hotel manager to get the
wedding ceremony arranged with a local JP. It was all set
for the next morning at 11.00 at a place called the Chapel
of Eternal Love.

'It's only for a few minutes,' he said, with one hand on
my shoulder.

'Darling, I don't mind. It sounds lovely.' I couldn't help
myself and started to laugh uproariously. Sydney looked
like a naughty boy who had broken the biscuit jar. He

joined in and it was a few minutes before we could recover, wiping the tears of laughter from our eyes.

Actually it was lovely. Quite charming. The JP had pure white hair, warm blue eyes. His wife played a little electric organ in the corner, two people from the hotel had come along as witnesses. I had suddenly felt very nervous, I was amazed at myself for even being there.

I had always been so cautious about everything – it would take me ages to make up my mind about a new dress, or a pair of shoes. I'd go through agonies if I decided it was time to re-paint a room. I would buy tins of different colours and paint large patches from each one on a wall, the room would soon look like a crazy-patterned quilt – and sometimes stay like that for weeks. Now – in a space of nine weeks – I had met a famous millionaire, become his mistress, temporarily abandoned my job to run off to Hollywood ... and was now getting married in Las Vegas, in the Chapel of Eternal Love.

We flew back to London from New York, where Sydney had arranged a few meetings in connection with his quiet take-over of the Lacoma Mining Company. I had spent the day we had there just walking round some of the wonderful stores: Sak's, Bloomingdale's, Lord and Taylor's. The range of goods available was staggering, the stores themselves quite beautiful. I was surprised too to see how reasonable many of the clothes were, many items actually cheaper than in London – yet Americans earned so much more. No wonder they had so many things.

I had several cups of coffee along the way, and would just sit quietly thinking about what I had got myself into. I hardly knew Sydney, I didn't even know where he had been born, what his parents had done. He wouldn't tell me. He'd just laugh and remind me he was the mystery man.

There was hardly ever time to ask him. He would always be talking to me, or to people he met on the plane, with great enthusiasm – asking them questions too. We had made four flights now, always first-class, and each time

Sydney got to know some of the other people travelling. He would find out what they did; he'd ask them their opinions. What did they think of Watergate? What did they know about Britain?

People asked him questions, usually businessmen who knew who he was. I remember one American, a senior executive with the airline in fact, talking to Sydney about Concorde. Sydney had shaken his head.

'A disaster from the beginning,' he had said, 'a triumph of politics and national pride over managerial common sense. When I heard the thing was to be built with two production lines, the British measuring in inches, the French in millimetres, I knew it would be a fiasco.'

Sydney loved Britain. He was seriously worried about the power of the unions; he truly believed that there were communist agitators at work, causing trouble – their one aim to destroy the country's economy and lead to a communist take-over.

'I believe in self-interest,' he would say, 'but an enlightened self-interest, a self-interest that respects the self-interest of others. It's the same premise as the Golden Rule.'

Capitalism was the natural way of life, he just knew that.

In many ways I did know him, I realised. I loved him, I was certain of it – how else could I have allowed my whole life to be changed overnight. I had literally been swept off my feet. Sydney said it was natural to have doubts, but I'd soon get over them. He pointed out that I had gone as far as I really wanted with the magazine; I should phase myself out gradually – then take a good period off and think about what I might like to do.

'I believe in a mid-life change of careers,' he would insist, 'otherwise you get a little too complacent, stagnant. It's good to get shaken up, to have new problems, new challenges. That's how we grow as people.'

I wasn't worried about what other people would think. I was certain a lot of my friends would raise their eyebrows and have great fun talking about me. I knew they'd be a little envious too – and that, I had to admit, delighted me. I had quickly found I rather enjoyed being a rich man's wife, it did make life easier. The first time I had been called Lady Clark was a shock – it had been the doorman at the Plaza. I'd had a late breakfast in the suite, as Sydney had gone off very early, then I decided to walk around New York. It was still cold, but the sun was shining. The doorman had touched the brim of his braided cap in a small salute. 'Taxi, Lady Clark?' I shook my head and thanked him graciously, the lady of the manor. It was lovely.

I told Sydney about it on the plane back to London.

'I know just what you mean,' he said. 'I still enjoy it – and it doesn't half make it easy to get reservations.'

What did worry me was the prospect of seeing Sydney's children, Jane and Charles. They were the only people whose possible reaction disturbed me. They were his flesh and blood; I wanted them to like me. I had met Jane just once, fleetingly, Charles at least twice. He was funny, very dry – a nice self-deprecating sense of humour. Sydney was concerned that he was lazy, just drifting along. He was bright enough: he had qualified as a veterinary surgeon in order to manage Sydney's race-horses. There were seven of these, all fillies, which would be the basis of the new stud. But that seemed to be the only thing Charles was interested in doing, and it didn't take much of his time.

Jane was quite different, still at university and planning to go to Harvard to take a master's degree in American Politics. I hadn't had time to form any fair opinion of her – though I did sense a brittle, nervy personality. My female intuition, for which I had a great respect, told me that I would have trouble with her.

It was something I'd have to face up to. Jane and Charles both lived with Sydney, though they were away a lot. They had little flatlets within the house, nearly self-contained. Sydney told me I wasn't to worry about them – they were quite grown up; they had their own lives to lead.

'I don't consider my children belong to me. I have no

rights over them. I'm only the physical catalyst that brought them into being; that doesn't give me any claims on them. I expect them to think of me in the same way.'

It turned out much as I expected. I hadn't realised that Sydney had telephoned Charles from New York. He met us at the airport with a large bunch of red roses and gave me a warm embrace and a kiss.

'Just don't expect me to call you mother' he had grinned at me.

I was grateful to him for the effort of coming out to meet us – ominously Jane wasn't there. She'd be at the house, Charles explained.

She greeted her father with a huge hug, then stuck out a hand rather formally to me. I went forward to give her a kiss, but I could feel her stiffen and realised I had made a mistake. She smoked three cigarettes in about the same number of minutes, then left, saying she had to meet someone. Sydney had gone straight off to make some calls and there was a moment's silence while I wondered what to do.

'Don't worry about Jane, Diana. She'll come round.' Charles waved an expansive arm towards the rest of the house. 'Come and let me show you the mansion, then I'll run you over to your place.'

Thank God for Charles, I thought to myself.

The next few months passed in a whirlwind of activity: I had to wind up the job at the magazine, help find my successor and see her started, arrange to sell my flat and dispose of all the furniture. Sydney insisted that I help him redo the whole bedroom suite so I'd feel at home there. He had had it done by an interior decorator about three years previously and was quite fed up with it. He wanted a sauna installed in the bathroom, so that and everything else involved took over a month. Sydney went back to the States twice more in that time, once to France, and twice to Rome. He must have been away for half of the time – his lifestyle was as he promised. He was full of energy – 'my animal energy' he'd call it. It was something he looked for in all his executives.

Finally, I moved into Sydney's house and our married life really did begin. I liked to cook for him, but meals could be hard to plan. I quickly had to learn to accept sudden changes of plans ... and surprises.

He was quite capable of calling at four in the afternoon to tell me to pack an overnight bag.

'We're going to Paris for dinner, I've got to see some people there – we'll come back early tomorrow.'

One Saturday night we did have a dinner I had cooked, just the two of us. But there was a surprise. I had been making small-talk, just asking him some questions. I had reminded him of the point he had made to me when we first met, that self-confidence was one of the secrets of his success. 'Of course, hard work is a part of that too,' I said.

'But what about luck?' – someone had said something to me that same day about Napoleon always asking of a general 'Is he lucky?' – 'Doesn't that play a part too?'

'Well, some people may say so,' Sydney answered, 'but one thing I do know: the harder I work, the luckier I get.'

Then he suddenly grinned at me and whipped out his wallet. With a great flourish he dropped two tickets on to the table. He explained it was why he had suggested an early dinner. The tickets were for a rock music concert that night at the Odeon, Hammersmith. A new American super-group was in town for one performance. They were called Nebraska. They wouldn't come on till after nine so we had plenty of time.

Sydney explained that he had never been to one. It was something many people did, so he thought we should go ourselves, just for the hell of it. And it was loud – the audience wildly enthusiastic. After a while I found myself carried along by the music and clapping along with the rest of them. Sydney seemed to watch the stage half the time, the audience the rest. He thought it was wonderful.

After about forty minutes the band ran off and the audience started shouting for more. I looked around and saw hundreds of people striking lighters or matches, the theatre looked like a giant Christmas tree. I nudged Sydney and pointed it out to him.

'It all started at Woodstock,' Sydney explained. 'Frank Zappa suddenly asked everyone to light a match just to see what it looked like in the dark. There were thousands of people there. It was an extraordinary sight. So it's become a sign of approval from a rock audience, like a crowd shouting for a bull-fighter in Spain to be given the bull's ears and tail.'

I looked at Sydney with amazement; he would always surprise me, I realised.

I knew I was learning from Sydney all the time, particularly about business – a subject I had always avoided in the past. I had never read the financial pages with all the jargon about price-earnings ratios, gearing and what-have-you. Don't worry about that, he'd say. They're just the tools used. He would quote from *The Little Prince*: 'For us who understand life, figures are a matter of indifference.' He could always make me feel better, less insecure.

He read voraciously, three or four books a week, three newspapers daily, six or seven magazines and periodicals weekly. He would constantly make lists of things he wanted Liz Walters to look out for in the papers and magazines he didn't read for himself from cover to cover. Every morning there'd be a pile of material for him on the gargantuan coffee-table in his office – red circles around the things at which he should look.

He was particularly fond of reading about American businessmen and had quite a library of books written about them and by them. He loved going to the States, though he had his criticisms too – he felt Americans just had to come to terms with their over-consumption.

'They consume a third of the world's energy, eat a third of its food – enjoy half of the world's income. It can't go on. But Americans have a great capacity to learn from their past mistakes. The ecologists, the conservationists – they're being listened to now. And because they're being listened to, some people will make a great deal of money out of new government regulations ... as with rhyolite,' he added with a grin.

He often talked about the need for flexibility in business; you had to listen to new ideas, constantly examine the old ones.

'Remember that Cadillac Seville we had from the second day in California – there's a perfect example of flexibility. General Motors set out to re-educate Americans on how they thought of cars: don't think of size, think of interior space and driving quality. They believed they had to do this; the big cars were "gas-guzzlers" and therefore bad news. So they came out with the Seville, marketed it superbly, and had a smashing success.'

Simplicity was another favourite theme of his. I've always remembered one example he used – on an occasion when I got a sharp reminder that he was mortal too.

We had had a long, leisurely dinner at Ma Cuisine, one of our favourite restaurants. It was only open for lunch and dinner from Monday to Friday and was so popular that even Sydney had to make a reservation three to four weeks in advance. In order not to be disappointed we had made a permanent booking of the first Friday in the month. If something conflicting came up a friend or someone from the office could always take our table.

It was one of our regular first Friday reservations – it was a warm, balmy evening in the early autumn and we decided to stroll home as it would only take about twenty minutes. Tommy had been given the night off so we would have had to wait or call a taxi anyhow.

We passed a grocery shop and Sydney stopped and gestured towards a display of soup tins.

'Do you know about H. J. Heinz?' he asked.

'Only about the 57 flavours,' I answered, my arm linked through his.

Sydney explained that when Heinz was a twelve-year-old boy in Pittsburgh, Pennsylvania, before the American Civil War, he discovered a simple truth that became the foundation stone of his success.

'And what was that?' I asked as we continued to stroll along.

The Heinz boy, it seemed, was allowed to use the family kitchen garden for his own efforts. He sold off what the family didn't eat, and found that his customers wanted far more of his home-made horseradish than he could turn out. That was it, the key: housewives would pay for convenience. By the time Heinz was sixteen he had four people working for him and three acres devoted to horseradish. Another marvellously simple but effective idea had come to him – he bottled the stuff in clear glass to show that it hadn't been adulterated with grated turnips.

Sydney laughed with pleasure at the thought. We paused at a corner before crossing when I felt his weight suddenly pulling on my arm. He had gone white; he complained of sharp pains across his chest. They wore off after a few minutes. I was able to hail a passing taxi.

Sydney made no protest when I called a doctor to come right over. He was always perfectly sensible about something like that; he thought he should be as careful of his body as he would an expensive piece of machinery in one of his factories.

The doctor examined him, then said it would be checked out in the morning – but it was probably a mild heart attack.

'I doubt very much,' he went on, 'if it's anything to worry about. It's just a signal from your body saying you're pushing too hard – ease up, give me a little break.'

I felt cold as I looked at Sydney, the thought of losing him was more than I could bear. It's just a warning, I told myself, don't panic. Just thank God it wasn't one of those sudden killing attacks that come from nowhere.

7

'I'm afraid Lady Clark is unable to take your call, sir.'

Put-down time, Jonathan Browning thought. He thanked the golf club steward and rang off. If Muhammed won't go to the mountain, the mountain . . . He picked up the road atlas sitting on the corner of his desk and worked out his route to the St George's. It wouldn't take long and he'd be certain to catch her when she finished her round.

It had been a purely routine call he had made to the photo library, asking for any photographs on file featuring the late Sir Sydney Clark. You never know, there might be some sort of lead. So many things in his career, some scoops in fact, had come from simple luck, from stumbling over something at the right time.

The photograph had been one of Sir Sydney and his first wife, Mary, coming out of a building, King's College Hospital. Some freelance had been hanging around the entrance in case anyone important or famous came in or out. It had never been used. It had just sat there waiting in a dusty file in the library.

He pulled his battered Fiat into the car park outside the golf club, enjoying its contrast with all the shiny expensive cars waiting for their owners to return from their games. He slammed the door, walked over to the car he recognised as Diana's, and settled down to wait. Waiting: the common lot of journalists and policemen.

He had held the photograph in his hand for ages back at the library, with good old Malcolm breathing down his neck, waiting to be patted on the head like the good retriever he was. The other photograph was on the table, just a snap of Sydney walking into a building – it didn't mean a thing. He remembered how his eye had dropped down to the date stamp: 14 September 1971. September 1971! Of course! He remembered now. He knew all those hours he had spent going through back issues in the morgue would pay off. Oh yes, September 1971 was a very significant month for friend Sydney.

Mary Clark had proved as formidable as her photograph had promised. She had nearly managed to kill Browning over the telephone line with a few well-directed word-bullets. Not only had she refused to answer a single question, but had managed a half-dozen threats as well. I'll hear more there, he thought to himself.

Diana was perhaps a bit of a long-shot. But you never know. She was really too close to her subject for her own good – journalists, like nurses, shouldn't get emotionally involved with their cases.

At last he saw the flash of blonde hair as Diana strode out of the club, some slave tottering under the weight of her clubs. She looked better than she had in Düsseldorf. She really was an attractive woman.

He watched her eyes narrow when she recognised him grinning at her as she came crunching over the gravel. She opened the boot of her car for the clubs to be put in and then walked to the driver's door.

'You're becoming a nuisance, Mr Browning.'

'Only "becoming"?' he bantered – with just the right touch of Irish charm, he thought. He proffered the envelope containing the photograph, hoping to catch her attention. But Diana ignored it and started her engine.

'I got a lift down here,' he lied. 'I rather hoped you'd give me one back.'

'Sorry!' Diana smiled tightly and drove off.

Browning watched her go. He didn't mind at all – the hook had been baited. Another 'chance' meeting the next day, a drink offered . . . it would work.

And it did. The pub was nearly empty; it was midday after

all. He brought the glasses over to the table.

'Lager. OK?'

'Do I get a choice?' Typical of the man, Diana thought.

'Don't be like that. I'm doing you a favour.' He sipped his drink, then put the envelope on the table. He watched Diana look at it, then look quickly away. He gave her another moment of curiosity, and at last revealed the photograph.

'That mean anything?'

Diana told him it didn't, and asked how he had the nerve to keep pursuing her when she had made it quite clear she really had nothing to say to him.

Browning pointed out that she didn't have to have her drink. He raised an ironic eyebrow at her defence that she was only trying to protect her husband's name. He tapped the photograph and told her it was King's Cross Hospital, the date September 1971. Diana was quick to remind him that was before she had even met Sydney; she knew nothing about an illness. Sydney had never mentioned it to her. Why didn't he try Mary Clark? Oh, he had all right, but he hadn't got anywhere there. Diana was still fuming and accused Browning of trying to find a story where none existed.

'But there must be a story in it,' Browning insisted. 'You don't go into hospital for nothing ... or do you? Did he?'

Diana ignored the obvious insinuation. She asked if Browning had any other photographs up his sleeve. He admitted there was another taken about the same time, but it didn't seem to mean anything – yet.

Diana looked at the photograph again, more willingly this time, and then sat back as if she had found the answer. It was really quite clear she explained: there couldn't have been a story attached, otherwise the photograph would have been used. There were always photographers hanging around Sydney – they were often quite a nuisance. Browning agreed it might possibly be that simple, but ...

Diana was sharp. 'You have a nasty, twisted little mind.'

'Call it what you like, love. I live by my nose.'

'Will you please stop calling me "love",' she snapped. Browning made a gesture of apology. 'Well,' she asked after a minute, 'what does your "nose" tell you then?'

Browning outlined a theory: Sydney could have organised a false illness, easy enough to do if you had the money to pay a Harley Street quack. The timing was very convenient after all – he was sick just in time to be unable to give direct, personal evidence to the Government enquiry into that Malta property scandal.

Diana was astonished; she thought he was contemptible, cynical – and said so.

Not cynical, Browning claimed, just experienced. He had been able to dig into it, to find some facts. Sydney had been admitted for three weeks, and he had come out fit and well. Browning had been able to establish that nothing had been done to him, or for him. The point was that Sydney was probably playing for safety, or rather insurance, just in case things went wrong. It was quite a common phenomenon. There were enough public figures who had fallen back on some sort of convenient sickness to make this theory believable.

Diana was now very annoyed. The enquiry had made it clear that Sydney was exonerated; she remembered that much from the newspapers at the time. Government enquiries are very thorough, and they are unprejudiced – unlike some petty-minded journalists she could name, with chips on their shoulders.

Browning's smile was doubtful, knowing even. 'What occurs to me is that Sir Sydney didn't even know he was innocent ... until the enquiry said so. Smoke without fire and all that. There must have been something to suspect or there wouldn't have been an enquiry in the first place.'

Diana wasn't sure how to handle the situation; she had been a professional herself and her interest was aroused – a fact Browning obviously knew, and was relying on. One part of her just wanted to get up and walk out, but another part kept her in the chair. Their voices had risen and the only other customer in the pub was watching and listening to them with open interest.

Browning lowered his voice; he claimed it was something that had to be brought out. It would be all too easy for some reviewer of her book, or his, to refer to the Malta thing, to hint that the business wasn't as rosy as had been painted. Another thing that made him very suspicious was that Tom Vyner had stood up in the House and defended himself, and his friend Sir Sydney, before anyone had accused them of anything ... either one of them.

'My mother,' he went on, 'a wise old country woman, did always say that attack was the best form of defence.'

Diana had the picture now: Browning clearly was fishing – he knew nothing else. He had a half-formed suspicion, little more, and he was trying to see if he could get some clue out of her. A suspicious mind was the occupational hazard of the journalist; she was well enough aware of that all right. There was no point in staying any longer.

She stood up to go and drew her coat around her shoulders, gave him a curt, cold nod. 'Please don't bother me again.'

This whole business was worrying Donald Sanders greatly, and there were *two* of them. He had, possibly, some control over Diana's, but none at all over Browning's. Clearly strings would have to be pulled, the question was which ones, when ... and how strongly? And then the two Lady Clarks were no little problem either – first Mary on the phone and now Diana coming to see him. Mary had been very firm, as always – both books had to be stopped, she insisted, and that was that. She expected him to do something about it. And now Diana wanted to ask him one or two brief questions about that wretched Malta business. Dangerous ground – he'd have to be careful.

Liz Walters buzzed through on the intercom: Diana was here. He picked at his perfect tie-knot, smoothed a few non-existent hairs on the top of his head and got up to welcome Diana. He decided to move straight to the subject of her visit, so, sounding very plausible, he explained that as a public figure Sydney was inevitably involved in official enquiries. There had been several over the years.

'I'm interested in only this one, at the moment.'

'*At the moment!* You do make it sound ominous.' He tried to make the remark lightly.

He proceeded to give her the background, outlining how Sydney had made a large – private, he stressed – property investment in Malta. They were mainly holiday properties, very attractive ones. When all the talk started about kicking the British out, property values fell dramatically. Sydney had had the good luck, or foresight, to sell out in one big deal just before. The banks had made large loans to Sydney, and the Malta properties formed the main bulk of his collateral. If Sydney had still held them after the fall in values, well, the banks would have called for extra and Sydney would have been too stretched to comply. But it didn't happen, Sydney escaped the disaster by the skin of his teeth. Some people said that Tom Vyner – whose wife Diana knew so very well – had abused his position as a minister in the Commonwealth Office and warned Sydney about what might happen. And a good thing for her, too, as her own money would have been greatly reduced; Sydney would have had very little to leave her.

As for that stay in hospital, the timing was quite fortuitous. Sydney had suffered from a succession of colds; he was run down and the doctors advised him to rest. A supervised rest seemed the only way of making sure that he did. That was all. Sanders didn't know who the actual doctors were; Sydney had used several – and in any case he treated personal things very confidentially, as Diana well knew.

Sanders paused, and then decided the time was right to suggest to Diana that her book – and the waves it would make – might have some unfortunate consequences. It wasn't just a matter of looking for the truth – it could affect her money, and his; it would hit Jane and Charles, Herr Keller in Düsseldorf even, all the various families involved. The people who worked for them. The pensioners, the investors. He could see he was impressing Diana.

'Life's never simple, is it? Never straightforward.' He pressed forward his advantage. 'Has someone been suggesting ... hinting at things? What's happened exactly?'

Diana admitted there was a man, a photograph. 'Yes, it was Browning. Does it matter?'

'One likes to know the strength of the enemy.'

Diana paused. 'I think he sees himself as a friend.'

The road ahead looked blocked for miles, it was amazing how London traffic clogged up whenever it rained. She had allowed plenty of time to get to Harley Street for the appointment with Dr Whytaker, but now she might well be late. The taxi pulled suddenly into a side mews and then into another main street; that too was jammed. Diana sat back and tried to relax. She smiled as she recalled Sydney's advice for just such a situation: 'Remember', he would say, 'it's stupid to get worried, upset or angry at something beyond your control. Count to ten, sixty, whatever, and think of something else.' She did her best. She thought about Charles. At least he had come up with the lead to Dr Whytaker, the man most likely to have looked after his father back in 1971.

Poor Charles – so bright and friendly, so much in the shadow of a successful and dynamic father. He was drinking too much, she decided. She would really have to try to get him out of that. Get him into doing something. He did seem to be drifting since his father's death. Mind you, she admitted to herself, I did too before this damned book project came up. To be honest, I sometimes wish I had never started, but at least it does keep my mind occupied.

Charles could be so bitter when he was drinking, that same bright social wit that made him so popular could turn very ugly. He had challenged her last night to reason out why Sydney had been so secretive all his life; there must have been good reasons why so few things were really known about him. It was what was known as 'the unacceptable face'. He'd make a good bet that Sydney hadn't needed a rest at all at the time of the Malta enquiry.

'There was never anything wrong with him. He avoided sickness as studiously and effectively as he avoided income tax.' Charles had been pleased with that *bon mot*, and had virtually giggled. He had been equally as cutting about Sarah Vyner, one of Diana's best friends. Diana found her good fun to be with and they always laughed a lot together. Sarah didn't seem to worry about anything, took nothing seriously, was gay and witty. Charles obviously saw a very different person. To him Sarah appeared ambitious, the power behind the throne – the throne being Tom Vyner. He even described her as greedy.

At last, the taxi found a clear run and soon reached Harley Street.

Dr Whytaker was an old-fashioned doctor, ample girth, three-piece suit, with a nice-looking gold watch-chain in the perfect position. Very avuncular ... and clearly determined to give out as little information as possible. It was quickly established that Donald Sanders had already been through to him to tell him that he might be hearing from Diana. To warn him, Diana thought. The facts came out as easily as impacted wisdom teeth. Diana ground away at him nevertheless.

He did say that Sydney had come to him in a pretty run-down state, no obvious physical symptoms – but he was nervy, losing weight, his liver seemed out of sorts. It had seemed the best thing to send him into hospital for a simple rest. With a busy and successful man that was sometimes the only way. As Diana pressed him further, he became evasive again, though admitting that hadn't been the end of it. But it was long ago really; Donald Sanders was concerned that he shouldn't distress her. Diana was now getting impatient and insisted that she be told the whole truth. She refused the conciliatory offer of a drink, but Dr Whytaker helped himself to a whisky. His next statement was startling.

'When he was discharged from hospital my dear, it was recommended that he should see a psychiatrist.'

Diana looked at him carefully. 'What was his problem? I mean, why a psychiatrist?'

'I'm no expert in these matters,' the doctor answered, 'but I believe it was diagnosed as depression.'

Diana asked if this depression, if any depression, could have been caused by any one thing. She was informed that depression was usually pretty deep-rooted; a particular thing might well be the catalyst, so therefore it seems to be the cause.

When Diana enquired who the psychiatrist had been, Dr Whytaker became evasive again. He had obviously given her all the information he was prepared to.

Browning was able to discover the psychiatrist's name quite quickly, but he didn't realise the significance of knowing it. It came as a result of that other September 1971 photograph which he had uncovered at the photo library – the one of Sydney entering a building. It transpired the building was in Wimpole Street. It was occupied by five medical people: four gynaecologists and a psychiatrist called Geraldine Tonks.

Browning discovered something else significant when he was buying a thank-you drink for Malcolm, his contact at the library. Malcolm had received a memo putting an embargo on all material involving the late Sir Sydney Clark – all enquiries to be referred to the executive director.

He asked Malcolm if he could try and find out why that memo was circulated, though he didn't have much hope of Malcolm getting hold of the real reason. He'd make a good bet that Diana was behind it, directly or indirectly. The other day the photo had lain on the table in the pub through their whole chat. She was bound to have noticed the photo library stamp on the back, so she'd know their name. A little influence in the right places and ... The really interesting question was why Sir Sydney was going into that building. It would hardly have been to see one of the gynaecologists – that left the psychiatrist ... very interesting!

Malcolm offered his theory: an abortion. Sir Sydney was trying to arrange it for some girl-friend. The psychiatrist would say the bird was too stressed to have the kid, then she'd pop next-door to get fixed up.

Browning laughed; he doubted it. Clark wasn't the type to worry about his women's problems. In any case it didn't really fit in with the King's Hospital photograph – there might well be a connection between the two.

Diana had decided a nice lunch and a chat with Sarah Vyner would cheer her up immensely. She could bounce her thoughts off her; that robust and practical common sense of Sarah's was bound to disperse a few clouds. She asked Sarah if she'd known about Sydney's depression, but when Sarah said no, Diana got the feeling she wasn't quite telling the truth. Just some instinct, but then she had that feeling about everyone connected with Sydney. She'd better watch it, be careful she wasn't becoming a little paranoid about the whole thing.

Sarah did remember Sydney being a bit off-colour, but that was all really. She didn't like people being ill. If Tom got so much as a cold she had to go away for a couple of weeks.

'I wonder if Tom would know?' Diana asked.

'He might. I doubt it though. Tom knows very little about anyone except Tom.' The remark was made with a light-hearted grin as Sarah nodded thanks to the waiter attentively pouring the last of the white wine into their glasses. The bottle of Château Beaucaillou 1967 had been opened when they first ordered; they were both looking forward to it.

Diana said she wanted to ask Tom some questions about the Malta business, but was quickly warned off by Sarah. Tom wouldn't want to talk about that – in fact there had been quite a cooling-off between the two men after the enquiry. Previously they had played golf nearly every weekend, and often during the week as well. But afterwards all that had stopped. She really felt Mary might be the best person to ask.

'I hardly know her. Besides, she doesn't like me.'

Sarah laughed. 'Mary doesn't like anybody.'

'That's true,' agreed Diana.

The wine was as good as they hoped and they laughingly discussed whether a Kir each, a half-bottle of Montrachet and a bottle of claret meant that they shouldn't have a drink with their coffee. They decided it didn't, and ordered two Grand Marniers.

Suddenly Sarah asked Diana how her journalist friend was keeping. Diana confessed herself confused as to why Browning should approach her at all about Sydney being in hospital at the time of the Malta thing. If he was on to something surely he would save it as a scoop for his book. He'd drop the bombshell then.

'Precisely, Diana. There obviously isn't a bombshell. He's just trying to provoke you into saying something about Malta, in the hope that it might lead him somewhere. If I were you, Diana, I'd ignore him altogether. Browning will soon get fed up and leave you alone.'

Diana doubted this. 'Browning isn't the type to give up easily.'

'Then anticipate him,' Sarah insisted. 'Just refer to it in your own book, something along the lines that at the time of the Malta enquiry your husband had unfortunately suffered from a recurrence of depression.' She stopped suddenly and lifted her already empty glass. There was a change in the atmosphere as Diana digested Sarah's last remark.

'Recurrence?' she asked lightly.

Sarah seemed put off-balance for just the briefest of

moments. She mumbled something about only suggesting how it could best be phrased to indicate that the illness or whatever wasn't just a timely excuse. Anyhow, it would mean Jonathan Browning would have the carpet pulled from under him.

'You make it sound very simple, Sarah. I don't think it is, though.'

Diana signalled for the bill and wondered again about that little voice telling her that Sarah Vyner, one of her closest friends, knew more about Sydney's depression in 1971 than she was prepared to admit.

She was anxious to discuss it with Jane and Charles when they both agreed to stay in for dinner with her a few nights later. She put the casserole into the oven, Swedish Lamb with dill she called it, and went to join them in the living-room. Jane seemed a little guilty when caught glancing through Diana's notes for the book, which lay on the desk in the corner. Diana smiled at her stepdaughter to assure her she didn't mind, then asked Charles to fix her a drink.

'I'll get them,' Jane offered hastily. 'Brother dear must be exhausted, running to and from the bottle all day.'

Diana protested that was unkind; Charles was improving. He saluted her with his glass. Changing the subject Jane wondered about all this sudden interest in Malta.

'Malta,' Charles lectured, 'a dreary lump of rock, weighed down by strategic significance and the George Cross.'

Diana looked at him resignedly. 'I take it back, Charles. You've not improved at all.'

When they talked about the now-famous illness, Charles doubted it ever existed at all. Jane thought their mother could have been responsible: she'd have made his life hell if there was any hint of a scandal likely to come into the open.

'She couldn't have cared less,' Charles commented, 'as long as the money still flowed in. It's the only thing she really cares about.'

'That's a rotten thing to say,' Jane snatched her drink from the coffee-table and dived into her handbag, looking for her cigarettes.

'Rotten, maybe,' Charles shrugged. 'True, certainly. She never once complained about Dad philandering. She accepted all of it. Years and years of it.'

He glanced at Diana, embarrassed that he might have gone too far and upset her – something he wouldn't like to have done. But Diana didn't even blink, she was sitting curled up in her chair watching the exchange carefully.

Jane was certain that Mary had felt upset about the other women. Why else did they split up? Charles looked closely at his sister: that was the first time anyone had ever suggested so. When Jane stuck to her guns, Charles reverted to what he claimed was his mother's mercenary attitude towards life. After all, she had made sure she came out of the divorce on top. Sure she would have been upset if their father had been disgraced – but only because it would have depressed the share price, led to her dividends being cut. It would have hurt her pocket, not her heart.

This dispute had gone on long enough, so Diana intervened. Since neither of them could give her a definite lead on Sydney's depression she said there was no point in discussing it further.

Both Jane and Charles were surprised to hear the word 'depression' – they would never have believed their father capable of it. He just wasn't the type; he could bounce back from any problem. Charles, as usual, added a stinger: if it was depression it proved that maybe Sydney had real feelings after all. He also maintained that, as far as information was concerned, all roads led back to Liz Walters. Diana sighed as she got up to usher them into the dining-room for dinner. She realised that she would have to face Liz again. At least last time it had led to Düsseldorf and the clues about Sydney's war-time life.

She thought there might be a better chance of getting on with Liz if she saw her away from the office. Perhaps she wouldn't feel to defensive, so protective then. Liz's concern for Sydney's memory seemed a misplaced maternal one; it was an analogy that certainly seemed to explain her attitude – the mother hen protecting her chicks.

But when Liz did come to the house, Diana felt that familiar feeling of insecurity. She didn't know why it should affect her, but it did. She knew Liz felt superior to her, looked down on her. Sydney was always telling her not to worry about what other people thought of her, just be herself, do what she wanted, and to hell with everyone else.

Liz refused a drink, the 'in-control' Diana went ahead and poured herself one. It was what she wanted, so why not? She still wasn't sure how to handle the meeting, how to begin. Simply, she thought and so stated that she had a problem. Liz said nothing, just sat and waited. Diana mentioned the three-week period in hospital in 1971 – but still Liz said nothing. Diana persisted, explaining that it had been suggested to her that the time in hospital was somehow connected with the Malta business.

Liz finally spoke – surely Diana had discussed this with her husband? Diana patiently pointed out, yet again, that it had happened long before she ever met Sydney. She and Sydney had too much to do to spend time talking about the past. She too could be proprietary about Sydney, she thought. She added firmly that if it did have something to do with Malta she would want to say so in her book.

'If you do, you'll make a great many more enemies,' Liz claimed.

'*More?*' Diana was surprised. Was this how some people regarded her?

Liz ignored the question and contented herself with stating that if there was any implication that Sir Sydney had acted on privileged information it could have an unfortunate effect. She wouldn't say if he had, but if things did blow up there were some major pension funds quite capable of withdrawing their investments, and that would be very difficult at this time.

'Because they're told the truth?' Diana was unconvinced.

'Truth is a very relative thing, Lady Clark, isn't it?' Liz replied.

In defence Diana outlined her plan for the book – as well as telling the story of Sydney's life she wanted to show people the high pressures and demands of a successful business life made on a person, that it wasn't all champagne and Ascot.

Liz was quite cynical about this, about what people really wanted to know. The real truth and the truth people wanted to believe in were two very different things.

Diana tried again to persuade Liz to help her. The woman had so much information she could provide if only she'd stop being so stubborn. Perhaps a timely warning? So she emphasised that it was all more complicated than Liz imagined: for if she herself didn't write about Malta, somebody else probably would. In fact she was certain of it.

Liz looked hard at her. 'Sir Sydney always believed that when anyone tried to force his hand they were in a position of weakness, not strength.'

'You mean this ... other person really hasn't anything to go on?' Diana asked.

'Has he? ... or she?' Liz shifted in her seat.

Yet again Diana appealed to her to please tell what she knew: about the illness, about Malta. But it was to no avail. Liz just stated firmly that all she knew about Malta was to be found in the official report. As far as the illness was concerned ... she knew nothing at all.

Diana knew her temper was about to flare. She did her best to remember Sydney's dictum about anger, that it was a waste of time and energy, and therefore stupid. She even poured herself another drink as a way of counting to ten.

'I don't believe you.' Diana felt surer now. It was time to get a few things cleared up. 'There's something wrong about all this and you, and some other people, won't tell me a thing. It's because you all still resent my involvement in Sydney's life. That's right, isn't it?' She slammed her glass onto the coffee-table.

Liz was startled, and actually tried now to be conciliatory. She explained that she, and some others, had worked for Sir Sydney a long time. They were used to asking few questions of him, so it was difficult to give answers to other people. It was perhaps as simple as that.

Diana wasn't appeased. 'I'd've thought you'd rather help than see his memory muddied.'

'It sounds to me as if you're the one who's preparing to sling the mud?' Liz snapped back, her own taut control breaking for a moment.

The two women glared at each other; the daggers were truly out. Liz slowly got to her feet, intending to go.

Diana stood too, took a deep breath and tried again. 'Can you tell me *nothing* about his depression?'

Liz walked to the door, then hesitated – as if making up her mind about some thing. She glanced at Diana. 'I know that he was unable to cope ... with the demands being made on him.'

'By whom?'

It seemed Liz wasn't going to answer, then: 'I think you should ask Mr Vyner that.'

Diana was puzzled. 'Why Tom? Was it the Malta business?'

Liz's reply was brief, 'I didn't say so, Lady Clark.'

'You know,' Diana said as Liz got ready to leave, 'I'm not sure which is more frustrating. A dead man who can't speak, or living people who won't.'

Liz merely nodded farewell and Diana stood in the doorway for a moment watching the brisk figure walking away down the street. Tom Vyner had rung just before Liz Walters had arrived; he could give her a few moments later in the afternoon if she could come by the House. Perhaps he really could give some answers. Someone had to.

Diana had been to the House of Commons several times

with Sarah Vyner when Tom had been going to make a major speech. They sat up in the Visitors' Gallery and she had enjoyed the whole thing enormously. MPs worked all the time; it was no wonder their marriages broke up, many turned to drink and a number did die younger than they should. Politics were absorbing of course, at least elections were – Diana always stayed up till the early hours watching the television as the returns came through. And not just British elections; she found the same fascination with the results of each American presidential election.

Sitting on the bench she had been shown to, she watched the MPs rushing by, some faces familiar from television. They all seemed to be in such a hurry. Then she glimpsed Tom Vyner coming towards her.

The actorish voice, with the ever-present hint of false sincerity, sounded out. 'Diana! So sorry to keep you hanging about.'

The Division bell would ring soon; he just had a few minutes. He launched into what sounded like a prepared statement on the Malta affair. How the enquiry had completely exonerated him, how he knew nothing of Mintoff's intentions until they had been made public – and by then Sydney had sold the properties anyhow. That's really all there was to it. Oh yes, someone may have said something to him; he had a lot of connections in Malta at that time. Someone from out there most likely – who'll probably never be known.

As far as the book was concerned, it was really of no more importance than a footnote at the end of chapter thirteen or wherever. The Division bell rang and Tom jumped to his feet. Saved by the bell! Diana thought irreverently. Just as he was about to go Diana suddenly switched to his early connection with Germany.

'How much did it cost to get you out?'

'Cost?' Tom came back towards her.

It was, after all, a very long time ago and he was only six. There had been money, but it was money offered, not asked for. The whole thing was a costly business, and dangerous. He wouldn't be here now if it hadn't been for Sydney.

'Which gave him quite a hold over you, didn't it?'

Tom was very annoyed. He told Diana, very firmly, that was a terrible thing to say. There were many people who owed their lives to Sydney – if they had money they gave some certainly; it all helped. If they didn't Sydney still helped them.

'How do you know that?' Diana asked quietly.

'It's what I've always understood – and I'm quite sure it was the case.' He turned on his heel and walked quickly away.

Diana was becoming much harder in her thinking about the book, and the information she wanted. So many people – Liz Walters, Dr Whytaker, Donald Sanders, Mary Clark – had been so evasive, uncooperative and obstructive that they had now strengthened her in her resolve. If she had to get tough, she would. Mary Clark was as good as anyone to start with, she thought, as she sat in the plant-stuffed room and listened to the woman's bossy tone.

'I'm baffled', Mary was saying, 'that you think yourself capable of putting this book, this biography together after such a short acquaintance with my husband. But then you journalists are all the same, aren't you? Flip judgements, with little information . . .'

'I am researching thoroughly,' Diana cut in, in a no-nonsense voice.

'And yet, one incident,' Mary went straight on, 'and you're lost. How many more are there?'

'Quite a number, I've no doubt,' Diana came back at her, 'but at least I'd like to get this one right.'

Mary started to pour out some coffee for them. The teapot looked very good silver, the cups fragile and expensive – as was everything else in the room. Diana felt she could now understand what Charles had been going on about.

Mary's next line of attack was a hint that there seemed to be something going on between Browning and Diana – it seemed her suspicion was based on the fact that she found the man's manner too familiar. Diana knew what she meant there.

The illness was a surprise, Mary later agreed; it was so unlike Sydney. The psychiatrist was some woman called Tonks, ridiculous name. Mary seemed to bear quite a grudge against the lady. Before the so-called therapy there had been nothing wrong with their marriage, but afterwards . . .

Mary's good news was that Browning had been taken care of in a very neat way. It was what Sydney used to call being kicked upstairs: Browning was to be made features editor of his newspaper, the price was to abandon the book. Diana was flabbergasted to say the least. She supposed she should be relieved, but she still had the problem of what to put in her own book.

'I'd like to write the truth. Whatever it is.'

Mary held out her hand for Diana's cup and carefully refilled it. 'That's up to you,' she said. 'But when you do find it, I think you may well prefer not to publish it.'

The truth – or at least Geraldine Tonks's version of it – was a surprise. The psychiatrist had quite willingly agreed to see Diana, and she had Sydney's file waiting on her desk when Diana came into the office. She was a brusque lady – what Diana's father would have called a 'blue-stocking'. Her suggestion was that the cause of Sydney's depression was probably a woman. Diana was amazed; she could have expected anything but this. This didn't sound like the Sydney she knew. She started to speak of Sydney's reputation as a lady's man – but was interrupted.

Dr Tonks theorised that the woman in question was probably stronger than the others, a dominating type, less of a victim. She would wear the trousers in the relationship, so to speak. And that might have been a threat to his manhood; he was used to doing the ordering. The pattern was familiar: first physical symptoms, then depression ... taking the form of impotence and general anxiety.

Diana found this almost impossible to accept. 'I find it difficult to imagine my husband either lovesick or henpecked.'

Dr Tonks explained that female dominance could be achieved in a variety of different methods, even blackmail.

What about Malta? Diana thought. She hesitated. 'I think he had ... other worries.'

'Well, he recovered rather quickly,' the doctor went on, 'which led me to suppose he had probably disentangled himself from the ... affair.' No, she answered Diana's next question, she had no idea who the woman was. 'It was never mentioned. He was not the most forthcoming of men, was he?'

That mystery was solved a few days later, on the golf course. Sarah and Diana had been discussing Malta, when Diana mentioned Tom's explanation that he couldn't have told Sydney about Mintoff because he didn't know anything.

'Oh, that's not true,' Sarah blurted out. 'How do you think I found out?'

Diana stared at the other woman. 'You?'

'Well, of course. Who do you think told Sydney?'

Diana was dumbfounded.

'I thought you realised, darling' – Sarah shrugged – 'I was involved with him for years – well, almost a year anyway. He was human, you know – in those days.'

Sarah laughed, a nervous laugh – an apology. 'Why do you think Liz Walters hates me so much?'

8

I had been talking to Sarah Vyner for at least half an hour, enjoying her naughty gossip and wicked stories. The phone rang again as soon as I had put the receiver down. I hadn't moved from the desk.

'Darling,' Sydney said, 'it's all clear. They've done the final checks. Everything is 110 per cent OK.'

'You're not surprised,' I laughed. It was absolutely expected but I still felt a great sense of relief flooding through me.

'No, no,' he said, 'but it's nice to have it confirmed. More good news – I've been able to put things back or forward. I'm clear for the last two weeks of May and the beginning of June. It'll be a great time to be in France.'

It had been nearly a year since Sydney's heart attack. He had been quite shaken by it; he really had been one of those people who hadn't had a day's illness in his life. He took up the doctors' suggestions with the same enthusiasm he took up a new business project – watched his diet, exercised regularly, cut back on his drinking, cut his smoking to one cigar a day. Almost every weekend Tommy drove us somewhere into the countryside where we would spend hours walking along the public footpaths. We loved the Sussex downs and gradually worked our way along every suggested walk.

It seemed logical to buy somewhere in the country, somewhere for the weekends – but with a home office for Sydney too. His business interests were so far-ranging now that he really didn't have to go into Berkeley Square every day. All he needed was to be near a telephone. A place in the country would mean a tennis court, a swimming pool, some stables for us to keep a horse each. I had loved riding as a girl and found Sydney enjoyed it as well.

'If we found the right place, with enough space, your race-horses could come in the off-season. The change of air and surroundings would do them a world of good.'

Sydney agreed enthusiastically and we looked at everything on the market. Southdown Manor was perfect – it was just within a few miles from Glyndebourne too. That was important as we meant to use the Manor as a place to receive regular business guests from all over the world. Many of them would love being so close to the opera, especially the Germans. A lot of the southern race-meetings were within convenient travel distance too, yet central London was not an hour and a half away by car – even quicker by train. Part of the reason for our trip to France, aside from taking a simple holiday, was to find and hire a young chef. We thought we would do a gradual, gentle tour, driving ourselves – having only one meal a day in a recommended hotel or restaurant. We wanted to visit some of the wine châteaux in the Loire Valley, Bordeaux and Burgundy, in order to taste on the spot and meet some of the growers. We were going to buy quite a bit too – to stock up the new wine cellars we were building at Southdown Manor. We meant to lay down supplies for twenty years or more in the next six months.

'It's good investment sense, too,' Sydney would point out.

The trip was wonderful – the longest period we had ever enjoyed with just the two of us alone. We crossed to Cherbourg then travelled down to Nantes so we could head through the Loire Valley and then on to Dijon. From there we made our way right down through the Burgundy country, then through the Côtes du Rhône area. From Avignon we cut across to Cannes to stay for four days at the Carlton. Sydney wanted to be there for the last days of the film festival.

We then travelled right across to the Atlantic coast and back up to Cherbourg through the Bordeaux area, where we made many wine-buying stops. From beginning to end the trip took exactly three weeks. We had driven several thousand miles and spent £16,000 on buying wines, most of which – particularly the red – we couldn't start drinking for five, even ten years. We broke our intention of eating just one meal a day by having lunch several times – so we had twenty-five meals altogether. I was amazed and delighted to find that I had actually lost one single pound during the whole trip. Twenty-four of the meals ranged on a scale from excellent to superb. We ate at some of the great restaurants of France: the Barrier in Tours, Frères Troisgros in Roanne, the Pyramide in Vienne, the Moulin de Mougins in Mougins – they were all worth the journey. We kept a daily diary so we could remember every meal in detail, and also what the growers said about each wine we had bought.

Our final meal was at the Hôtellerie Lion d'Or in Liffre. I scribbled busily with my pencil.

'Sydney, forget the wine for Southdown, and the hotel and all the petrol – we've spent nearly £1,500 in restaurant bills alone. My God, come the revolution and we'll be the first to swing on the lamp-posts!'

His eyes crinkled, 'I'll die a happy man. This has been the best time of my life.'

We talked and talked throughout the whole trip – I think Sydney learnt every single thing I had ever done or known. We discussed our plans for Southdown at great length, and what I might do after they were completed. It would take a year to get it all together, we felt. Sydney talked for hours about the future of Clark Holdings, where it would go, how it should grow. He felt he had some of the answers for the problems facing Britain and wondered how he could implement them.

For a moment I worried that he might be thinking of going into politics – for that to come on top of his normal activity could be killing. The memory of the heart attack, that warning from the heavens, came back strongly. But Sydney laughed – an MP had so little power, so very little influence. No, the answer might be some sort of research institute, from which papers could be produced – the sort of thing Nelson Rockefeller had done in the States.

Looking back on this trip I realised that Sydney had never referred to his childhood, his early life – in fact he hardly ever went back more than a few years. He just wasn't reflective in that way. I did remember one thing he said about his childhood, about the only thing he ever did mention voluntarily. We were having croissants and huge cups of steaming café-au-lait in our hotel suite in Cannes. Sydney always had a glass of fresh orange juice as well, wherever he was.

'I visited the Tropicana plant in Florida once,' he said. 'In a giant cold warehouse they have piles of great slabs of frozen orange juice. They squeeze the oranges when the crops come in, then store it like that so they can send the juice all over the States all year round. They just melt it down as needed ... They looked like gold bars stacked to the ceiling.' He finished his glass, then put it on the table. 'Do you know, I was fourteen before I ate my first orange.'

I tried to ask him about it, just where it was that he had eaten it.

'No, that's it,' he said. 'That's the day's clue to the Sydney Clark mystery.'

'More like the year's clue,' I flashed back.

One day while in Cannes we decided on an early lunch, as we were going to see a film première that evening. We drove the Rolls over to the Oasis, at La Napoule just along the coast.

We had started with ducks' liver in aspic, then had oysters in a light champagne sauce, followed by salmon pastry with chervil. While we waited for the main course, I asked Sydney about the research institute – what sort of papers would it produce.

Sydney said the first one might be on North Sea oil, what to do with the revenue. Even though the research institute wouldn't be set up for a while, he thought he might commission a private paper soon after we got back to England.

'It's the perfect sort of thing for Southdown. We could have three or four experts down for a long weekend, give them some great meals, superb wines and hammer something together. I could then distribute it around some of the right people.

'As long as you approve of it,' I suggested with a grin.

Sydney admitted he did have some definite ideas, but others he was still formulating. 'Look, we're not Kuwait – with a tiny population. All the oil revenues from the proven finds, spread over every person in the country, comes to about £2,000 a head.'

'How many heads?' I asked.

'Some 56 million. No, the money doesn't go far when you think of it like that. But it is a bonus – we should use it as a catalyst, something to spark off a transformation of our economy into something like Germany or Japan. Those countries were in ruins twenty years ago – look at them now.' Sydney felt particularly strongly about personal taxation and exchange controls. People need incentive; they need to reap the rewards of their talent, of their hard work, he would say.

'If I hire a new top executive I always offer the same deal: he'll get only the salary he's getting in his present job, but he'll have a piece of the action. It's never failed. No one has ever said no – because it's the right incentive!' If exchange controls went in the right sort of atmosphere, it wouldn't lead to a flow of money out of the country; it would lead to a new investment empire, like we had in the nineteenth century; it would lead to the creation of wealth – not the dispersal of it.

Listening to him explain these sort of things made me feel as if I understood them. The sea was as smooth as glass as we crossed back to Southampton. It was warm, with hardly a breeze, and we spent the whole trip sitting in the sun on the upper deck, so we were quite glowing by the time we got to the other side. As soon as we had gone on board we went along to the restaurant, where we ordered sausages, bacon, eggs and chips with lashings of toast and hot sweet tea. It was so good we didn't speak for about fifteen minutes while we gobbled it up . . . anyone would think we hadn't eaten for three weeks.

We sat on the wooden bench, enjoying the sea air – not saying much, just holding hands. I've always remembered that time, it really was the last time we had together alone, before that terrible day.

Sydney had always a great deal to do; he had never been away from his businesses for as long as three weeks before. I had to go down to Southdown quite a lot with the architect and Laura Samuels. Laura had been suggested by Charles. Her main job was as a stylist on television commercials – she arranged the clothes, the settings and so on. She was one of those people who knew where to find anything. Her help was invaluable.

On one such occasion Laura and I stayed at Southdown overnight. Next morning we were enjoying a second cup of coffee after breakfast, out on the terrace, when the telephone rang. Laura went in to answer. She came back to say it was for me. Her smile seemed weak and forced. I knew something dreadful had happened. There was a pile of painters' ladders and things in the hall. I noticed every old drop of paint in sharp, sharp detail as I picked up the phone.

'Hello.'

'Diana, it's Donald . . . Sanders.'

'It's about Sydney, isn't it?' I put my hand to the wall, I felt dizzy yet my mind was clear. I could see, hear, feel everything with a stunning clarity. A film was going through my mind with maniacal speed, but the figures were moving in slow motion.

Sydney was dead. He had gone to Leeds for two days of meetings, so had stayed overnight. He'd left an early call, to be woken with orange juice, coffee and some toast. The waiter had knocked, then opened the door with his pass-key – Sydney had instructed him to do so in case he was in the shower. But the room was dark, the curtains pulled. The waiter realised something was wrong, and rang down for the manager. Sydney was still in bed. He looked – they said – as if still asleep.

It hadn't been his heart at all – a massive brain haemor-rhage, a small clot. Pressure had built up – then a sudden explosion. He had died in his sleep. He would never have known, or felt, a thing.

Sydney had left detailed instructions of what was to happen if he died suddenly or was killed. It had been well planned; everyone had some instruction – even Jane and Charles. However, there was nothing for me – it had all been set up by Donald Sanders about a year before I had even met Sydney. At that time he never thought seriously of marrying again. And then, after we had married, it never occurred to him to rethink because of me. Dying just hadn't seemed possible to him, I suppose. His will didn't even mention me by name: the last one had been drawn up soon after he and Mary had been divorced.

There was just one clause saying that in the event of his remarrying etc. his new wife would receive a set per-centage of his estate and an annual income, to be 'inflation-proofed'. Donald tried to explain it to me, but it took ages for it to seep through. My stake in Clark Hold-ings was worth about £2,000,000 at present market prices. Aside from the dividends on that, I would get the equivalent of £25,000 a year; and there was about £300,000 in cash, plus the London house, to be shared with Jane and Charles.

It didn't mean a thing to me. I went through the mo-tions mechanically, everyone was very kind, I was perfectly polite in return. The doctor had given me some sort of tranquillisers and I took one every four hours. It was al-most a dream world I moved in; I remember people saying things to me and not having a notion of what they were talking about.

About a week after the funeral, Ellen asked me about the pills, suggesting maybe I shouldn't go on with them. That night I flushed them down the toilet. Instead of the odd, sweaty, dry-mouthed sleep I'd been having, I found myself wide awake around three in the morning. I just lay in bed thinking and remembering. I had had everything – and now nothing. We had not even celebrated our second wedding anniversary.

The next morning I waited till just after nine – then I called the estate agent in Lewes and told him to sell Southdown.

9

Diana had been having trouble sleeping. The doctor suggested she try a medium-strong valium every night – just to relax the nerves. She had been reluctant at first, remembering the zombie-like state she had been in in the days after Sydney's death. But the doctor stressed that they were great tools if used in the proper way and not abused. Diana found that one at night, with a cup of hot chocolate just before going to bed, did help her greatly. She was sleeping soundly, though it did take a few minutes to come to again after Ellen brought in her breakfast tray – with the post and the newspapers. It was a Saturday, so she had slept later than usual. It was just past ten when Ellen knocked gently on the door and entered. Diana pushed herself up on the pillows and made ready for the tray. Ellen placed the post on top of the newspapers.

Diana took a sip of her orange juice and glanced up to see Ellen standing beside the bed, still holding one letter. She looked a little uncomfortable.

'What's that, Ellen? Overspending at Fortnum's again?'

Ellen smiled weakly. 'Well, no. It's addressed to Sir Sydney. It's been passed on from the office ... it's from Spain. I could send it back for Miss Walters to deal with.'

Diana frowned at the mention of the name and held out her hand for it. She'd deal with it.

Ellen delayed for a minute or two, then left the bedroom. Diana wasn't going to give her the satisfaction of witnessing the opening ceremony. She wasn't feeling in the best of moods.

The letter had been written in convulated English, with

all the flourish of the continental business style. Diana read it twice before she took it in.

It seemed to be about a flat in Mojacar, which Sydney had seen and bought last September. He had asked for certain work to be carried out. Apparently more was needed and the writer, who was the agent concerned, wanted instructions. The letter ended in the hope that Lady Clark was well.

Diana shut her eyes for a minute and tried to think back to September. She certainly hadn't been to Spain with Sydney. Nor had he for that matter, as far as she knew. She quickly pushed the tray aside and left the bed, pulling on her dressing-gown as she strode from the room. As expected, she found Charles lounging in the sitting-room, balancing a coffee-cup on his chest as he worked his way through the *Sporting Life*. He was planning to go off to Lingfield races later that morning. Diana thrust the letter at him. Charles read it through – then looked up at Diana. '*Non satis*, he needs to work on his English some more.'

'Damn the language, Charles. What's it about?'

'How should I know. I've never been to southern Spain.' Then he realised what Diana was concerned about. 'Ah, I take it you weren't there last September?'

'No, I wasn't.'

There was a silence while Charles thought. The best suggestion he could come up with was that Diana ring his mother.

Diana doubted whether that would be of much help, but went over to the telephone and dialled the number. Charles pointed out that the phraseology of the letter could be taken to mean several different things … it didn't actually say that this 'Lady Clark' was with him in September.

There was no answer, Diana dropped the phone on to its cradle and picked up the letter again. 'Look here, at this bit … "taking up residence" … I mean, the meaning of that's pretty clear, isn't it?'

Charles shrugged, it was all a complete mystery to him.

The letter bothered Diana for the rest of the weekend. She was due to see Donald Sanders first thing on Monday morning, so was reluctant to call him at home in case it looked like she was making too much of a fuss. There might be some perfectly simple explanation for it all. After all, asking after a man's wife was fairly normal behaviour. Only her suspicious mind made it seem more.

On Monday she reached the Clark Holdings building early and ran into Sanders in the reception area. As they waited for the lift she told him about the letter from Spain. He said he knew nothing about it.

'You know Sydney, Diana. He was a law unto himself.'

'But surely you'd know if it was a company flat, something to do with the business?'

Sanders was watching the floor numbers light up as they ascended, seemingly not listening very carefully.

Diana tried again. 'Could the company have bought it? Assuming it exists, of course!'

Sanders turned to her at last. 'Oh, do you think there's a mistake?'

Diana confessed she was thoroughly confused. She had checked Sydney's diary for the month. His only trip abroad was to Rotterdam, for an economic conference. They fell silent as they got out at Sanders's floor. He went through his morning routine of greeting people, then asked for some coffee to be brought into his office.

Once the door was closed he asked Diana if he could see the letter, glanced through it, and handed it back to her with a smile . . . as if he had the answer.

'Lucky girl, aren't you?'

'Lucky?'

'A flat in the sun you knew nothing about!'

Diana sat down and tucked the letter safely away in her bag. To her it seemed it was a flat she wasn't meant to know anything about. She shook her head at Sanders's suggestion that nothing could be more ideal, a nice little bolt-hole in sunny Spain.

'Donald, what about this "taking up residence"? That doesn't sound temporary to me.'

Sanders sat down behind his desk and glanced at Diana. Maybe she was jumping to conclusions again – a little too quickly?

Diana controlled her impatience. 'But, Donald, the lawyers have said nothing about a flat. It wasn't listed in the estate.'

Sanders echoed Charles's line – ask the first Lady Clark; but if Diana was worried about Sydney having been in Spain with another woman, she should remember that the letter didn't actually say there was a woman there. Asking after Lady Clark was probably just normal politeness. Sydney may have mentioned Diana to the agent; in fact he was bound to have done. There was really nothing more Sanders could do to help.

'Donald, at least try to find out if it *was* a company flat. Apart from anything else I need to know what the legal position is.'

Sanders sighed, then agreed. 'What about Liz? She knows all the secrets . . . past *and* present. Take your coffee over to her office?' He leant back in his chair and thought for a minute. 'Diana, there is something – a possibility at least. Perhaps he bought the place illegally, without Treasury approval. Go carefully.'

Diana nodded; it could be a very reasonable explanation. She picked up her coffee cup and walked towards the door. 'I don't suppose Liz was in Spain last September, was she?'

Sanders gave an ambiguous smile. 'Good heavens, Diana. What a thought! That's something you'll have to ask her.'

Liz Walters was engrossed in some heavy-looking business documents as Diana poked her head around the door. Her door was always left open – Liz liked to watch the coming and goings. She likes to watch everything, Diana thought to herself.

'Good morning, Liz. Do you know anything about this?' She took the letter out of her bag again and plonked it down on the desk, and Liz started to read it. 'After all, you know more than anyone else.' There was a sudden slight frown of concentration on Liz's face. 'About Sydney's various secrets, I mean,' Diana instantly regretted her bitchy tone of voice. Liz glanced up coolly, then returned to the letter. She read it a second time and silently handed it back to Diana.

There seemed little or no chance of information coming from this woman, but Diana wasn't going to give up easily. She pointed out that Sydney's diary indicated only one trip abroad that month – to the Rotterdam conference.

'I know,' Liz said at last. 'I was with him.'

'Were you? For how long?'

Liz didn't answer, just pressed her intercom button and asked for some coffee.

'What happened, after Rotterdam?' Diana persisted.

'Sydney had a private arrangement, if I remember. I could look it up.' She gave Diana a brief smile. 'I returned here.'

Diana tried to elicit what she meant by a private arrangement, but Liz claimed she couldn't say more.

'Can't say ... or won't say?'

Liz only gave an enigmatic smile.

'Well, would looking it up tell you anything?'

'I doubt it. When Sydney wanted to keep something to himself, he was very good at it.'

Diana was feeling thoroughly exasperated. 'Lots of us seem to have that talent, Liz.'

Liz got up and closed the door to her office. She looked like she was going to make a major policy statement. Her voice was calm and reasonable.

'Look, Diana, my relations with Sydney were confined to his business life, whatever else you want to think. He rarely discussed private matters with me. In fact, almost never.'

Diana finished her coffee. 'Well, *I* didn't go to Spain last September.' She could hear the petulance in her voice. 'I'm therefore wondering who did.'

Liz relaxed a little. She looked over Diana's shoulder and re-read the letter. The wording was ambiguous – wasn't it?

'Conveniently so?' Diana suggested. 'Liz, may I ask you? Were *you* aware of the flat? I certainly wasn't.'

'I can have it checked through our overseas property people—'

'But that's not what I asked, Liz. I asked if you knew of its existence!'

Liz evaded the question. There was such a great number of pies in which Sydney dabbled – she really couldn't recall. Perhaps it was one of those many little deals Sydney constantly got involved in. Hardly a week or a month went by when he didn't buy something, some property, some shares, and then sell a little bit later. He was a great believer in buying something he felt was undervalued, then selling it the next day.

She reminded Diana of those two occasions last year he had bought young fillies at auction, then sold them a few hours later because he had been offered an immediate twenty or twenty-five per cent profit.

'It was his Midas touch, Diana. This flat could have been the same thing. He bought it, telling the agent he was going to live there from time to time, when he had no intention of doing so. He probably thought he would make a quick profit in a matter of months.'

Diana nodded, there seemed some sense in what Liz was saying. 'Will you at least look into it, to see if you can find out anything at all?'

'Of course. Let me just make a note of this agent's name and address. I'll let you know what I can dig up ... if anything.'

Diana thanked her. She'd be with Sanders for an hour

or so, then back at the house late in the afternoon. As she reached the door, Liz asked if there was any news on what Jonathan Browning was up to. Diana shook her head gloomily. 'No, and I think that's something else to worry about.'

Jonathan Browning was on to something, of course. That same day he was having a second meeting with Roy Barnes, a long-distance lorry-driver who spent his time driving enormous container lorries all over Europe. Browning asked about the trips he had made to Rotterdam some four years before. Barnes explained that his number of journeys into Rotterdam were controlled: he had to get a permit for each trip . . . and he could only get so many of those a year.

Browning pressed him further.

'Well, it did mean I couldn't do half the work I wanted . . . not unless I could get through Rotterdam without having the docket stamped. If it wasn't stamped I could use it again, see. Two trips instead of one; maybe even three or four – if I was lucky.'

Browning's next question was about the cargoes he was carrying.

'It was mostly dairy produce,' Barnes answered.

'Which way?'

'How do you mean?'

'Export or import,' Browning explained.

Roy Barnes scratched his ear; it turned out it was both ways – all to do with the Common Market and the butter mountain business. Daft bloody system!

'Why Rotterdam?'

Barnes glanced shrewdly at the journalist. He said he thought there was a bit of 'how's your father' going on. 'Know what I mean. You could get away with the docket business there, more often than not.'

Browning offered him a cigarette, then asked casually if the butter run wasn't for the Clark Corporation?

'Don't ask me, old son. It's years back now. I just do the

work, don't I? If somebody wants something carried, I'll carry it.' He glanced at his watch, it was time for him to get back on the road.

Browning thanked him for the chat, then watched the lorry pull on to the highway. He grinned happily, he was feeling very pleased with himself . . . he was going to get some good stuff on old Syd this time. His next port-of-call would be the Clark offices, and a try at Ms Liz Walters. These icebergs could be well worth melting, sometimes.

The use of a casual threat or two, the promise of a story in the next day's paper proved enough to get him past the receptionist and into Liz Walters's office. Not that she was going to prove at all helpful, she was obviously determined to avoid answering a single question.

Browning tried to bluff. He told her he'd find all the information he wanted: it was a matter of a couple of days or a couple of weeks. It was up to her. All he was trying to do was to cut a few corners. Liz Walters smiled at him quite amicably; she was enjoying herself. She told him quite simply that she couldn't answer his questions. She also remarked that, in her experience, when journalists talked of cutting corners what they usually meant was that they were looking for a way to avoid the truth.

Browning tried to maintain the bluff, but without much hope. 'OK,' he said, 'if I get it wrong I can always blame Sir Syd's unhelpful friends.' He offered the Irish-charm grin.

Liz Walters drew herself up, her expression severe. For a moment Browning had a fleeting memory of Sister Mary all those years ago.

'I was Sir Sydney's personal assistant, Mr Browning, as you very well know. I now work with Donald Sanders. It is my duty to protect the interests of the corporation, not to supply the gutter press with salacious misinformation.'

Browning made a show of heavy mock surprise. 'Did I say salacious?'

'Whether you did or not . . .' Liz went on primly.

Browning interrupted her. 'Actually, all I was wanting to know was something about lorries.'

Liz was startled. 'Lorries?'

Browning made a few joking references to the old boy's womanising; the public had surely had enough of all that.

Liz ignored the humour. 'Just what do you want to know about lorries, Mr Browning?'

He turned serious for a moment. It was about lorries in and out of Rotterdam. In '73 and '74 Syd had quite a few of them trundling backwards and forwards across the Channel. He watched her carefully for any reaction. Then: 'You didn't know, of course!'

'Sir Sydney was often involved in business deals that had little or nothing to do with this office.'

'There must have been some paper-work done somewhere.'

'It is usual in commercial transactions.' Liz sounded pedantic.

Jonathan Browning tried to find out who might have done this paper-work; surely she had some idea. Perhaps Lady Diana Clark might?

'Is it necessary to distress Lady Diana with questions about things she knows nothing about?'

Browning's instincts quickened. 'Distress?'

Liz Walters explained that Diana and Sydney weren't married in 1973, so how could she possibly know anything of his business operations at that time.

Browning leant confidentially across the desk and gazed closely at her. 'And that'll distress her, will it? Upset her? If I mention lorries, she'll turn rather strange – gnaw the carpet or something?'

Liz looked at him calmly. 'Isn't upsetting people your purpose?'

Browning stood up again. 'I tell you what I'll do. You give me the name of Syd's contact in Rotterdam, and I won't go near the dear lady.'

But Liz Walters was unmovable. Sir Sydney had travelled all the time, all over the world. He had contacts everywhere. She really wouldn't know which particular contact he meant.

'Mr Browning, I'd suggest you come armed with rather more specific information, and a few genuine questions, if you want this office to be of any help.'

Donald Sanders suddenly appeared in the doorway, he apologised for interrupting – claiming he had thought Liz was alone.

'She is now.' Browning nodded curtly and left the office.

Sanders raised his eyebrows at Liz. 'Well, well. He seems a little put out. I knew he was here, of course. What a nuisance he is. What was he trying to find out this time?'

'Just peering for dirt, as always.'

There was a pause as Sanders looked around her office. 'Ah, this Spanish property thing,' he said at last. 'The one that Diana's come up with – mean anything to you?'

'I haven't had a chance to look into it yet.'

'I hope it's not going to give us a problem.'

'What do you mean?' Liz asked.

Sanders chose his words carefully. 'The Treasury people ... nowadays they seem more, ah, vindictive ... mischievous anyway. More so than they used to be. I hate to think we'll get one of those dawn raids, all those men taking away their black plastic bags full of papers.'

Liz thought for a moment, she nodded in agreement with Sanders. 'I don't think it was company cash, you know.'

Sanders pounced. 'You do know something.'

Liz ducked and weaved. 'I believe it was ... personal.'

Sanders smiled; he was satisfied. 'Well, let's leave it at that then. I mean, there's nothing I can do is there? Let me know if I can be of any help later on – if you need some, of course. Moral support perhaps. Diana can be somewhat ferret-like at times.'

After Diana had left Liz's office she had gone straight over to Philip Wilkins. She showed him the letter and told him

'The thing is, unless there was a strike or something, I was always booked through Rotterdam.'

Tim Croxley immediately pointed out that that was odd: it was neither the cheapest nor the shortest way.

'Exactly, Tim,' Browning stressed. 'That's why the whole thing stinks.'

Roy Barnes continued his story. The usual thing is you're hired to carry a load, you're told where to pick it up, where it's to go, and by when. The actual arrangements are left entirely to you. But not with the Clark people – with them it was specific sailings, in and out of Holland. Even though sometimes it meant having to wait half a day. The other thing was that there always had to be a sticker on the cab window, they were absolutely insistent on that.

'In and out of Rotterdam, always stick this flaming bit of paper up in the corner. Green it was. With a red stripe. Nobody ever seemed to take any notice of it, never was required by the paper-work. God knows that was complicated enough.' He accepted Browning's offer of the other half.

Tim Croxley clearly established that as Barnes went in and out of Rotterdam he managed to get through without having his transit licence stamped.

Browning clapped his hands with affectionate sarcasm. 'Well done, Tim. That's the whole point. Always the same place. Fixed times. Same official.'

Barnes nodded vigorously in agreement. 'Nearly always. Sometimes you had to wait a while if the geezer was busy. It used to nark me a bit. But what could you do? You couldn't get away with it with any of the others. Only him ... I mean, it was obvious. He was on the fiddle. Somebody was dropping him a hand-out.'

Croxley glanced at Browning. 'Clark, I suppose?'

Browning smiled. Did it need an answer?

Roy Barnes didn't know the official's name, or even if he was still there. He hadn't been to Rotterdam for two or three years.

The three men all drank deeply, another round was ordered. Croxley turned to Browning. 'It's worth looking into. I'll have a nose around. But even if it does gell, it doesn't prove anything about the Common Market.'

Browning laughed. 'Couldn't care less, me old mate. It's old Syd Clark I'm after.'

Roy Barnes looked at the two journalists nervously. 'Look, there's going to be no hassle, is there? I don't want no trouble.'

Browning reassured him. 'Don't worry, son, your name'll never be mentioned.'

The driver wasn't easily pacified. He did have a living to make after all. He wouldn't go into court or anything like that.

'You won't have to, that I guarantee.' Browning reached into his pocket and took out a sealed envelope. 'Here's the first half as promised. If it all checks out, you'll get the second in a week or two.'

Barnes had another two drinks, then left saying that he had to be off early in the morning with a load to take to Austria. The two journalists talked on about the seeming fiddle. Croxley couldn't understand why a million-pound businessman like Clark would get involved; how much could it mean to him? A matter of thousands maybe?

Browning was unperturbed. 'It's the mentality of the man – he was a gambler, you see. A thousand here, a thousand there . . .'

Croxley wasn't really listening. He was almost thinking out loud . . . 'You know, if you told me he was working something with vegetable oil, that'd be something else.'

'Vegetable oil?' Browning had no idea what he was talking about.

'Yeah – well, there were some abuses in the early Common Market days. It had to do with importing and exporting to non-EEC countries.'

Browning shrugged; maybe that was part of it. Who knows? No one ever looked into the flaming trucks. Good old Roy Barnes knew no more than the words on his pieces of paper.

'Anyway, Tim, I don't think I agree with you about the few thousands. If he was shifting the tonnage back and forth regularly, in thirty trucks, maybe even more, he could have netted a tidy old sum.'

Croxley ordered another round. Maybe the man was against restrictive laws. He was trying to find ways round them ... for the sake of increasing trade.

Browning slammed his glass down. 'Listen, I don't care what his motives might have been. He was crooked, however you look at it ... and that's what I'm after.'

Diana Clark had often wondered about the relationship between Sydney and Liz Walters. She felt it was natural to do so. Liz was an attractive woman, yet there seemed to be no man in her life. Sydney had been quite a womaniser, as he had admitted to her when they got married. It would never have occurred to her to doubt his faithfulness to her during their marriage ... except for this business over the flat in Spain. If only Liz was more forthcoming, trusted her more.

When she got home from Philip Wilkins's office she asked Ellen what she thought of Liz Walters. Ellen didn't say much at first, just commented that it was a funny question. Diana told her what the letter, the one from Spain, had contained. Sydney had obviously bought a flat for someone to live in, probably quite soon.

Ellen looked at her sympathetically. 'And you think that someone is Liz Walters?'

Diana sighed. 'I don't know, Ellen. Could it be her? I mean, would Sydney want to set her up in a flat? Does it seem likely to you? You saw them together over the years, many times.'

Ellen interrupted her sharply. 'Do you know what I think, and always have done? .. He wasn't very good with women.'

Diana was amazed. After a moment she laughed. 'I must

say, that's not the opinion I had formed.'

Ellen explained, somewhat awkwardly, what she meant. He was a clever man, of course, but he never could get away from his background. He never felt quite comfortable, not underneath. Oh yes, he was a good host, very popular and all that. But he felt he always should have a clever woman with him. What he should have had was a good, solid, hard-working, perfectly ordinary woman with no pretensions.

My God, thought Diana, Ellen's had a crush on him for years. She's talking about herself as the right person for Sydney.

Realising what she was saying made Ellen smile reassuringly at Diana. 'Mind you, you were good for him. Things were quite different after you came along. But you're an ordinary person at heart, same as me ... Well, you are, aren't you? Not like Miss Elizabeth Walters.'

'That's quite a speech, Ellen. And what about her?'

Ellen looked puzzled. 'I don't know really. She's an unknown quantity. There's lots say that there was something between her and, you know ... But what I always felt – why didn't he marry her, after he got his divorce?'

Diana felt a sense of relief. 'Yes, I've wondered about that, too.'

They both turned as they heard the front door open, then Charles ambled in.

'Hello, hen party ... or can any cock join in?'

Diana welcomed him and poured them all a glass of brandy.

'I'd like to arrange a dinner party,' she announced.

Charles looked at the brandy glass in his hand. 'And that's worth this snort of VSOP?'

'Ah well, there will be just four of us – Philip Wilkins, and Liz Walters.'

'Good Lord,' said Charles and took a large swallow of his brandy.

Ellen looked at Diana in amazement. 'Are you trying a bit of match-making?' Charles went on. 'Her and me?'

'She's not unattractive, Charles,' Diana laughed. She looked over at Ellen 'If it's in any way an embarrassment...'

'No, of course not. She knows I keep house for you, after all.'

Charles looked from one woman to the other. There were undercurrents here, he realised. 'What's all that about?'

'They used to work in the office together, as you know. We were just talking about it.'

Charles looked bemused. 'Well, of course I'll come, Diana, if you really feel you need me ... Diana, it's pretty obvious you're thinking of Liz as the Lady of Spain.'

Diana shrugged. 'Your father and she were very close – she was involved in all his deals. They were often away together.'

Charles laughed. 'Not in a million years, my love. The woman *worked* for him, that's all.'

Diana's voice was emphatic. 'They were away together last September.'

Women! Charles thought to himself. They can be like a hound worrying a dead fox. He began to feel a little annoyed with Diana. 'So it's going to be one of those parties, then, is it? The truth game between courses! It doesn't sound like a very good idea to me.'

'But you'll come?'

'I've said I shall, so ...'

Diana smiled. 'Well, let's just see what happens, shall we? She may not accept!'

Liz Walters did her best to dodge the dinner party invitation – Tuesday was no good, nor Thursday. Well yes, a week Friday would be fine ...

The evening did not go very well. From the beginning the conversation was stilted, forced. Everyone trying a little too hard.

It turned out that Liz went to Greece every year for her

holiday. She loved the islands particularly.

Charles's quick wit couldn't resist the obvious. 'Lesbos, you mean . . . somewhere like that?'

Diana glanced sharply at Charles. Naughty boy! Liz Walters, however, took the question as perfectly straight-forward.

'My favourite', she said, 'is actually a very small place called Psara. Quite difficult to get to, but well worth the trouble.' And so the conversation continued – through dinner, the sweet course and on to the cheese. As the wine flowed, Charles was able to relax completely. He talked amusingly of his role in life as a wastrel, a chinless wonder, without a social conscience. He suddenly directed a question at Liz: 'What about you – I mean, where are you going with your life?'

Diana, the perfect hostess, suggested that Liz had done pretty well already. Charles went on to explain what he meant was: What next? What was open to her?

Philip Wilkins took up the bait. 'Yes, the Stock Exchange has its women brokers. And you? Chairman of the Board, something of that sort? Or should I say Chair-person?' Everyone laughed.

Charles asked about marriage, the effect that had on a woman's career? Diana quickly protested that it shouldn't make any difference at all . . .

'I agree,' Liz broke in, 'but then I made my choice about that long ago.'

'Choice?' Charles questioned. 'Is that the word? I wouldn't have thought so. You don't have choices where biology rules.'

Liz looked at him for a moment. 'Charles, you surprise me. Marriage has little to do with biology these days.'

Charles took her point. 'But commitment, whatever you like to call it, does start with biology.'

Liz gave a slightly smug smile. 'I think I can survive without entangling myself in someone else's biological needs.'

'And if the perfect person appeared? Tomorrow?'

136

Liz spoke quietly. 'It's my belief that women do have that choice. I'm not sure that men do. Not yet.'

Charles walked around the table, refreshing everyone's glass. Then he asked Liz to explain what she meant.

She took a deep breath. She was clearly about to describe the keystone of her personal philosophy. 'If a woman chooses a career, she can elect not to marry; or to get involved with anyone. Her career – not someone else's – becomes her life ... Now can you honestly say a man is capable of such a clear-cut, hardline choice?'

Charles still couldn't see her point. 'Hasn't he always been?'

The burden of Liz's argument was that if biology ruled anyone, it was the man. It was men who cling on to the old primeval urges. A woman is different – she can say 'No, thank you'. Nor was that an admission that a woman couldn't manage both a career and a marriage. 'It's men who are bad managers. That's why they demand so much attention – when they are married.'

Liz paused. She realised she had the floor, but she felt committed. 'Charles, too many men are like you ... thinking that women are incapable of any kind of genuine achievement in their own right ... as if our only way to success is through the chairman's bedroom.'

The silence was awkward. Liz knew she had touched on something about which everyone at the table had either thought or spoken. Even Ellen, busily clearing the last of the cheese plates, had frozen. She dropped her challenging stare, and made some effort to return to being a polite guest. 'I suppose that's why I'm so attached to Greece. After all, it was the first nation to realise and protest against the subjection of women.'

That seemed to be the end of that.

'Lovely meal, Diana,' Philip Wilkins stated. Liz echoed him. Diana suggested coffee and brandy or whatever in the lounge. As they pushed back their chairs, she asked Liz if she had had a chance to look into that Spanish flat ...

'Yes, I did.' But she said no more.

Charles and Philip Wilkins watched the exchange warily. There was a long pause.

Diana said she'd love to see it. 'Where is Mojacar exactly?'

'Near Lorca, I believe,' Liz answered.

'Is that in the south?'

'South-east. A little above Almeria.'

Diana became a little too effusive. She talked about the delicious mystery, this lovely flat. Someone quite mysterious was going to move into it. Perhaps a complete stranger, perhaps someone they all knew. She turned to Wilkins.

'Sydney, apparently, bought some flat in Spain and gave it to someone . . . and no one has any idea who.'

Wilkins made a gesture of bewilderment. He was embarrassed by Diana's drawing him into the charade.

'I adore Spain,' Diana went on. 'All that sand and sun.'

Liz said that much had been spoiled for her – the tourism and all that. It made it rather trendy, rather boring. Then she looked hard at Diana.

'So I'm afraid – whatever you may have thought – that it won't be me moving to Mojacar. It's not my kind of place at all.' Her smile was sweet.

So was Diana's. 'It hadn't occurred to me that it would be you, Liz.'

'No?'

'Sydney's taste, at least in his private life, seems to have been for animated, impulsive, vivacious people. That's not your style either, is it?' Diana instantly realised she had gone too far. She started to babble about a nice Sandeman '63 port she had asked Charles to decant for them, even though it might be a year or two before its prime.

Liz Walters looked pointedly at her watch. 'I ought to go.'

Diana protested: 'Surely, not yet. Besides you haven't told me what you've found out, about the flat.'

'Very well. Sydney did buy it – but not for the Company.' She looked at Wilkins. 'Though I'd have thought

Mr Wilkins would have found that out by now ... Sydney bought it in the name of Walters Holdings.'

Liz enjoyed the variety of expressions on the faces of the listeners. She told them that it was something he did from time to time when he wanted his name kept out of a deal. He had done it, for instance, when he bought Langton Road, where his father had lived.

The dinner party was clearly over. Liz insisted she must leave. She had to get up early to go down to the country for the weekend. Diana saw her to the front door, then came to join the two men in the drawing-room. Charles had poured them both some of the port.

Philip Wilkins greeted Diana with a smile. 'You could almost hear the blade whistling into one's back every time that woman smiled.'

Diana laughed as she sat down and asked Charles to pass her port. 'You must admit, though, she was rather good – the way she stood up to you two like she did.'

Charles commented drily that Liz wasn't exactly unaware of what Diana was up to.

'Yes, I know,' Diana agreed. Then she apologised to Wilkins for inviting him with an ulterior purpose: 'I just wanted to get a man's reaction to her.'

'She's very intelligent, very capable,' he replied. 'But she doesn't attract me, I must say. I find her rather frightening. She makes me feel mentally inferior, at least she makes me think she believes I am.'

'I know just what you mean,' Diana replied. 'But tell me – any news from Spain?'

'No more than you heard from the lady herself. The agent was surprised when he saw the name on the property deeds – you know, now that we do have that name there are a number of other deals coming to light, all over the place. I'm afraid there are going to be some awkward financial questions to deal with.'

'What about this mysterious, prospective tenant?'

'Nothing yet. Maybe in a day or so.'

A few days later Tim Croxley was able to report his findings back to Jonathan Browning – they were disappointing. It had been possible to match the arrival times the lorry driver had given them with the customs officers' duty rosters. There certainly was one man who stood out as a common factor. He was the only one working then who was on duty every time Roy Barnes had come into Rotterdam.

At this Browning was elated, but his smile soon disappeared as he saw the grimness of Tim's face.

'Here's the bad news, old son. This man – look, here's his name,' he passed Browning a piece of paper, 'retired last September. Then a week later he got killed in a car crash. A lorry hit the cab he was in.' Browning let this news register for a moment. 'Christ! It's so bloody frustrating. I know I've got Clark on this one . . . but I need the proof.'

Tim Croxley grinned. 'Is it a biography he's writing, I ask myself, or a charge sheet.'

'Very funny, Tim. It's all right for you, but I'm into big money with this book. Big money and big dirt.'

Tim apologised. He agreed there was obviously a big fiddle going on. Millions of green pounds going astray. But there seemed to be no way to prove that Sydney Clark was involved.

'Unless I can twist Roy's arm.'

'Come on, Jonathan. You heard what he said, he didn't want to get involved . . . and you did promise to keep his name out of it.'

Browning signalled for some more drinks. He looked down at the long Dutch name on the piece of paper. 'It's not on, is it? You don't get killed on the day you retire, for God's sake.'

'Well it wasn't the same day exactly – it was about a week later.'

'What's the difference?' Browning raised his eyes to the heavens, or at least to the roof of the pub. 'Syd Clark's even got Him sewn up.'

Tim Croxley sifted through his notes again. He revealed that the dead man's colleagues had said the man was going on a cruise as soon as he retired. Maybe he might have saved all his life for it – apparently he was a bachelor. But there was a good deal of cash on him. His passport too, but little else. No addresses, no travellers' cheques. There seemed to be no relatives either, or close friends. 'Where do you go from here, Jonathan?'

On the Wednesday after the disastrous dinner party, Diana was in Donald Sanders's office when Liz buzzed through to say she had some news on the Spanish flat. The two of them quickly crossed the hall to Liz's office. She showed them a letter that had just come in. It seemed Sydney had bought the flat as a business favour, 'for services rendered'. A Spanish lawyer had a letter to that effect. Sanders rubbed his hands. 'Good, that's that ... rather rubs out your unsavory theories, Diana, doesn't it?'

'I'd hardly say the mystery was solved, Donald.'

Sanders said at least it was clarified; anyhow he was satisfied. He had to go back to his office, so he gave a cheery wave as he left the two women.

Diana asked Liz whether she couldn't have already given her that piece of news herself.

'No. I couldn't. As I've said before, Diana, Sydney had a lot of secrets he kept to himself. Even from me ... and it didn't make for the easiest of working relationships either, I may say.' She picked up her internal telephone, then groaned.

'They say Jonathan Browning's here again. Apparently it's very important: to do with Sir Sydney.'

'Do you mind if I stay?' Diana asked.

Liz smiled quite warmly. 'Of course not.' She gave instructions for him to be sent in.

Browning raised his eyebrows in surprise when he saw who else was in the office.

'Ah! Two birds, as they say. Well, Miss Walters, it's about lorries again.'

141

'I thought I'd said all there was to be said on that subject the last time you were here.'

'Not quite all. I've found out what the great man was up to, you see. He had a little scheme going with a customs man in Rotterdam.'

Neither woman seemed surprised or distressed to hear this news.

'I even know the man's name.' Again there was no reaction.

'I wouldn't want to get the facts wrong, in the book. So perhaps you could give me some dates.'

Liz Walters clasped her hands on the desk in front of her. She reminded Browning that she would give no information unless he showed he had evidence of genuine knowledge.

Browning tried hard to bristle with confidence. 'Oh, I can do that, all right. I'll give you the name. You tell me where and when Sir Sydney met him.'

Liz frowned. 'I'm not clear why you want to know if, as you say, you've already established a connection between Sir Sydney and this man.'

Browning sighed, then spread his hands in defeat. 'Never mind. Forget it. I wasn't winning on this one anyhow.' He looked at Diana. 'I've been chatting up container-drivers. Blokes your husband had under contract ... One told me of a regular little fiddle, in Rotterdam. About someone who was exploiting loopholes in Common Market legislation.'

Diana arched an eyebrow. 'You make it sound rather petty. Are you sure my husband would have been interested?'

'I know he was. Unfortunately the man, Van der Soest, was killed in a car smash a few months ago. Name mean anything?'

Both women shook their heads. They had never heard the name.

Browning turned to go. 'Never mind, something else

will turn up. The Clarks of this world don't stop at Rotterdam.'

After Browning left, Diana picked up the Spanish letter and handed it back to Liz. They grinned at each other.

10

Diana's next dinner-party was a few weeks later. As Ellen cleared the plates and the remains of the toast and guacamole, Charles launched into an elaborate Jewish-dialect joke, naming his father as one of the participants. Diana watched him with an amused expression, Jane looked impassive and unamused. Donald Sanders was diplomatic, Liz Walters slightly uncomfortable.

Charles's Jewish accent was quite good. Diana and Sanders laughed easily, Liz's reaction was a tight smile, while Jane continued to look stoney-faced.

Sanders glanced at Jane. 'It was quite funny, you know.'

'Have a care, Donald.' Charles was still flushed with his success. 'She still hasn't found a replacement figure for her father fixation.'

Jane looked at him disdainfully. 'When did you join the National Front?'

Charles laughed sarcastically, then a flash of inspiration came: 'I took over Dad's life membership.'

He could feel the atmosphere change; his wit had crossed the line into bad taste. But Charles was completely unrepentant. 'Oh dear, have I overstepped the mark?' He couldn't have cared less.

Diana lifted an eyebrow. 'Didn't you intend to?'

Charles lifted his wine-glass to her in a semi-mocking, semi-admiring admission of defeat. He took a large swallow.

'I'm afraid Donald and Liz bring out the worst in me.'

Liz looked at Diana; her voice was a bit too loud. 'Well, obviously you must have invited us for a reason. I wonder when you'll tell us what it is.'

Charles grinned villainously, and tried his German accent this time. 'You still haven't squirmed for quite long enough.'

The pad down at the vegetable-market end of the Portobello Road couldn't have been a greater contrast to the luxury of Diana Clark's dining-room, with its silk canopy making it look like something from the Sheik of Araby. The furniture was old and unmatched; the walls covered with alternative society posters. In one corner a young man was working on a long table covered with silversmith tools. A large girl was sitting on some cushions on the floor, listening to the music. She was smoking a carefully prepared joint, she was at peace with the world. She hardly seemed to be listening to the lean young man, very brown and with a neatly trimmed blond beard, who was thumbing through the London A–D telephone directory.

'You know how many S. Clarks they got in here?' The voice was American. The girl was American too. 'Anyhow, the lady won't be listed,' she said. 'There's a special operator for unlisted numbers. You could try that.' She took a drag, then held the smoke deep in her lungs before she slowly released her breath. Then she handed it up to the man, who took it and began to take a long drag himself.

The girl stretched luxuriously. 'They'll ask her if she'll take the call ... but why the hell should she, Gerry?'

Gerry was making a Japanese tea-ceremony of it: several small puffs then a long, long, slow pull. 'She's gonna have to. 'Cos I'm not going to stop ... until she does.'

Diana and her guests were on the sweet course. She had decided that the time had come to tell Liz Walters and Donald Sanders why she had invited them.

They seemed taken aback at her opening remarks. Sanders was amazed, or pretended to be: 'Deliberately obstructive? Good God – no!'

Diana's tone was challenging. 'Are you claiming that

145

you've always been completely open and frank with me?'

Sanders started to protest, but Liz cut across him. 'No! She's right. Why deny it?'

The whole table argued for a few moments, the frustrations of the last few months rising to the surface and bubbling over. Liz turned to Diana, a high colour on her face.

'Just because you're married to him – what rights do you think that gives you to poke and pry? *None*.' She looked away for a second. 'I had more of him than you. And for longer. We had a life together – nine, ten, eleven hours a day. We talked about things that he would never dream of discussing with you. Shared things he wouldn't share with you. He's dead ... and now you expect me to turn all these memories over to you as if you had some sort of right. Well, they're *my* memories and I don't see why I'm under any obligation to share them with you.'

There was a stunned silence. Everyone was amazed at Liz's uncharacteristic and emotional outburst, by the vehemence of it. Liz looked down at the table, then asked if she could have a glass of water. Diana moved to the sideboard and poured one out. She brought the glass back to Liz, and made an attempt to re-establish her ground. 'I'm a writer; researching the subject for a book.'

Sanders echoed her quiet tone: 'The fact is, you're obsessed by him, Diana. The book's become an excuse ... and obsession hardly encourages objectivity.' Then he became pure diplomat. 'If Liz and I have seemed less helpful than we might have been, I'm sorry. It's because we've been concerned that you might put the wrong emphasis on things. Inevitably certain actions ... well, on the surface ... they might appear underhand ... unethical.'

'Illegal?' Diana's voice was crisp and sharp.

Sanders was unabashed, and went straight on to say that that could indeed be an impression. Unless one understood the context in which that action was taken. And that was difficult to explain to a newcomer. It would be like explaining a new VAT booklet to a layman.

Diana was angered by Sanders's bland condescension. She hated that; in her view, his behaviour and Liz's was simply explained by their determination to save their own skins. They were the Kitchen Cabinet after all; they had the influence – they could steer Sydney.

Donald and Liz spoke together: Donald denied it; Liz said someone had to.

Charles was enjoying their discomfort, a broad grin on his face. Jane snorted that the two of them were the 'unacceptable face of capitalism'.

Sanders felt distinctly hounded: 'And what about your father?'

Diana decided that the time had come for her to explain why she had invited them to dinner; then the telephone rang and she paused, until she heard Ellen answer it.

'The chapters of the book,' she announced, 'covering your dealings with Sydney are finished. Tonight I'm going to give you both copies, which I'd like you to read ... and then I should like to know if you intend to sue.'

She rose from the table and offered coffee and liqueurs in the sitting-room. She did not see the quick, wary glance exchanged between Sanders and Liz – but she could feel it. And it made her smile.

Ellen stopped her on her way to the sitting-room to tell her that a Gerry Dole, American voice, had rung. It meant nothing to Diana; she shrugged. As Sanders and Liz followed her in, Diana went over to her desk. She picked up two folders sitting on top. She gave one each to them and asked how they wanted their coffee. They both ordered black, and sat down holding the folders, as if they had been served writs.

'Supposing ...' Sanders hesitated, 'that there are things we're not too happy about?'

Diana was quite calm, and confident. 'Then it all becomes rather heavy, doesn't it? Solicitors, injunctions, publicity ...'

The word *publicity* hung heavily over them. Then Charles brightly suggested a brandy. But Liz had had enough. 'I don't feel like anything, thank you. I think I'd just like to go.'

Sanders rose at the same time. 'That means me too. I'm her taxi,' he explained. The telephone rang again as Diana started to show them the door, but Ellen must have been somewhere where she couldn't answer it ... it rang and rang. Finally Diana couldn't ignore it any longer and answered it herself.

The soft American male voice commented that she was a hard person to get hold of, that there was something they should talk about, something of great interest to her. Diana asked him to clarify himself, eyeing Sanders and Liz, who were watching her with open interest and curiosity.

The man on the phone just stated that they should keep it between themselves for the moment. Diana was about to put the phone down when he stopped her.

'Hang on, lady. Just listen to this. If you think you were only the old man's second wife, you're wrong ... 'Cos what I know makes you number three.'

Diana paused then she said: 'It's a little inconvenient to talk now. Ring back in fifteen minutes.'

After seeing Sanders and Liz off into the night, she paced the room anxiously waiting for the phone to ring again. She picked it up on the second ring and took down the rendezvous instructions – near Marble Arch, at lunchtime the next day.

She had been told to look for the 'guy' selling silver belt-buckles at the Marble Arch underground station. The only possibility was a long-haired man sitting with a girl, both in dark glasses, seemingly oblivious to the world passing by them.

Diana approached them. 'Excuse me, are you Gerry Dole?'

The man laughed and shook his head, the girl got up and smiled in a friendly way.

Diana felt a little irritated, and a little confused. 'He said if I came here . . .'

The girl nodded. 'That's right, come on.' Diana hesitated, it all seemed a little cloak-and-dagger for her. But the girl gave her a lovely smile: 'I'll take you to him,' she said.

Diana hesitated, then followed after her. She didn't notice the man take off his glasses and watch intently for several moments to see if anyone was following. Satisfied that there wasn't, he began to dismantle his display. Diana had to run to keep up with the girl's fast pace. She didn't seem quite so languid now.

'This's all rather elaborate, isn't it?' she complained as they paused beside a folk singer strumming a guitar and singing a plaintive little lament.

The girl gestured, 'That's him.' She smiled again at Diana. 'Nice to have met you.'

The singer finished his song, then unslung his guitar and picked up the leather cap on the concrete, with a few coppers glinting dully. He half held it out to Diana, who just stared at him.

'The song?' he shrugged. 'Or the way I sang it?'

Diana gave a 'teeth-bared' smile. 'Both. Actually.'

Gerry Dole was quite unoffended and led the way to the central area above-ground, with the fountain and a bit of greenery. She could hardly hear him above the roar of the traffic around Marble Arch.

He told her about a German woman called Eva Bosch, who was married in Berlin in March 1938. She had got out of Germany in 1939 and come to America. He had met her a few years before in a funny-farm in California, where he was working to escape the draft. He had got very friendly with her. She gave him a book, *The Magic Mountain* in German, just before she died. Sometime later he had been looking at it and discovered a marriage certificate stuck under the back fly-leaf. It said she had got married to a guy called Sydney Clark. Meant nothing to him, not until he read in *Time* magazine about some big British financier dying. So he wondered, and started checking. Bingo! Diana's Sydney Clark and the Sydney Clark in Berlin were one and the same man.

Diana said she would want to double-check the story. If it was true she'd certainly be interested in buying.

'How much do you want?'

Gerry Dole told her she'd better not hassle. He could go elsewhere … he was looking for the best offer over ten thousand pounds.

Diana was shocked. 'Don't be absurd. Even if it's authentic, it's hardly worth fifty.'

Dole nodded and smiled. 'Except that Eva and your husband were never divorced.'

Ellen could tell something was up the way Diana banged into the house, carelessly throwing her coat on to the nearest chair. She walked over to her desk and picked up the now-heavy folder containing the pages of the book so far. She shifted it in her hand as if she was weighing it. 'Trivia,' she muttered under her breath. Ellen tried to tell her that Jonathan Browning had rung; so had Marjorie Reynolds from her publishers. But Diana didn't want to talk to either one of them.

'What on earth's happened?' Ellen asked in a bewildered voice as she picked up Diana's discarded coat.

'I'm not altogether sure,' sighed Diana. 'Be a darling and pour me a drink will you?' Diana picked up the phone and dialled a number; when she was connected she asked for extension 383.

She quickly told Morris Birley that she wanted a favour. She wanted him to use his Foreign Office influence to find out if a woman called Eva Bosch had married an Englishman in Berlin in 1938.

As she rang off, Ellen handed her a sherry. Diana's face confirmed what Ellen had hoped was only a bad guess.

'I don't believe it,' she said.

Diana was just managing to be wry. 'I'm trying not to.

Have a drink with me. Ellen, it's even more complicated than that. Worse. So not a word.'

Donald Sanders and Liz Walters had both read their copies of the manuscript as soon as they got to their homes after leaving Diana's house. They managed to clear their morning appointments the next day so they could discuss it.

Liz felt that she actually came out of it better than Sanders, and that was not saying much. But one thing was certain for both: Diana wasn't going to get away with it.

'I don't know that it's actionable,' Sanders said; he ignored Liz's disgusted sniff. 'She's very experienced with words.'

Liz was scathing. 'You and I both know solicitors who could successfully find libel in a wedding invitation.'

Sanders was worried about the publicity: widow hardly out of mourning and they were clobbering her with writs – which was exactly what Diana was counting on, Liz suggested.

'She's also counting,' Sanders said in a matter-of-fact voice, 'on the fact that most of it is basically true.'

The intercom buzzed. The secretary's voice told him Lady Clark was on the line.

Sanders glanced at Liz, then told the secretary to put her through. He flicked a switch so Liz could hear the call as well.

'Diana' – Sanders was the consummate liar – 'My dear, I haven't even read it yet. I'm sorry but ...'

Diana wasn't thinking about the manuscript. She wanted to know if Sanders could recommend a private investigator. At first he suggested cynically that she look in the Yellow Pages, then he relented and admitted that Sydney had used someone once or twice – he raised a puzzled eyebrow at Liz's near-frantic wave of her hand.

'In Victoria. Gough and somebody ... Gough & Bennett, that's it. Well, as long as you don't turn them loose

on me. Or Liz.' A somewhat barbed joke, he felt. Liz shook
her head; she really wished Sanders had not given Diana
the name of Gough & Bennett. But she was not going to
say why. She rose to go. 'Donald, let me know when you've
decided what you think we should do about this wretched
book. Only let's not leave it too long, shall we?'

Diana was surprised by the Gough & Bennett offices. She
realised that what she had expected was a seedy private-
eye's office, from a lifetime of Hollywood films. This office
was very modern and elegant: subtle tones of brown and
beige, steel and black leather furniture – smoked glass
tables. She found herself sitting opposite a well-dressed
man of about forty. Mr Gough seemed to be ex-public-
school, maybe army, SAS or something like that. He
looked physically powerful. And ruthless. The shape of his
nose indicated that he had taken up boxing for a while as
a younger man.

He was explaining that he had never actually met Sir
Sydney; the business was always conducted through his
personal assistant – a very efficient and charming lady.
Diana asked if there had been much 'business'?

Gough smiled delicately. 'Whatever there was ... still
enjoys the same degree of confidentiality you'll find extended to yourself.'

Diana realised she was now meant to explain what she
wanted. She wondered where to begin as she watched
Gough obviously switch on a recorder. She started by saying she wanted to find out about someone ... a Gerry Dole.
She wanted to know as much as could be discovered. All
she could tell was that Dole was young, early thirties at
most, and American. He had worked once at a mental
hospital in California; he played the guitar. She didn't
know his address; he was in London at the moment ...
she had reason to know that.

'Oh yes. If you can find where he worked in California,
I'd like to know if there was a patient there, at the same
time, called Eva Bosch ... And then I'd like to know if

he's ... how can I put it, if he's ... vulnerable.'

Gough's interest was sparked. The hunter's gleam came into his eyes. 'You know that our services are not inexpensive?' He gently reached forward to switch off the recorder. 'Particularly if we need to do things which might be ... slightly illegal.'

Diana's voice was quiet, flat. 'Money isn't a problem.'

Diana wasn't the only person Gerry Dole had contacted. He had done his research very well and knew there would be other interested people. Jonathan Browning for one – newspapers could pay a lot for this sort of thing. And then there were the two children, Jane and Charles. The fact that Sydney had never been divorced meant that his marriage to Mary was bigamous; they were illegitimate. How would this fact affect their trust funds?

Jane and Charles determined to raise some money as quickly as they could. Their problem was that they could realise very little in their own right. Jane wouldn't come into control of her money until she was twenty-five, Charles had to wait until he was thirty – it was a lack of faith in him by his father he had never really minded before.

Jane's response was to approach Donald Sanders, as senior trustee, to ask for three thousand pounds – in order to buy a new car, she said. He pointed out to her that she already received some four thousand pounds a year as an allowance – married men with children had to live on that. And she lived rent-free: no food bills, no rates, electricity or gas to worry about. Sanders enjoyed his moment greatly; he had had to live with her sneers for a very long time. Finally Jane stomped to the door, crackling with anger and frustration.

Sanders had the last word. 'You'd better learn to hate the privilege that money gives you as much as the way it was earned, or you'll make a pretty pathetic socialist, my dear.'

Jane slammed the door as she went out, leaving Sanders

smiling for some moments. It was beginning to look like a very good day for him.

Charles's solution was one of direct action. It was easy enough to sell the car. Tommy Meadows helped him get a fair price. The silver would be, well, just borrowed for a few weeks. There were no dinner-party evenings planned for some while, so it wouldn't be missed.

Unfortunately, Ellen happened to walk in just as he was searching for those George III pieces his father had once told him were the choice of the collection. His excuse about looking for a clothes-brush sounded lame even to him. Ellen had looked at him very oddly as he left the dining-room.

Later he and Jane were arguing fiercely about the respective merits of their efforts when Diana walked in on them.

'Do you know,' she said, 'I can hear you two halfway down the drive. What's it all about anyway?'

Jane's sudden inspiration of saying they were arguing about a flat Charles might buy, and Jane's share, didn't convince Diana. She felt rather tired, so she wasn't too pleased to hear that she had a visitor—Jonathan Browning. He had already been given a drink by Ellen, but Diana topped it up. Browning quickly told her he knew about Gerry Dole, and the supposed marriage certificate. Presumably the idea was for them to bid against each other. Browning was having a stringer in Germany check it out. Dole could be a con-merchant. She must be doing the same thing? Might it not be a good idea if they pooled their resources?

Diana gave him a small, perceptive grin. 'Why? Can't you afford his price?'

'I'd rather not have to,' Browning answered, then went on to explain that was why he had come. He was seeing Dole tomorrow. Browning wanted to know if he and Diana could work out a deal first.

Diana was careful to be casual. 'Where are you meeting?'

'South Bank, outside the National.'

Diana asked him if he would publish. Browning had to say he would. Sir Sydney Clark bigamously married for thirty years ... he couldn't ignore that. He put it to Diana that she couldn't either, if she was honest.

Diana reminded him that it didn't directly affect her. She married Sydney in 1976. Eva Bosch had died in 1975. Her marriage was absolutely legitimate ... but it could affect several others: Jane and Charles, for example.

This didn't bother Browning greatly. 'Most kids seem to get by without inheriting millions. You and I had to.'

'We weren't brought up to expect it,' Diana remarked coolly.

They continued to argue the pros and cons, the responsibilities of the biographer to tell the truth. Eventually Browning left promising Diana that he would give her a ring when he had actually seen the certificate.

Diana thoughtfully finished her drink, then dialled the number Gough had given her in case she had any new information. She quickly told the man that a journalist called Jonathan Browning was meeting Dole the next day somewhere by the National. Yes, she had Browning's address. Gough was pleased.

'Well now, I think we can safely say we're in business ... Yes indeed.'

The Gough & Bennett operation worked beautifully. The girl had picked up Browning as he left his flat and followed him to near the meeting-place. She had guessed correctly that her best vantage-point was from the pedestrian walk on the Hungerford Bridge. The long-distant view-finder on her camera could keep close tabs on Browning's meeting with the girl. She was able to follow him through the view-finder to where Gerry Dole was waiting – the silversmith had no chance of carrying out his assignment: to look for signs of anyone following Browning. The Gough & Bennett girl was able to get in six quick exposures within seconds of Browning meeting Dole. It was no problem to stroll casually near to where they were talking, and then to follow Dole as he left.

Dole led the way back to the Portobello Road. The girl was dressed in jeans and a donkey-jacket, a voluminous tote-bag slung over one shoulder. She looked totally at home in that area. She observed Dole go into the house. There could only be one flat above the shop. She walked by, then stopped and scribbled the address on a scrap of envelope taken from her pocket. She walked back to the door and rang the bell.

The girl who answered the door was the same girl who had escorted Browning to the meeting at the National.

'Hello, I'm Janice Cox,' the Gough & Bennett girl stated. 'About the dog.' The American girl looked puzzled, then Janice explained she had rung about the Labrador puppy, the one advertised on the notice-board at work. There was only a bewildered reaction ... Obviously, a mistake had been made. Would it be possible for her to use the phone?

So it proved easy to gain entry.

Gerry Dole was delving through his rucksack, seemingly sorting out what needed washing and what didn't. He looked at Janice with great interest as the American girl explained there was a mix-up over some addresses: she was looking to buy a puppy and was going to make a call to see if she could get the correct address.

Janice was a superb actress. She dialled her own number and then waffled on pretending to ask someone to look for a certain piece of paper. She smiled nervously at Dole once or twice, she was attracting his interest, which pleased her – it would make the job easier.

She hung up, to find Dole on his hands and knees, barking – then sticking his tongue out and panting heavily.

Janice laughed. 'They can't find the number. So I'm never going to solve it, am I?' She started to move towards the door, taking her change purse out of her bag to pay for the call.

'Forget it,' Dole said, then gestured towards the kitchen. 'Hey, we don't do dogs here, but she does great pizzas.'

Janice gave him just the right touch of a seductive smile, and said she'd be delighted to stay.

After his meeting with Dole, Browning had gone to the first telephone-box he could find and called Diana. They met in a pub near her house, Diana thought it would be better than her house, with Jane and Charles likely to come in any minute.

Browning bought a pint of beer for himself and, without asking, a dry vermouth for Diana. He told her that he didn't read German, but the piece of paper had certainly looked old and authentic. Unfortunately there was no way Dole would let him have an expert examine it.

Diana played with her glass. 'I don't believe he lied,' she said. 'He couldn't have lived with a lie like that. It wasn't Sydney's way.'

Browning's voice was almost gentle. 'But can you prove it?'

Diana looked at him sharply. 'You've decided, haven't you? ... Guilty.'

'Running out of options.' He sounded almost regretful. 'Adds another dimension to the man.'

Diana gave a slightly bitter laugh and remarked that it was easy enough to convince yourself of something if you wanted it so. She didn't know what she was going to do, but when she did decide it was going to be her decision and no one else's.

Janice Cox was delighted at the way the assignment was going. The atmosphere was very relaxed and Gerry Dole had already told her a great deal about himself. He had been talking mainly about his travels around the world.

'It must have cost a fortune – flying all over the world!' Her voice sounded innocent enough, but it was a probe. How did he pay for it?

Dole and the American girl looked at each other and

giggled. 'He's got a credit card,' she said. 'He always uses credit cards.'

Janice pretended not to understand, then glanced at her watch and commented on the time. She got to her feet with an obvious show of reluctance; she had to go.

Dole got up too, and said he'd walk her to the tube. He winked at the silversmith as he shut the door. The message was clear: don't expect to see me till the morning, folks.

Diana's own investigations weren't going very well. Morris Birley rang through; nothing had turned up in Germany. But that didn't prove anything – records could have been shifted around, or destroyed, because of the war. The truth probably would never be known.

She was about to give Ellen the news when Charles walked in and asked if he could borrow her car for the morning. Diana was surprised to hear that his was in for a service.

'I thought you'd had that done, a week or two ago.'

Charles seemed a bit ill at ease. He mumbled something about a part not in stock; the garage had to wait for it.

Asking him to remember it was her car, not his, that he was driving, Diana tossed him the keys. After Charles left she was about to tell Ellen the news from Morris Birley at the Foreign Office, but she could see the other woman was worried.

'Ellen, I can tell something's up. What is it?'

'I think he's not being honest with you.' It was as if Ellen instantly regretted her words. She hesitated. 'It's just ... I understood that he'd sold it.' She explained that Tommy had told her; he had gone with Charles to make sure he got the best price. And there was something else she felt Diana should know.

'There's a quantity of antique silver missing from the dining-room.'

The two women stared at each other for a minute, then Diana quickly walked from the room down to the garage, just as Charles was about to climb into her Mini.

'I've changed my mind,' she said coldly, 'in case you try to sell this one as well!'

Charles stood still by the car. 'That perfidious little runt,' he said bitterly.

Diana crossed her arms and stared at him. 'If you're referring to Tommy – he didn't tell me.'

'Told someone though, didn't he?'

When Charles explained that he had needed the money, his flippant tone annoyed Diana.

'Look, I don't like being lied to,' she said, 'and I don't like thieves very much either.'

Charles sagged against the car; so she knew about that too. 'I only pawned the silver. I didn't sell it,' he offered as some sort of consolation. He refused to tell Diana what sort of trouble he was in, just that he owed the money to a fellow. He allowed her to jump to the conclusion it was a gambling debt. When Diana called him idle, indolent, irresponsible, Charles just shrugged.

'Get the silver back,' Diana stated in a quiet, flat voice. 'I don't care about your car, but the silver doesn't belong to you. If your creditor isn't satisfied, tell him to come and see me. The balance can come out of your next year's allowance.'

'Don't leave a chap much dignity, do you?'

Diana was ice-cold. 'Is stuffing family heirlooms up your jumper what you call dignified behaviour?'

Gough's file on Gerry Dole was impressively full of papers and photographs. He told Diana that Dole didn't seem to have an actual police record, but he had masses of credit cards he used to travel around the world. The only trouble was that he never paid the bills – there were at least three investigators looking for Dole on behalf of major American credit-card companies.

Diana wanted to know what kind of person Dole was – if he deserved what she might have to do to him.

Gough thought for a minute. 'Usually my operatives

don't meet our clients. It helps to protect your anonymity, you see. But the young lady responsible for this has got to know Mr Dole remarkably well.' He pressed his intercom switch and asked the receptionist to get Janice Cox to step in for a moment.

When Janice walked into the office she was looking at Gough and didn't see Diana. Then Gough asked her for a thumbnail sketch on Dole. Janice turned towards Diana and, for the briefest of seconds, a look of alarm crossed her face. She recovered well.

'Er, he can be a lot of fun. He's very selfish. Amoral. Opportunist ... but charming, quite gentle. I don't think he means any harm to anyone, but he does leave a trail of mayhem behind him.'

Diana looked closely at the girl – there seemed to be something familiar about her.

'Haven't we met before?' she asked. The girl said she didn't think so. She glanced at Gough, who had just realised his error. There wasn't a thing he could do about it.

'It was when I was selling my flat,' Diana went on. 'You came and looked at it three or four times. You wanted to take a lot of measurements, to see if your furniture would fit ...'

Janice shook her head. 'I'm sorry, I don't remember.' She gave a quick smile and left the room. Gough tried to smooth it over.

'That's happened to me so many times. You're absolutely convinced, and yet ...'

Diana cut across him. 'It was her. Did my husband hire you to investigate me?'

Gough shook his head.

Then Diana remembered. 'Of course. All his business was conducted through his assistant. Liz Walters. Bitch ...' Diana rose to go.

Gough put up his hand to stop her. 'Before you go,' his voice had become very formal, 'I think you'll be interested to see this.'

He pushed across a photograph, obviously blown up, of Gerry Dole. He was talking to Jane Clark.

In the taxi back to the house, she felt guilty about the way she had spoken to Charles in the garage. It was quite clear now what he had wanted the money for. When she got home she found Jane and Charles there together. She told them about Dole approaching her – and they told her their story. They had hoped to scrape together enough money to buy the certificate and then to burn it. Diana said how distressed she was that they hadn't come to her, but they explained that they just didn't know how she would react.

Inevitably they discussed what they might do now. Jane and Charles were worried that Diana would use the information, which could seriously affect them. The Trust Laws tended to be puritanical. Who was to know what some clever lawyer might pounce on? Diana now felt wretched; she was having a tussle between her conscience and moral honesty. 'If the book isn't going to be honest ... there's no point in going on with it.'

There was a long pause.

Charles was bleak. 'Well, that's it, then.'

'You don't give a damn about us!' Jane accused her.

Diana was very unhappy. 'But I do!'

Charles went to the door. 'Don't waste your breath,' he said over his shoulder.

Jane followed him, then looked back at Diana. 'I'll go on the streets to get the money before I let you get your hands on that certificate!'

As she rang the doorbell at the Portobello Road house Diana felt she had worked out the best answer to Gerry Dole: a compromise package of some cash and some threats.

Dole seemed quite surprised to see her. Diana explained that she hadn't ten thousand pounds available. Dole

snorted in disbelief – neither did Jonathan Browning ...
nor her stepchildren.

'I'd be willing to give you two thousand, which you'd
be well advised to accept.'

Dole looked up at her. 'Or else? Come on, lady. You
keep hinting at something. Let's have it.'

Diana indicated the American girl watching and listening. She pointed out that his friend's visas had expired
eighteen months before – if immigration caught up with
them, need she say more? As for Dole himself, he was
wanted for fraud. Her offer of two thousand was therefore
very generous.

'Or you blow the whistle on us?' There was a smirk on
Dole's face. 'That's really nice and dirty.'

'No dirtier than what you were doing.'

'All I was doing was holding a sale,' Dole defended
himself.

The American girl was getting nervous and urged Dole
to tell the lady what had happened. Diana began to feel
a little uncertain – the American seemed so confident, so
unworried by her threats.

Dole grinned at her. 'Would you say it looked like I'm
getting ready to split?'

Diana looked down at the packed and bound up rucksack with a dawning sense of unease.

'Wanna know why?' Dole went on. ' 'Cos you're too late,
lady. I already sold it.'

Diana went straight home. Her first thought was to ring
Jonathan Browning. She knew it couldn't have been Jane
or Charles who had paid up. Browning was quite cool, and
slightly sarcastic. He claimed it had nothing to do with
him.

Diana put down the phone with a puzzled expression,
just as Ellen looked in to announce that Liz Walters had
arrived.

Liz Walters seemed apprehensive. There was now none of

that self-confidence that had used to annoy Diana so much. She apologised for just dropping in like this. As a matter of fact she had driven around the house several times before she decided to risk it. And it wasn't about the book.

'Ah, of course, You've been speaking to Mr Gough,' Diana supposed. 'I thought he might call you.'

'I want to explain.'

Diana asked if she please would.

It wasn't easy for Liz. She tried to explain that she had done it for Sydney really. She had wanted to protect him. That was her job. Perhaps she had overstepped the boundaries.

Diana almost laughed. 'You mean you mistrusted his judgement. So you thought you'd double-check.'

Liz was very embarrassed. 'I suppose . . .'

The two women talked further, though it was very painful for both of them. Liz tried to explain that she only had Sydney's best interests at heart, but Diana resisted this. Her feeling was that Liz was trying to protect her investment in Sydney. Behind every great man . . . ?

Angrily Liz pointed to the manuscript on the desk. 'Everything you've said about me in that book is maliciously inspired. I wonder how you'll treat *this* story?'

'I won't treat it at all. It's not important enough. And it didn't involve Sydney. Whatever's in the book is the truth. It's my duty to write the truth.' Even if it was not complimentary to Sydney, she hadn't shirked from it. Diana hesitated as she remembered her confused state of mind over the supposed marriage certificate Dole possessed. She still didn't know quite what she would have done with it if it had come into her hands.

She reaffirmed that she was telling only the truth. If she took that policy towards Sydney, she could hardly do less with Liz.

Liz's voice was soft. 'Don't you think it's a little unfair using the same yardstick for the living as the dead? You can't hurt the dead ones.'

Diana thought for a moment, influenced by what Liz was saying. It was reasonable enough certainly. 'I'll ... look again at what I've written.'

A hint of relief crossed Liz's face.

The matter of the mystery buyer of the certificate was cleared up when a cheery Charles breezed in later that afternoon.

'Who else should a chap turn to than his own dear mother. Some blood is thicker ... after all.'

Diana decided to ignore the slight barb. She rang Mary straight away.

Mary had bought the certificate for far less than the ten thousand asked, but then she had been able to tell Dole the good news about Diana hiring private investigators to find out about him, so he really hadn't much choice. Then she had burnt it. She found out from Dole – once the money was safely in his possession – that the marriage had been purely one of convenience, to help Eva's family get some of its money out of Germany. Eva Bosch had been Jewish. The marriage had never been consummated, so Mary assured Diana.

Diana was about to say goodbye when Mary asked a sudden question.

'What would you have done with it?'

Diana swallowed hard. 'I'd have destroyed it.'

11

The small man seemed nervous. He had been standing for hours watching the entrance-door to the small block of flats. He was awkwardly holding a long package wrapped in brown paper. His eyes were constantly on the first-floor windows, where the curtains were still closed. He had been waiting for Charles Clark for four days outside the Clark House; then finally Charles had turned up in a taxi. He was laughing and suntanned, with a pretty girl and expensive-looking luggage.

The man was just getting close enough to make his move as Charles dumped two bags inside the door. But before he could react, Charles had popped out again and jumped into the taxi, in which the girl was waiting. Then, it had moved off.

The small man just had time to catch the girl's instructions: 36 Queen's Gardens, Bayswater.

Luck had been on his side when he reached Queen's Gardens. There was a small balcony at first-floor level, and Charles and the same girl were standing there in the late-afternoon sun, drinks in hand.

The man decided to wait . . . it was a long night. He had planned what he was going to do. A glance at the name-tags beside the bells had told him the girl's name was Suzanna Michaels. He had written this carefully on a label tied to his package – and the address.

Everything worked out perfectly. A middle-aged lady had come to the door and stopped to sort out the morning post. She was only too willing to open the door to him and point the way up to the right flat.

The girl had opened the door, dressed only in bra and panties – a T-shirt in one hand. The man was embarrassed, the girl amused.

'Yes?' she asked.

'Sorry,' he said glancing at her, then looking away again quickly. 'I've an important message for Mr Charles Clark.'

'But how did you know he was here? You're not a divorce detective are you?' She laughed. 'And I thought he was a single man.'

'No, no,' the man answered, then inspiration struck, 'Lady Clark gave me the address. Mr Clark left it with her yesterday. He was expecting me, you see.'

He looked harmless enough, she thought. How very strange. She shrugged and opened the door for him to come in.

'Make yourself at home. I'll just go and see if the master is awake.'

The girl pulled on her T-shirt as she walked towards the bedroom door.

The man mouthed a 'thank-you'. He looked around the room as if he wasn't sure of his next move. He noticed the door had a highly-mounted mortice lock. He suddenly reached up and turned the key; removed it and pocketed it. He then walked around the room several times, trying each of the armchairs. All the while he kept hold of the long brown package. Just as he was about to settle on a straight-backed chair by the desk, he jumped to his feet, went over to the windows, and pulled the curtains shut.

He then resumed his seat, propping the parcel on his lap. He felt for something through the paper with his right thumb. He found what he was looking for and rested his thumb in position.

Charles came into the room, still rubbing the sleep from his eyes, a bath towel wrapped around his waist. He was very brown.

'Who on earth are you? I never left this address.'

'Mr Clark, ah ... I'm very sorry, but you're kidnapped.'

Charles looked at the little man with amazement, then

shook his head with a disbelieving smile. 'Are you an urban guerrilla?'

'Please don't make jokes. I'm here to right a terrible wrong. Your father cheated one of the best men who ever lived out of £50,000. Unless you give me the money, I'm going to blow my brains out with this shotgun.' He gestured with the long brown parcel.

There was something so sincere in his tone that Charles was inclined to believe him. He sat down gingerly and remarked that he didn't usually carry that much money on him.

'I am not a fool,' the man continued. 'You are to pick up the telephone and call Mr Sanders. Tell him what I've just said and that my name is Timothy West. He is to call Archdeacon John Francis and tell him the whole situation. The Archdeacon knows the story. We'll wait here until Mr Sanders rings back.'

Charles was very intrigued. He turned to the girl with an apologetic smile. 'I think I'd better do as I'm told, Suzanna.

She nodded, biting her lip as she glanced back at Timothy West. His face was wet with perspiration; he was either very nervous or very warm. She heard Charles dial a number, identify himself, and ask to be put through to Donald Sanders at once.

It took him a little while to make Sanders grasp the facts, then to agree to do as requested. He dropped the phone and looked over at West.

'He's checking you out, as you asked.'

West nodded nervously. He gestured to his sweater. 'Do you mind. I'm a little hot.' He gripped the package between his knees and pulled off his polo-neck sweater, revealing a clerical collar underneath.

Suzanna shot Charles an enquiring glance. He shrugged in reply.

West looked at Charles. 'You can get dressed if you like.'

'He's showing off his suntan,' Suzanna tried a smile.

'Picked that up on holiday, did you?' The man was being very polite. The Caribbean, Charles explained.

West said he had wondered where he was. 'I've been waiting for four days now. The sun's lethal out there I've heard say.'

'Thirteen degrees north of the Equator,' Charles agreed. They exchanged a few more pleasantries. Then Charles made an attempt to ease the tension.

'This is ridiculous,' he laughed, 'you don't really mean to use that shotgun, do you?'

'I assure you that I do.'

Sanders had been stunned by Charles's phone-call. His first thought was that this was one of Charles's inane pranks. But then look what had been going on in Italy over the last few years. He himself had often said that the kidnapping trend might come to London one day. It could be the real thing; he daren't take a chance. He jabbed at his intercom.

'Get me the address and phone number of an Archdeacon John Francis – someone at the Church Commissioners' office might be able to help.'

It took only ten minutes to trace the Archdeacon. He was based in London, it turned out, and Sanders gave him all the information he had.

'What can you tell me about this Timothy West? Is he dangerous?'

'He's one of us. I mean he's a curate,' the Archdeacon replied. 'I had no idea he was so disturbed. I knew he was distressed – that's why I suggested he took a six-month sabbatical at Masham Abbey. I'd like to make some telephone calls. Can I ring you back?'

'Better yet,' Sanders said, 'I can be with you in twenty minutes. I'd rather talk outside this office.'

'Quite. We'll see you shortly then.'

Sanders rang off and got up to leave, just as Liz Walters walked in.

'I hear you've found Christ, Donald.'

'Whatever do you mean?' he asked, edging towards the door.

'Urgent requests to reach archdeacons. On the road to Damascus, are you?'

'Just something I have to do.'

'Donald,' Liz looked at him knowingly, 'after all these years I can tell when you've got something up your sleeve.'

Donald held out his arms and shook them. 'Look not one single solitary card. 'Bye, bye.'

Liz looked after him for a moment, then calmly walked over to Sanders's desk and looked down at his note-pad. Sanders was an inveterate note-taker, he scribbled constantly during every telephone call.

Timothy West was getting very anxious.

'Do you think Mr Sanders will fulfil his obligations?' he asked Charles.

'Yes I do. Your Archdeacon may be hard to find. We'll just have to be patient, I think.'

'It shouldn't take him long to contact the Archdeacon. He's not trying to fool me, is he?' West suddenly became very agitated. He looked at Charles. 'You don't think you can fool me, do you? Like your father?'

Charles was immediately aware of danger and tried to placate the man with a gentle, reasonable tone of voice. Isn't that how the police got a would-be suicide off a window ledge? He told West that Sanders had probably gone to see the Archdeacon in person. He'd probably have rushed home to change his suit and shirt – very particular about his appearance was Donald. Charles then switched to their recent holiday, going into great and detailed description of what they had done. Gradually West relaxed. I must get him to talk too, Charles thought to himself; that'll keep his mind off the telephone.

'What exactly is it that my father did, I'd like to know?'

West nodded. 'I think you should.' He explained that he had been the curate at a church in Chiswick. The vicar was a wonderful, saintly man. Tom was his name. Tom had always dreamed of running an orphanage. He had felt that the big, rambling vicarage was ideal, and eventually he convinced the Church Council to give permission for this – if he could raise the necessary money. He did get some, but then the local authorities came in with their demands: thousands would be needed. Tom had gone back to the Church, but they couldn't help. In fact they wanted to sell the vicarage, but Tom had to agree.

Charles was startled. 'They needed the vicar's permission?'

'Yes, he was an incumbent, you see. He had the right of possession for life.'

'They've changed that now, of course.'

Suzanna spoke out: 'Like a sitting tenant, you mean. That's what I am here in this flat.'

West nodded, and then went on with his story. Charles's father wanted to buy the land to build offices. He promised to donate £50,000 for Tom to build his orphanage, if he agreed to move out. West persuaded the vicar to accept, and to give his permission to the Church Council to sell to Sir Sydney Clark. They had moved out; the builders had come in and knocked down the vicarage, erecting a small block of offices in its place. But the £50,000 had never been paid.

Sensing that he might become agitated again, Suzanne suggested that she fixed them something to eat. Her neighbour across the hall had done some shopping for her to come back to after the holiday. Scrambled eggs, bacon, toast, coffee? Charles and West agreed readily.

'I must say, I do feel rather hungry,' West admitted.

The meal put everyone into better spirits. The three of them talked very affably though West continued to hold on to the shotgun. He had been telling them how he had become redundant. Curates were on a three-yearly contract. When they went to a new vicar they could be given six months' notice.

Charles asked why he had been given notice.

'The new vicar didn't understand – how much the orphanage meant.'

Tom had died of a broken heart, and he, Timothy West, had been the cause. It was the gossip of the parishioners. When the orphanage didn't appear, people began saying that Tom had taken a back-hander – from Sir Sydney. He looked at the two of them earnestly. 'All I want to do is to clear his name and to build his orphanage.'

Charles crossed the room to take some matches off the mantelpiece. 'There's just one problem, the way I see it. Inflation. You're not going to be able to build the orphanage for fifty thousand pounds.'

The telephone rang.

It was Donald Sanders. He asked for Timothy West; the Archdeacon wanted a word with him. The Archdeacon spoke very kindly to the little man.

'Timothy, this is not the way to go about things. We'll have to have a talk you know. Now Mr Sanders is here with me and he is very upset that there should have been a misunderstanding with Sir Sydney Clark. On behalf of his company he is prepared to make a donation of £50,000 to help establish a new orphanage. We must all sit down and discuss it.'

There was a long pause.

'Hello. Timothy, are you there?'

'Yes, Archdeacon. I need time to think. May I call you back in a few minutes.'

The Archdeacon agreed, and rang off. He turned to Sanders. 'He says he needs time to think. He'll call back in a few minutes.'

'But what is there to think about. I have agreed, after all.'

'I know, I know', the Archdeacon said placatingly. 'I think we'll just have to wait.'

He gestured for Sanders to sit down. Some tea was coming soon. Almost immediately the Archdeacon's wife, a pretty grey-haired lady, came in with a tray laden with a pot, cups and saucers, a dish of biscuits.

'I'm afraid I'm going to have to leave you with the tea. I have to go out.'

Sanders had stood up. 'Thank you for bothering.'

'Not at all,' she smiled. 'But as you're standing, perhaps you'll play Mum and pour. John's quite useless – I'll never understand how he manages communion.'

The Archdeacon took his pipe from his mouth. 'Practice.'

Mrs Francis moved from the room. 'Well, I do hope you sort out this terrible problem of poor Timothy. I can hardly believe it.'

The telephone rang and the Archdeacon pounced across the room. The conversation seemed a little one-sided, the Archdeacon saying little but yes, that he understood. He put down the telephone and turned to Sanders.

'I'm afraid the price has gone up.'

'What!' Sanders was incredulous.

The Archdeacon itemised the rising costs of building materials, land, interest rates, etc. – something about a percentage of multiple interest since the agreement was made with Sir Sydney. 'I'm afraid I couldn't follow it – just not my territory. And I really didn't think Tim knew about such things.'

Sanders slumped back in his chair. 'Charles!'

'Yes, he did say that Charles knew all about it.'

'His father's son' – Sanders groaned, and the Archdeacon looked at him curiously. 'Charles is stage-managing his own kidnap and increasing his ransom.'

'More than increasing, I'm afraid,' the Archdeacon stated. 'He's asking for one hundred and fifty thousand pounds.'

Sanders looked aghast. 'I was prepared to pay the fifty, to accept that the company had a responsibility, but this . . .'

The Archdeacon's eyes twinkled almost wickedly. 'Why were you prepared to give the fifty thousand pounds? Because you didn't want the true reasons for a curate's suicide spread over the newspapers – or because you wanted him to have his orphanage?'

There was a long, long pause before Sanders responded. 'Perhaps because it'll help when I'm trying to chat up St Peter at the Pearly Gates.' His smile faded quickly. 'Sorry, a bad joke.'

But the Archdeacon enjoyed it hugely. 'I must remember that,' he laughed.

Mrs Francis entered the room, dressed in a leather jacket and carrying a motor-cycle crash helmet.

'I'm off now, darling. I do hope you sort things out. 'Bye, Mr Sanders.'

Sanders looked after her in astonishment. The Archdeacon didn't seem to notice anything. 'Archdeacon, I'd better get back to my office. May I ring you in a little while?'

'Yes, of course. By the way, Timothy said he wanted the money by nine tomorrow morning. He's an innocent – he doesn't even know the banks aren't open at that time.'

Sanders found an irate Liz Walters pacing his office when he walked in. He nodded coolly to her. Before she had a chance to speak he pressed his intercom switch and asked for the company cheque-book to be brought in.

'Donald,' Liz said, flashing a piece of notepaper from his desk, 'would you mind telling me what this is all about?'

'Nothing to worry about.'

'Nothing to worry about! I gather that Charles has been kidnapped, there's a fifty thousand pound ransom demanded, mention of a 12-bore shotgun, and you say there's nothing to worry about!'

'Absolutely nothing,' he repeated.

'Look, I know you don't have much time for Charles, but if he's in danger I simply won't allow you to play the cool, ruthless businessman.'

Sanders shrugged, and moved round to take the chair

at his desk. Liz was obviously very angry.

'I'm going to call the police.'

'And say what? . . . I'm afraid I won't back you up with the police. After all, you know nothing.'

'Exactly – well, are you going to call Diana at least?'

'She's having a well-deserved holiday. I'm not going to disturb her with this nonsense.' His secretary came in with a cheque-book. Sanders reached for the pen on his desk. 'Will you please counter-sign.'

'That's a blank cheque', Liz protested. 'Do you expect me to sign a blank company cheque?'

'But I thought you were the one so concerned about Charles's health?'

Liz tried to explain that she needed to know exactly what was going on, she wanted to be able to judge if Sanders was handling it properly. Yes, she was prepared to call in the police – it was the correct thing to do. He was not to try and trick the kidnappers; Charles's life was in danger.

Sanders picked up his telephone and suggested that Liz call Charles; she'd find him very well and happy. The 12-bore shotgun she'd found out about by spying at his papers wasn't intended to shoot Charles. Now, would she please counter-sign the cheque.

'Not until you tell me what's happening.'

'I'm doing a touch of embezzling.'

Liz was exasperated. 'My God, Donald, you're so bloody pompous.'

Sanders was stung, his eyes glinted angrily. 'Let me spell it out for you. Charles, dear Charles, whose well-being you're so worried about, is putting up the price of his own ransom. The kidnapper, a curate' – Sanders touched his neck to indicate a clerical collar – 'is going to blow his own brains out, not Charles's. He's doing all this because Sydney took it into his head to con a vicar and make a killing on the property market.'

He paused, giving Liz a moment to let it all sink in. Then he asked her if she still wanted to call in the police, or would she sign the cheque and let him and the Arch-deacon handle it?

Liz nodded, took the cheque-book and pen, and signed.

'Is there anything I can do?' she asked.

'Forget about it. I'm worried enough for all of us ... and don't take any calls from Charles. He'd enjoy thinking everyone was involved. Have them transferred to my car for the next hour.'

Timothy and Charles were getting on famously; the shotgun was leaning in a corner of the room, momentarily forgotten. The two of them were sitting at the dining-room table, papers spread around. Charles was punching the buttons of a small calculator. Suzanna was stretched on the sofa, listening to them and smoking a cigarette.

'You'll need at least £150,000,' Charles said, 'then there's the running costs on top.'

'I can raise those on charity,' West suggested.

'No, we'll not have any do-gooders involved here. Mrs Donald Sanders can look elsewhere. She's a charity freak, you know. And we mustn't be too dependent on charity. There must be a guaranteed annual income on top of grants: £50,000 well invested would be right ... so that's £200,000 we'll ask.'

Suzanna walked over to the table, a worried expression on her face. 'Don't you think you're going a little over the top, Charles?'

He turned on her angrily, 'Why don't you go and buy some beer?'

'You go,' she snapped back.

Charles agreed and strode over to the door. He found he couldn't open it and turned to West, who suddenly realised, apologised and dug for the mortice key in his pocket.

'I'll be back in fifteen minutes,' Charles said.

'I know you will,' Timothy smiled.

After Charles had left, Suzanna asked West about the shotgun. It had belonged to his father, he replied, who was a farmer. It was wrapped up in brown paper because he found the sight of guns offensive. But he'd use it if he had to.

Suzanna came to the table and sat down next to him. She asked why he hadn't got a job in another church.

'The Sheffield Report – the Church has to deploy the clergy. They'll be losing about 160 men in the London area alone. There's no job for me.'

'Is it because of what happened with Charles's father?'

West shook his head, then stammered that he was heartsick. He couldn't get rid of his guilt feeling over the advice he had given to poor Tom. The Archdeacon had been terribly kind – that's why he had asked Sanders to ring him; he knew the whole story. But then he had realised that he had to help himself, and that's why he was here.

He looked keenly at Suzanna. 'Why are you here? I told you you could leave.'

Suzanna suddenly smiled at him. 'Like you, I've suddenly realised I have to help myself.' She began to explain exactly what she meant, how she felt about Charles; how her greatest rival, of course, was Diana, but Charles didn't know this or wouldn't admit it to himself.

Charles was enjoying himself. He whistled as he walked to the off-licence; he winked at two pretty French girls tripping by. The telephone-kiosk at the corner gave him a sudden inspiration.

He'd give good old Donald a ring, tell him the news about the ransom going up to £200,000. The office transferred him to Sanders's car. The man himself sounded apoplectic.

'What the hell do you mean playing these games, Charles? Just keep your nose out of it and leave it to me. Fifty thousand was the price, and that's it!' The pips went. Sanders turned puce with anger.

Charles returned to the flat in merry mood, and greeted West heartily. West glanced towards the kitchen where

Suzanna had just gone to see what she could organise for supper, then beckoned Charles to come closer.

'Who's Diana?' He whispered.

Charles looked at him curiously. 'Why do you ask that?'

West looked very earnest. 'Because Suzanna cares for you and if there's another girl in your life I think you should tell the truth.'

Charles's cheery mood evaporated. 'Diana is Lady Clark, my stepmother. Not even that, I suppose; my own mother is still alive ... she's just my father's second wife.' He explained that he had always been fond of her; they got on wonderfully well. That was all – so Suzanna had got it a little wrong.

There wasn't a chance to say anymore. Just then Suzanna waltzed in, triumphantly brandishing a container of frozen spaghetti bolognaise sauce she had just found in her freezer.

The meal went down swiftly. Charles pulled another tin of beer towards him and pulled off the tab. 'Absolutely delicious. My compliments to the chef.' He noticed West was staring gloomily at his plate.

'Don't worry about Sanders. He'll pay up by the time I've finished with him. Like playing a trout.'

Suzanna got up and started to clear the dishes. West jumped to his feet to help, but Suzanna told him to sit still – it would only take a minute. Charles waved a languid hand of appreciation, but didn't actually find the words for an offer of help.

West watched him for a moment. 'Why do you despise your father so much?'

Charles looked surprised. 'I don't.'

'Perhaps envy's a better word.'

'I envy him nothing and, thank God, I inherited nothing from him ... except his money.'

Timothy plunged relentlessly on – wasn't it Charles's problem that he couldn't compete with his father? There was no way he could be richer, more powerful, achieve more. Woo and win Diana for that matter.

T.—9

Charles pushed his chair back from the table angrily. 'Are you trying to get back into practice or something? On me? Confession and all that.'

West looked immediately abashed, 'I'm sorry, I didn't mean to intrude.'

There was a long silence. Charles walked over to the window and looked out. When he turned back to the room he was wearing his usual cheery grin.

'It really isn't fair, you know. Every other kidnap victim would have cordons of police round the house. All I've got is one dog hosing down a lamp post.'

The Archdeacon seemed very worried when Sanders arrived. He explained that he had reached the Abbot at Masham Abbey, where Timothy West had been staying. Apparently poor Tim was totally unbalanced. Ever since he had learnt of Sir Sydney's death he had got worse and worse.

'Well, he doesn't seem to be doing anything threatening,' Sanders said.

'Charles is obviously free to come and go when he pleases.' He told the Archdeacon about receiving the call from a pay telephone.

'Mr Sanders, I implore you to tell that young man to be careful. Some small insignificant thing could tip the balance of Tim's mind and then ... he doesn't deserve it.'

The Archdeacon walked over to his desk and refilled his tobacco pouch from the large jar. He continued talking about Tim – a man gets ordained, he serves five years of his seven as curate. Just two to go before he takes over as vicar. His vicar, the only man he truly loves, dies. He blames himself, because of the business with Sir Sydney Clark. Then he's sacked; there's no place for him. His guilt builds up so much that he loses his faith, a terrible thing for a simple man like that. So he takes his life out of God's hands and decides to fight his battle alone ... The trouble is that his only enemy is himself.

Sanders was silent for a moment, then he looked up at the Archdeacon.

'Charles is the enemy now.'

The Archdeacon agreed. 'The game he's been playing could turn very nasty very suddenly.'

'It's strange,' Sanders said thoughtfully. 'Charles is also fighting his own battle, and he is his only enemy, too.'

Suzanna, Charles and West were finishing the last of the beer. Suzanna wondered why Sir Sydney had never paid the money. West couldn't understand either; he had believed he would.

Charles spoke up in defence of his father: old Syd, he agreed, probably couldn't have cared less about the orphans; he'd have told them just to get on with their lives, the way he had done. What had happened was quite simple – he'd just forgotten.

'About fifty thousand pounds?' West's voice was awe-struck.

'Peanuts to him,' Charles stated emphatically. 'Tell me, did you ever ring him to remind him?'

West shook his head. 'Well, no. It didn't seem right.'

'That was your mistake. He was a very busy man. You should have rung him three times a day to remind him. Fifty thousand? He'd forget that in five minutes.' Charles stood up and stretched lazily. 'But Mr Sanders isn't going to forget. We're going to make a fair old hole in the company pocket between us now.'

The telephone rang. 'That'll be him, right on cue.' Charles went over to answer. He listened for a bit, glancing at West several times. 'Don't be daft. That's a load of balls and I'm not falling for it. It's two hundred thousand pounds or nothing. Don't confuse money with your own emotional problems, Donald, just pay up.'

Charles slammed down the phone, then put a hand on a worried West's shoulder. 'Nothing wrong, he's just squealing – trying to get off the hook.'

'I'm not sure this is right.' Timothy clasped his hands together and sat down.

'Tim, have you forgotten why you're here?' Charles's tone was pure leadership: the officer urging his men over the top, into attack. 'You're owed that money and you're going to get it. This is business, big business. And big business means dirty business. Leave it to me, it's my ball game.'

'But Mr Sanders did accept the original sum and I think ...'

'Don't think. Just leave it to me. You couldn't build a chicken-hutch for fifty thousand.'

'Rabbits are what go in hutches,' Suzanna remarked drily.

'There you are – I may know nothing about chickens and rabbits, but I do know about money. Believe me, Tim. We're going to make them pay for what they did to Tom.'

He clapped an arm around the man's trembling shoulders.

Sanders and the Archdeacon decided that, having warned Charles to be careful, the best thing to do was to go along together the next morning. Charles was determined that his best tactic would be the Chinese water torture: drip, drip until the victim gives in, or goes mad. He remembered the granite stairs in his college at Cambridge: each step curved in the middle by the weight of tens of thousands of feet over the centuries.

Sanders took the last call soon after 1.00 in the morning. His wife had gone to sleep in the other bed beside him; he had lifted the extension quickly so she wouldn't wake.

'I'm warning you, Charles. You're sitting on a time-bomb so stop fooling around ... No, your constant phone-calls aren't bothering me. I don't sleep at night.' After he had rung off Sanders stared at the telephone for a minute, then took the receiver off the hook. He tried to sleep but, predictably, tossed and turned. He always had done though – it was why they had decided to have twin beds years ago. Not that there seemed to be any point in a double-bed anyway, Sanders sighed. He thought of the Archdeacon and his wife; I bet they had a great time when they were young – open, healthy people. They're not constipated Christians like my dearly beloved Karen.

Charles didn't sleep either. Suzanna had gone to bed. Timothy West was sleeping on the sofa, a blanket tucked around him. His worn shoes lay on the floor. He alternated between lying peacefully and twitching like a child having a troubled sleep.

Charles decided it was time for another drip, drip, and rang Sanders's number. The engaged signal made him smile, and he called the operator with a very plausible story as to why he must get through.

The operator's loud buzz down the receiver startled Sanders awake just as he had finally managed to drift off. He picked it up and snarled down the line: 'Get the hell off this bloody phone.'

It was enough to wake Karen, who asked what was going on.

Sanders pulled on his bathrobe angrily. 'This time Charles has gone too far, and that's it.' He moved to the door. 'I'm sick to death of all this dirt I've had to clean up since Sydney's death. Damn the man! I've had enough. Let that silly curate blow his brains out all over Charles's wall, for all I care. He can mop it up himself.'

'It's having to pay the money that's really riling you, isn't it?' Karen asked quietly.

Sanders's shoulders sagged. 'I'll pay the money – the two hundred thousand. I don't give a damn about that. I've just had it up to here being tarred with the same brush as Sydney Clark. I'm not him, I'm Donald Sanders.'

'Is that better than being Sydney Clark?' Her tone was acid.

'I'm me!'

'And what is that? So you're nothing like Sydney? You never pulled a fast deal for a quick profit? Talking to an archdeacon doesn't canonise you, you know, my dear.'

'Don't sneer, my darling. You can always send your fur coats to a jumble sale.'

Karen sat up and asked angrily about his fancy ladies – what about their fur coats? She knew what he got up to in those late hours at the office, all those business trips. Sanders looked at her with his mouth agape; he sat down on his bed.

'My darling wife, you are unbelievable.' He looked up at the ceiling. 'Make it come true, please. Karen, if Marilyn Monroe came up to me stark naked I couldn't do a thing.'

They stared at each other, then the telephone rang.

'Charles! Hullo, how are you? ... I'm fine. In fact I've never felt better ... Why? ... Because I've decided to pay you the two hundred thousand pounds. I'll be at the flat with the Archdeacon precisely at nine. Goodbye.'

Charles was anything but elated as the three of them sat over large cups of coffee. 'I smell a rat, that's all.'

'But if he's agreed, it's marvellous.' Timothy's eyes were dancing.

Charles shook his head. 'He's got something up his sleeve – I know him. When they get here just let me handle it. Right?'

'Why are you so mistrustful?' Suzanna asked. 'Wouldn't you trust yourself in the same situation?'

'Because Sanders has agreed to real money and he's no fool. Two hundred thousand! It's mad.'

'What do you mean?' Tim asked nervously.

Charles had moved to the window and looked out. He smiled as he saw the big black car pull up outside the building. 'Here they are now, just leave everything to me.'

He watched the two men climb out of the car and make their way across the street. He could just see them on the pavement below as they paused and talked for a bit, then the buzzer sounded.

Charles rushed across the room and picked up the door-phone. It was Sanders. He asked for Tim to be put on, so the Archdeacon could talk to him. Charles, suspecting some sort of trick, said he wasn't sure about that.

Sanders' voice was crisp. 'I have a cheque right here, Charles, for two hundred thousand pounds, as agreed. Now please put Tim on to talk to the Archdeacon.'

Charles waited for a second. 'There's just one thing, Donald. I didn't do all this for nothing, you know. So whatever you've got up your sleeve don't think you're cutting me out of the deal.' He turned to hand the phone to West. The little man had taken a step back, his face transfixed with horror as he stared at the smiling Charles.

'Judas!' he rasped. 'You were hiding behind your father's shadow. He's fooled me again. But you can't buy me this time ... nobody can ever buy me again. You can keep your filthy money.'

He dashed across the room and seized the long, brown paper parcel. Charles and Suzanna watched, frozen, as West sat down in the desk chair and put his mouth over one end. He searched for the trigger with his right thumb.

Quickly, but softly, Suzanna moved towards the man. 'Tim, I want to say goodbye.'

This was enough to stop him momentarily. It gave enough time for Suzanna to reach him and bend over his head, kissing him gently. But she held her position; if West pulled the trigger he would kill her too.

Charles watched in horror, the moment seemed to go on and on. Then slowly, almost painfully, West lifted his head from the shotgun. He gazed up at Suzanna, tears running down his face.

He looked down at the shotgun, then laid it on the floor beside him. He got to his feet and, without glancing at either Charles or Suzanna, walked to the door. He opened it just as Sanders and the Archdeacon arrived, panting from their dash up the stairs.

The Archdeacon put his arm around the man and gently led him out. 'Come along now, Tim, it's all over now.'

Sanders stepped into the room and looked silently at Charles; his eyes glinted contemptuously. Finally he spoke: 'You've excelled yourself this time.'

Charles's face seemed to have hardened; it looked more mature. 'I am like my father, aren't I?'

'Yes. But unfortunately you haven't grown up yet.'

Charles nodded. 'I know, I've behaved like a kid. Somehow sorry doesn't seem enough to say, but I mean it.'

The two men looked at each other.

Charles turned to Suzanna. 'I need some fresh air. Feel like a walk?'

She nodded, and moved to join him.

'Where is it?' Sanders asked. 'The gun.'

Charles pointed to the parcel on the floor.

Sanders's temper burst. He strode towards the parcel. 'That's it? You've put me through hell when all the man had was a ...' He kicked it as he spoke ... the sound of the shot deafened them. A large glass floor-jar lay shattered in hundreds of pieces; the chest of drawers behind it was pitted with little holes. No one said a word.

12

Diana was gradually coming to terms with the conflict she had felt between herself as biographer of Sydney Clark, and herself as his widow. She continued her research calmly and with determination. She even managed to bring herself to be charming to Mary Clark and to overlook the efforts Mary had been making to get both her own and Jonathan Browning's books stopped. Mary had agreed to come over for some drinks, and to bring some photograph albums with her. During her time with Sydney, Diana had hardly ever asked Sydney about his first marriage, nor had he asked about her own marriage with Brian. It had been an unspoken pact between them. But now she felt a genuine curiosity to know more. Even if it didn't lead to much material for the book – at least, it would tell her more about the man.

The two women had come across some photographs of Sydney on the beach in Monte Carlo in 1960. Jane and Charles were there too, quite small children. Mary remembered it had been virtually impossible to get Sydney to take any sort of holiday – the only reason they had been in Monte Carlo was that Sydney had some business there. The photographs were deceptive: in those two weeks Sydney had managed to come to the beach with the children only twice. Charles had suffered more than Jane because of this relative lack of attention from their father. He was always trying to impress his father, to get him to notice him. This meant Charles tended to overdo things, then Sydney would get very exasperated with him, which only made Charles worse. Mary mentioned the time Charles had dropped out of Cambridge – though later he had taken up veterinary studies – and Sydney had blamed her for spoiling and overindulging the boy.

'Dear God,' she went on, 'if he had only once been a father to him.'

This interpretation of Sydney's behaviour as a father puzzled Diana; she herself had witnessed the great affection between him and each of his children. Besides they had, both of them, opted to stay with Sydney after the divorce. It was a mistake to mention that to Mary though; she clearly saw it as an accusation.

'Like everything else,' she said defensively, 'Sydney thought he could buy himself out of it – out of being a proper father, I mean.' As an example of this she mentioned the large trust funds he had settled on them in 1961. She obviously relished her suggestion that because these were so big, Jane and Charles hadn't needed to think of contesting Diana's share of Sydney's estate. But that was the end of his responsibility, as Sydney saw it: they were taken care of financially ... that was enough.

Diana thought she'd change the subject. What this bitter and malicious woman was saying was totally at odds with the man she knew, the many conversations she had had with Sydney about Jane and Charles. She poured out more gin-and-tonics and asked Mary if it had never been proposed that Charles join his father in the businesses.

Mary shrugged. She claimed it was Sydney's view that the lad had to find his own way, just as he had. 'Except Charles never had the advantages of a handy World War.'

Later they came upon a series of pictures of various people visiting the country house. It was business entertaining and quite a chore. Sydney had a German expression for it: 'Säuefuttërn' – sort of pig feeding. It didn't affect Charles much, he was away a lot at boarding-school. But Jane had always resented it. Diana was coming to the conclusion that every memory Mary conjured up was so prejudiced as to be totally useless. She just knew Sydney would never have used a phrase like 'pig feeding'; he was a great believer in getting to know people he was doing business with, and was quite exhilarated by what he learned from them. It would never have been a chore to him, though it obviously had been for Mary. She felt a pull in her heart as she remembered the wonderful plans they had had for Southdown. She quickly got up and rang down to Ellen for some more ice.

Jonathan Browning knew that Jane went to classes every Monday and Thursday evening at the Yoga Centre, Floral Hall, just behind Covent Garden, now that she was doing a special short-term course at the London School of Economics. He hung around the small foyer, planning to catch her as she came out. The lady at the desk eyed him once or twice as if wondering what he wanted, so Browning asked if the courses at the Centre were only Iyenga – and was given a clutch of information sheets as his reward. They gave him a reason for hanging on as he sorted through them.

Jane recognised him immediately. Browning attempted mock surprise when he heard his name called out, and hesitated a 'Miss Clark?'

The power behind Jane's slap made him stumble back a foot or two. 'Bastard!' she snapped at him.

A very fit young lady, he thought ruefully, as he rubbed the side of his face. He was well aware of the shocked faces of Jane's fellow yogis coming out of the room behind her. He turned to the lady at the information desk. 'See what I mean about Iyenga? Never quite gets that absolute tranquillity.'

Jane started to leave. She glared back at Browning. 'Don't expect an apology.'

'I'd prefer the chance to explain what I've been saying about your father.'

'Slanders ... a dirty smear campaign.'

Browning resisted the impulse to argue, and tried his super charming smile. 'Well, do I get it? The chance?'

Jane shrugged indifferently, but nodded agreement.

Browning ushered her out the door and across the street to a little pub. Her request for orange juice indicated her refusal to accept the occasion as a social one.

Browning took a swallow of his beer and launched into an earnest explanation of his search for the truth, for that's what it was. A smear campaign, on the other hand, was a process of contrived character-assassination – usually for political ends. Jane's father was being held up as the stainless philanthropist, the commercial wizard in saint's raiment. But there was definite evidence to the contrary, and the public had a right to hear that evidence.

'I challenge,' Browning finished his statement, 'that convention which says the grave should be a refuge from the truth.'

Jane's first comment was that Browning was dead glib in his defence, even eloquent. Sincere too – but then witch-hunters always were. But there was another way of describing it: zealous. But a zealot could only see things in black and white; he'd start with the conclusion and then find the facts to prove it.

Browning took a few more swallows of beer; he was getting the girl to talk. So far, so good. The next step would be to get something stronger into her, loosen the tongue maybe.

But Jane refused the offer of another drink, picked up her yoga mat, and was ready to go. Yoga was performed on an empty stomach, and she was off home to eat. She said she wasn't interested in a Chinese meal, nor a lift – the tube would be faster. Yet Browning's persistence was hard to refuse and she soon found herself being persuaded into the dirty old Fiat. As Browning got behind the wheel he suddenly got the feeling that she had intended to agree to the lift all along – that perhaps he wasn't as much in charge as he thought.

He kept asking questions as they drove through the evening traffic, and gradually he got her talking about herself. Her ambition was to go into Parliament one day. Browning enquired what radical bills she'd be bringing in: doubling police pay? Deportation of non-whitish immigrants?

Jane responded to the taunt with fervour, ticking each item off on her fingers as she listed a wealth tax, nationalisation of banks, tighter controls on cartels and share dealings ...

Browning was wry. 'Don't forget abolition of the Lords.' He grinned at her. 'Fashionably anti-capitalist, aren't you?'

'There are plenty of abuses to put a stop to.'

'Ah. And who should know better than you, Miss Clark.'

Jane nodded. 'Who indeed.'

'She was only a tycoon's daughter, but she wore a red shirt to the bank.'

They continued the verbal sparring until Browning dropped her at the house, but the atmosphere between them had changed. There was now a strong undercurrent of mutual attraction.

Browning leaned out of the car window. 'You do realise we're on the same side – it's the late chairman Sir Sydney Clark I'm after. Not your daddy.'

Jane stared at him for a moment, then nodded in what seemed to be acceptance. As she fumbled with her key at the door, Browning gave a cheeky beep-beep with his horn and sped off.

On the drive back to his own flatlet he felt well pleased with himself. Good progress had been made. This particular line of enquiry had started when he had received that surprising call from Charles Clark, offering to sell him some juicy information. For five thousand pounds. Greedy sod! The hint was that it had something to do with the trust funds set up for both him and his sister. Well, then – if Charles knew things, Jane might too. Handled the right way he could get for nothing the same information Charles was prepared to sell.

And there might even be a bonus – the lass was very beddable.

He'd need to work fast though. The fact of *Post* pulling out of the book would leave him short of funds. His agent had suggested that a nice sample chapter containing a new scandal, if shown to the Sunday newspapers, could lead to a fat advance. This could be just the thing. Jane's spouting of left-wing jargon was bound to help; he could play on that quite a bit.

He weighed the pros and cons of trying to make contact with her again as soon as possible – then decided that if it was going to work, it would work as well whether he tried again the next day or the next week. He had discovered her lecture and tutorial schedule – it would be easy enough to 'run into' her tomorrow, he thought.

She didn't seem very surprised when he did, just looked him up and down rather slowly. 'Surprise, surprise.' She started to move off, but Browning stopped her with a hand on her elbow.

'I thought we might resume our interrupted chat.'

Jane had with her an aggressive, hairy friend who tried to intervene on her behalf.

'Careful, Len,' Jane warned, 'it may look ineffectual, but armed with a pen it can get really vicious.'

Browning persevered, and won. Jane climbed into his car. As he pulled away, he waved a triumphant V-sign out the window at hairy Len.

His smile disappeared when Jane insisted she must get to know more about him before she talked further on the subject of her father.

They drove into Hyde Park, where they decided to leave the car and walk around a bit. Like most people Browning couldn't resist talking about his favourite subject, so he told Jane about his divorce – how it had come as a result of his work, the hours he had to keep, continual money problems. His addiction to the stock market hadn't helped – but, mind you, if some of his stock market gambles had come off his wife would have stayed with him for ever.

He put on his most charming smile: 'You know what

they say: inside every financial journalist there's a frustrated financier.'

Jane broke into a wide grin. 'So that's it. That's why you're conducting this vendetta against my father: he succeeded where you failed.'

Browning was stung. 'No one succeeds the way he did, not legitimately. Not without the back-handers and the shady deals.'

Jane looked at him sharply, and told him it still sounded like sour grapes. Browning asked if her mother would have stuck by Sydney without his great success. Jane replied that Mary would never have married him in the first place if he had not been successful.

They sat for a while on a park bench.

'You know,' Browning said, 'your mother obeyed the investor's golden rule ... she got out on a rising market.'

Jane was silent for a moment. Then she confessed that Browning was right about the back-handers, the shady deals. She had spent a few vacations working as a sort of PA to his PA; she had learned enough to know what was going on.

Browning was exhilarated; he knew he was getting on to something now. Softly, softly, he said to himself. Casually he asked her about the charity endowments.

Jane insisted that those were perfectly legitimate, but of course the need for private charitable patronage shouldn't be there, not with a proper welfare system. What her father had been doing really was buying himself tax-free prestige and a king-size ego trip.

Browning grinned. 'Now that's one quote I'd dearly like to use.'

Nevertheless he was growing concerned that nothing concrete was emerging, nothing to spice up that specimen chapter. Perhaps a catalyst was needed? His mind made up, he asked Jane if she would like to talk over a meal later that night; she looked at him appraisingly for a moment. 'OK,' she agreed. She was very much surprised to see where they were going a few hours later when

Browning's directions brought them to the entrance of the Sporting Club. She gestured to her 'New Left' clothes; they were hardly appropriate.

Browning laughed. 'Come on, you'll be a riot.'

'They'll probably fumigate me.'

As she hurried off to the ladies room, Browning took a seat at a side table.

For all her left-wing chit-chat she was still a typical woman, he reflected. Her first thought was to rush off and mend her make-up.

'You took your time.' The voice sounded petulant. 'I began to think you weren't interested.'

Charles Clark was standing by the table, nervously playing with a handful of chips, juggling them from one hand to the other. Good, Browning thought, here's my little catalyst, right on time.

Charles was thrown off balance when Jane came up to join them. He began expostulating about her being there with Jonathan Browning – the man dedicated to destroying their father's name and reputation. Jane retorted that, given the right approach, it could be worthwhile – he shouldn't forget their father had screwed the system for every penny he could. Charles grabbed her by the arm and called her a silly little LSE swot who was being conned out of her mind by a muckraker.

'Come on, he's a lost cause.' Jane swung round on her brother for a final bitter retort: 'If the book does nothing else, brother dear, I hope it shows how our system throws up parasitic chinless wonders like you!'

Browning got up to follow her, spread his hands in a there-you-go gesture to the deflated Charles, winked at him, and then hurried on to catch Jane up. She didn't say anything as he led her to a pub down the street; there she demanded a large brandy.

Seeing how quickly that one had gone down, he immediately ordered a second and brought it to her. 'A bit strong back there, weren't you?'

'Go to hell! You set that up, bastard. You knew Charles

would be there. That's how you people work, isn't it, part of the technique, stir things up? Christ, what a filthy job!'

Browning didn't mind. He just grinned in acknowledgement, joking that maybe he ought to lodge a claim to his union for occupational contamination. As far as engineered confrontations were concerned, they only worked if the ingredients were right, if the antagonisms were there to be exposed. Jane shook her head. Charles was a victim of his trust fund – hundreds of thousands of pounds he never did a hand's turn to earn. That was why he was a mess. That was one of the reasons she wanted to get into Parliament, to fight the inheritance laws. Father had set them up with a quarter of a million in the early sixties, just before the requisite death-duty loopholes were closed. The fund was worth four times as much now.

Browning shrugged. 'So what? Those trusts were perfectly legal.'

Jane knocked back her third brandy and winked conspiratorially at Browning. 'Except that father couldn't afford it – couldn't raise a quick couple of hundred thou without . . . well, pulling a crook.'

He could feel his pulse rate quicken. He casually asked Jane if she'd like another one. She shook her head; better have something to eat; she should go home.

Thinking she looked a little unsteady on her feet, he helped her towards the car. Her body pressed against him as they walked; there was no resistance to the arm around her shoulder. His fingers accidentally touched the fullness of her breasts, delayed a moment – he was very aware of the feel of the smooth young thigh against his leg. This is it, Johnny Boy, he exulted – double-bonus time!

Jane peered up at the unfamiliar building. 'This isn't home.'

'It is to me. You did say you were hungry.'

She looked at him, then opened the car door to get out. 'It had better be good.'

'Oh, it'll be that,' Browning promised.

It was hardly a flat, but more than a bedsitter. One large room, lined on three walls with shelves of books – a kitchenette in one corner, a double bed in another. A small bathroom/loo area was boxed in behind one of the shelf-lined walls. It looked like a bachelor pad and a work-place; there was a neat arrangement of filing cabinets with a large slab of plywood spread on top, the whole piece lined with white formica. A profusion of files, neatly lined up, filled one section. Next to them sat a small electric typewriter; beside it two old marmalade jars filled with sharpened pencils – one jar with ordinary lead, the other with various coloured ones. It was a warm, lived-in, friendly place.

Browning walked over to the smart music-centre on one large shelf. He chose a cassette and placed it in the tape-deck. Jane put on a déjà-vu expression, as if she was expecting some old-fashioned mood music. Her face changed and hardened as she heard the remembered voice boom out. Browning quickly turned down the volume.

It was her father: '... sounds arrogant,' he was saying, 'but I reckon I'd make a better job of running this country's economy than our present Chancellor.'

Another voice, obviously an interviewer, came on: 'With a controlling interest in what? ... over twenty different companies? – you could be said to have the broader experience.'

Browning explained the tape was from the Bush House archives: May '76.

Clark went on to talk for a moment about North Sea oil, then the interviewer said he wanted to ask a more personal question about the future. What would happen to the vast Clark commercial empire after his retirement?

'Who said anything about retiring?' There was an edge to his voice.

'There have been rumours ...'

'To blazes with rumours ...'

Jane crossed the room to punch the off button. She said the interviewer was obviously fishing about Charles. Just the personal aspect, Browning murmured, clearly in sympathy with the interviewer, as he walked over to his drinks shelf and fixed a brandy and soda for Jane.

He asked Jane about her money; she claimed it had affected Charles – so what had it done to her? Jane said it got in the way: the fortune-hunting syndrome, the question-mark over people's friendship. She had often been called 'poor little rich girl', sometimes to her face.

They were now sitting on the long settee in the middle of the room. Browning looked at his arm, just happening to rest along the back of the settee, behind Jane's shoulders. He felt as if he had returned to the back stalls of the local flea-pit, wondering whether he should, or shouldn't. Christ, I'm nervous he thought to himself – it's the generation gap. She'll probably call me a dirty old man. I should have gone on that diet; it's only ten pounds I need to take off. Pot's more lack of exercise than excess weight. Two days a week at the gym – it would take no time.

'So the lady has problems,' he stated.

Jane changed her position, so that she was facing him directly. She ran one hand through her hair. Her voice was teasing. 'There's always sublimation,' she said. 'You have to re-channel your libido into your studies ... Anyway, the LSE talent aren't much of a turn-on. All demos and pot.'

'Immature?' Browning finished his drink.

'Grindingly,' Jane answered.

Their eyes met, and held for that moment too long. The signals of sexual promise were exchanged.

Browning's voice took on a deliberate seductive tone. 'Sounds like good news for the professors.'

'Let's say the men.' Jane's eyes sparkled, danced. It was there: the challenge, the invitation.

Browning felt his confidence rocketing; his manhood wasn't doing so badly either. This was familiar territory; the excitement was there: of the discovery, the exploration to come.

He took her glass from unresisting fingers, put it on the

coffee-table and reached out one hand to the back of her head, then gently stroked her neck. Easy does it Johnny, he said to himself, and started to pull her towards him. She came with a rush, her arms around his neck, her tongue darting and probing. He groaned as he felt those lovely breasts in his hands. In spite of the space restrictions she was doing marvellous things with her pelvis. Must look into this yoga, he thought.

They finally broke for air.

'You were going to eat ...' Browning's voice was husky.

She stood up and reached for his hand. 'Priorities, Mr Browning – there's always breakfast.'

Browning shivered, then opened one eye. He could see that the window was wide open. Daylight was streaming in, and a very fresh breeze ... He remembered, took in the empty position beside him, and looked around the room.

Jane was sitting in some complicated-looking yoga position, very still, her eyes closed. She was wearing just a slip. He took in the curves of her body with some pleasure – it was better than waking to a glass of fresh orange juice.

He yawned. 'Good morning.'

Jane unfolded slowly, in correct yoga style, then looked evenly across at him. 'You've helped my paschimotanasana.'

Browning made an exaggerated gesture of propping open his eyelids. 'You've helped my proptosis.'

He heaved himself into a more comfortable position and grinned at her; he was feeling dead chuffed with himself. He watched Jane come to the bed, a serious expression on her face.

'Are you sitting comfortably?' She asked. 'Good. Then we'll begin.'

As Browning shifted to make room for what he thought was coming next, Jane walked over to the open window and leaned far out.

'Rape!' she yelled. 'Help ... RAPE!'

Browning leapt from the bed in one giant bound, half

tripping over the sheet he had dragged with him to cover himself. He pulled the window down and glanced out fearfully to see if anyone was paying attention.

'What the hell ... I suppose you thought that was funny.' He glared at Jane, who was now stretched out on the bed looking very pleased. Still clutching the sheet he hopped over to the hook where his dressing-gown was hanging. He groaned as he heard the familiar hoarse voice from the stairwell.

'Mr Browning!' It was the Deacon Dragon.

'It's nothing, Mrs Deacon,' he yelled through the door.

'Nothing?' The voice sounded nearer, was she mounting the stairs?

He opened the door slightly. 'That's right, just a joke.'

'Not how it sounded from down here.'

Jane came up behind Browning and leaned over his shoulder. 'One of his little games, Mrs Deacon. I'm sorry.'

After a long pause, the voice moved away. 'Games? ... Disgusting!'

Browning pulled Jane back into the room, slammed the door and angrily demanded to know what was going on.

'I wanted you to know how it feels,' she said – Browning looked at her questioningly, 'I'm talking about my father ... his memory ... my feelings.'

She crossed the room to fill the electric kettle, then continued explaining. If she had screamed down the stairs, Mrs Deacon would have come hurrying up and found her naked, her clothes strewn about the place. And because Deacon would only want to believe the worst about Browning, she would have made an immediate assumption. The fuzz would be brought in – a young girl ... and he twenty years older at least. What would have happened then to his reputation as a crusading journalist? It was no different from what Browning was doing to her father. If she shouts *rape* people will believe her. So what happens when Browning shouts *scandal* to a TV audience of millions?

Browning was quick to protest that he was not scandal-mongering. The public have a right to know – about Sir Sydney Clark's business methods, his integrity over taxes, company regulations ... the lot. He was going to fulfil that right.

'Come off it,' Jane tapped him on the chest with a long finger-nail. 'It's a thin line, you know – where "right-to-know" ends and scoop-hunting begins. Divorced man, failed stock-market punter – you need a scoop like a vampire needs blood.'

Browning was about to protest, but she was right, and she was the best chance he had at the moment – so he bared his fangs, grabbed her with mock ferocity and applied deep mouthing kisses to the base of her throat.

She mock-swooned ... then responded with some real kisses of her own.

'What next? Rubber, whips – a bit of bondage?'

Browning suddenly broke off, as if struck by a sudden pang of conscience. He confessed to Jane that Charles had called him about a week ago, offering to sell him some information on the trust funds. Some real dirt. That was why he had turned up at the Yoga Centre, picked her up outside the LSE.

'And why I'm in your bed now!'

'That I didn't, couldn't have planned.'

Jane went back to the kitchenette and poured herself some more tea, seemingly in deep thought. Then she whirled round on Browning in abrupt decision.

'Charles is a creep ... he's not going to sell, to you or to anyone.'

'Well, not at his current asking price,' Browning said wryly.

'Not at any price,' Jane's voice turned businesslike. 'Senior trustee: Donald Sanders. Date registered: April Fool's Day 1961. Total combined capital: two hundred and fifty thousand pounds.'

She suggested to Browning that he get pencil and paper to write everything down. He was only too pleased, and sat down eagerly – pencil poised. The story was simple. Sydney needed the quarter million fast in order to establish the trust funds before the laws changed, but he didn't have the ready cash. So he got Betsy Cross, Liz Walters's predecessor, to register a private company, Castle Fundings, with an issued capital of ... a quarter million.

The cash came, on paper that is, from Clark Holdings Ltd. Castle Fundings promptly made a capital loan, of a quarter million, to ... Sir Sydney Clark. It was used to establish the two trust funds. The trustees, i.e. Donald Sanders, invested the trust's entire capital in: Clark Holdings.

'Routine "recycling".' Browning tapped his pencil on the note-pad. 'The whole thing was a paper exercise.'

'Exactly,' Jane nodded in agreement.

'And, in the process, your Daddy ... with the complicity of Donald Sanders ... committing a flagrant breach of the Trust laws.'

This was it! Browning had to force himself to resist the temptation to yell whoopee. Instead he thanked Jane rather formally.

She lit a cigarette. 'Rather this way than have my Judas of a brother sell out for blood-money.'

'You don't care much for Uncle Donald Sanders either, do you?'

Jane sniffed disdainfully. 'A typical city shark ... establishment operator, and survivor.'

Browning held up the note-pad. 'I doubt he'll survive this lot.'

Jane left Browning's flat and went straight to a lecture. She missed lunch in order to fit in a couple of hours' library work for her next essay before an afternoon tutorial. By the time she got home she was famished. Ellen prepared her a marvellous cold supper: ham, salad, two hard-boiled eggs and some of her own mayonnaise, some grated carrots and cheese too. And a percolator of coffee – she always loved the smell of newly-ground coffee beans. She had put on a record at high volume, the Hosanna from the Bach B-Minor Mass. She shut her eyes and luxuriated in the glory of the music and the voices; then she sensed the presence of someone else in the room.

Diana was watching her. 'Jane, I didn't know you were here.' She walked over and turned down the sound.

This annoyed Jane intensely. The house had been her home, Diana was the intruder. There was an awkward silence; she felt Diana was trying to say something.

Eventually she asked if Jane had missed breakfast.

'Dinner as well, actually,' Jane answered. 'I hope you don't mind.' Her voice was slightly sarcastic.

Diana tried to be friendly. It was a relief, she claimed: 'Seems to me the only time one sees the anorexia generation really tucking in these days is when they're pregnant.'

This was a little close to the knuckle for Jane. She hadn't been prepared the night before. 'I'm too greedy for anorexia and too busy to get pregnant.'

Diana sat down in the chair opposite her. 'Not too busy to gad around the clubs with Jonathan Browning.'

Jane finished her coffee, then pushed the tray to one side. She stared coldly at Diana.

'Was it the *Tatler* you wrote that gossip-column for?'

Diana reminded her coldly that it was hardly a month since Jane had been suggesting they should be sueing Browning; now she was going around with him. The telephone rang. Neither made a move to answer – eventually it stopped. Presumably Ellen had picked it up.

Jane shook her hair behind her shoulders. 'As it happens, Jonathan's rather fun ...'

The call was for Jane: Donald Sanders asking what on earth she had been telling Jonathan Browning. The fellow had just been in his office, insinuating there had been shennanigans in the setting up of the trust funds, evading death duties, bending the Trustee Act regulations. He had been sent off with a flea in his ear. 'But he's been talking to someone. Was it *you*? ... What have you been telling the damned man?'

'Nothing to land you in gaol. Don't fret.' Jane could feel her confidence ebbing away.

'I suppose you think it's clever to meddle in these things. Well, you could regret it ... if you value your father's reputation.'

'If Browning wants to look into those trusts, he has every right to,' Jane snapped, and broke the connection.

Diana enquired what was going on. Why was Donald Sanders ringing her about the trusts – and Jonathan Browning? Ellen was just picking up the tray when Jane pointed a finger at her.

'If you want to know about the trusts, ask her. She's one of the trustees.' She left the room.

Ellen quickly tried to follow her – but Diana just as quickly crossed the room and put a gentle hand on her elbow.

'Are you?' she asked.

'I really never thought to mention it.' The hint was that it really wasn't any of Diana's business. Reluctantly she told Diana that Donald Sanders was the principal trustee; Liz Walters had been appointed one too, about five years ago, when Betsy Cross had moved to Portugal ... and Mary Clark as well, of course. Diana thanked her and went to the telephone, rapidly dialling Mary's number. She now knew it by heart.

At first Mary was reluctant to talk about it, then explained why. Sydney, and others too, had been tipped off by a man at the Treasury about pending changes in the Trust laws. A man called Wilmot. Too many people had rushed to set up trusts at the last minute; it was obvious that information had been leaked. Wilmot was traced and, in the usual tradition of the Civil Service, tendered his immediate resignation – which was quietly accepted.

'Sydney was hardly the villain of the piece,' Diana pointed out. 'He didn't do it for personal gain. It was for the children, not for himself.' It had been seventeen years ago, after all. There was no question of any threat to the actual trusts.

They exchanged goodbyes. As she rang off, Diana turned to Ellen, 'It's really not that damning ...'

Ellen was obstinate. 'Best let sleeping dogs lie,' she pleaded.

Sanders hadn't been the only source Jonathan Browning tried to check out on the details of Jane's story. He believed it completely – but his whole journalistic training had taught him to check, re-check and then double-check. Sanders had seemed a little too confident for his liking; a small, distant alarm-bell was ringing. Browning tried to ignore it, and started banging away at his little electric typewriter.

His insurance was to call his old mate Rhys Williams in Cardiff. He owed Browning a few favours, so he could repay them with a visit to the Registrar of Companies, just to check a few details: Castle Fundings, should have been registered about March 1961; some basic facts on Clark Holdings too, and the trusts themselves.

The specimen chapter was going really well when the telephone rang. Browning let it go on for a minute while he finished a paragraph of deathless prose.

It was Rhys Williams, as cheery as ever – but his news was not. There was nothing on a Castle Fundings established in early '61, nor any other private company registered by a Betsy Cross ... a complete blank.

Browning tore the paper out of the typewriter with his free hand and scrunched it into a ball. 'Damn ... damn, damn!'

Rhys bounced on. The trusts were pukkah, but something else didn't fit in with the story he had been given – Clark Holdings wasn't registered until the following year, June 1962.

Browning thanked Rhys for his help. He said he'd buy him a beer when he was next in London. Then he went and poured himself a very large whisky. He remembered old Joe Falk back in Sheffield ... 'Like God said, lad, be sure and check thy facts.' Thank you, Joe, he thought and raised his glass in silent toast. A fit-up. The little bitch would have sent me up the creek without a boat, let alone a paddle.

He was on his second large drink, wondering what on earth he could deliver in the special chapter he had promised 10% Wally in the morning, when there was a tentative knock on the door.

'Jane! What ill wind's blown you in?'

She looked at him with an uncertain frown for a second, then thrust out a copy of *War Cry*. 'I told your Mrs Deacon I was a Witness.' She scampered into the room holding a cluster of books and a foil bag of still-steaming kebabs. She was showing them triumphantly to Browning when, with a cold deliberation, he slapped her hard across the face.

'One I owed you ... Cunning little vixen, aren't you?'

Jane glared at him, then stepped back, rubbing her cheek and staring at Browning with a mixture of anger and apprehension.

He took a step towards her. 'All that rape mallarkie. You're the rape artist around here,' he jabbed a finger at her, 'and it ain't the kind you can lay back and enjoy.'

Jane eyed him carefully, with her hand still to her face, biting her lip.

'So you reckoned to take me,' he continued; 'con me with a load of libellous rubbish about offences under the Trustees Act. Did you think I'd really rush into print without checking?'

Jane grimaced in resignation. 'Blast you.'

'Why? For guarding against the risk of a court action? Feed me a lot of lies about old Syd and Uncle Donald fiddling the Trust laws, then sue me for defamation when I tried to publish it.'

'Well, it was worth a try.'

Browning poured himself another drink, then raised his glass to her ruefully. He agreed it was a try worthy of her old man.

'No, no, no,' Jane shook her head vehemently, 'he'd have succeeded.'

Browning shook his head – Syd would have had to buy off everyone in sight: his mate in Cardiff, the Registrar of Companies. He said he supposed Charles's phone-call was a put-up job too ...

'It was.' Jane shouldered her bag and moved to the door. 'Well, Jonathan. Thanks for the memory.'

Browning grinned at her. 'If nothing else we improved your paschimo-whatsit.'

'Maybe we could work on my Pranayama some time.' She matched his grin.

'Like now?' Browning leered.

Jane shook her head. She wanted to get to some lectures. Browning stood still for a while after she had left. He patted his stomach thoughtfully, then pulled it in as he stood straighter. He looked like a man who had just made a new resolution.

Jane's self-confidence was further shaken when talking to Diana a few days later. She had been explaining, somewhat defiantly, how she had tried to fix Browning. She had given him some rubbish about the Trusts, quite plausible it was too ... but unfortunately, Browning had checked it out.

'Of course,' Diana said. 'Whatever else he may be, Jonathan Browning's a pro. Let's hope you haven't put him on to the real scandal behind those trusts.'

'What?' Jane stammered in surprise.

'Why do you think Donald Sanders was in such a lather when he rang you?'

Diana went on to explain about poor Mr Wilmot from the Treasury and his wagging tongue. Anyhow, now Browning had probably been scared off that particular line of enquiry so, thanks to Jane, Diana had the scoop to herself.

'You're going to use it in your book? You can't!'

'Why not?' Diana said she felt it showed Sydney in

quite a good light, anyhow. Should she edit the facts to suit Jane's image of her father? She suggested the next time Jane tried to pull a similar stunt, she should ask her for a word of advice. 'Jane,' she went on, 'isn't it time to drop the wicked stepmother bit? I mean, we are on the same side. We both loved him, after all. We're probably the only two who really did.'

13

Charles and Diana were laughing as they climbed out of the car; it must have been a good night out. As Charles fumbled for his keys, they dropped on the pavement. He mimed being drunk as he scrabbled to find them. Neither noticed the burly man watching them from across the street. He was smiling.

When they finally got into the house, Charles poured out two large brandies. Once again he wished Diana a very happy birthday.

'You have to admit,' he said after an appreciative sip, 'Dad did keep you to himself on your birthday.'

Diana nodded in agreement. 'Sydney seemed to have quite a thing about birthdays in general.'

Charles was about to ask her to define this elliptical remark when the telephone rang. Diana picked it up.

She heard a man's voice, urgent, breathless. He asked her if she was on her own; whether he could come over right away. Looking at Charles, she said that she was alone, and, yes, he could come.

'Why aren't I here?' Charles asked as Diana put down the phone and looked at him with a quizzical expression.

All Diana could tell him was that the caller had described himself as 'The Pineapple Man'. He was coming right over.

'When did you get into the fruit business, Diana?' Charles laughed.

Diana seemed to be thinking out loud. She mumbled something about a telegram – that it must have been the telegram. Then, remembering what she said about being alone, she urged Charles to make himself scarce, but to remain within earshot, just in case. At first Charles was reluctant to move, but Diana pleaded that it might be important; he must get out of sight. She had told her caller there was nobody here.

'I'm nobody . . .' he shrugged. Rather forlornly he muttered, 'In vino veritas.' He held his glass to the light.

Then the doorbell rang.

Charles quickly took up a position on the winding staircase. It would be impossible to see him without mounting the first step. Where he was squatting he could hear every word from the sitting-room; he could reach it in a second or two.

Diana opened the door to a broad, continental-type man – furtive-looking, in fact. He identified himself as the caller on the phone, and stepped into the house, with a quick glance over his shoulder as if he thought someone was following him. There didn't seem to be – but neither he nor Diana noticed the burly man still across the street, in the dark shadow, with a puzzled look on his face. Diana's visitor seemed familiar to him, but he couldn't quite place him.

Diana took the man – The Pineapple Man, she wondered to herself – into the sitting-room. She offered him a drink, but it was refused with a curt movement of a hand. 'I don't drink.'

'Not even on birthdays?' Diana asked as she put her own glass down, unfilled.

'Many happy returns,' the man offered.

Diana asked him how he knew it was her birthday. The Pineapple Man nodded at the solitary birthday-card sitting on the mantelpiece. Diana commented that he was very observant. She asked if he knew her husband was dead. He did know, and he had come because he had information Diana would want.

'Not the sort of information you could put in a letter?' Diana questioned.

'In my business nothing is ever written down, Lady

Clark.' The Pineapple Man appeared glum, and tired. Diana felt herself in no physical danger – in fact, she found herself feeling rather sorry for him.

'I see,' she said, and wondered how to go on. 'I can assure you that we are alone, that nothing will be written down.' She smiled in an attempt to put him at his ease, then asked why he called himself The Pineapple Man.

'Your husband did.' The voice was flat, unemotional. 'That's why I'm here.'

She realised now that it was a code name, in answer to her cable.

The man leaned forward in his chair, he spoke sharply. 'Your husband owes me. He marked me and he owes me the rest of my working life.'

Diana had first thought it was blackmail; now it sounded like some kind of debt, or even revenge – perhaps it was a mixture of all three. She glanced towards the hallway where Charles was concealed and began to regret that she had allowed this so-called Pineapple Man to come into the house. How could she get rid of him?

She stated firmly that even if the man had ever worked for her husband in the past, he was owed nothing. Sydney was dead and that was the end of the matter.

The Pineapple Man became obviously agitated, and referred to a big, very big, business deal. The legality of it was questionable – it would be very damaging to her husband if the part he played became known; if the type of goods involved and bought was discovered.

Diana drew herself up. 'I will *not* be blackmailed!'

The man seemed very angry for a moment, then made an effort to calm himself. Diana listened quietly as he continued his story.

He described how he had completed his end of the deal all right ... But then everything was lost. He had been labelled a Pineapple Man – that was a man marked, a man never to be trusted. And that was what the late Sir Sydney Clark had done to him.

'Maybe there was a reason,' Diana suggested reasonably.

'There was all right,' the man agreed. 'He was trying to protect his own image.'

Diana protested that Sydney had loved people talking about him.

'About busting sanctions, and selling strategic American electronic equipment to the East?'

The man was quite wrong, Diana assured herself. She remembered Sydney's near-phobia about communists: he ascribed any labour problems in the businesses under his control to them. That was how they were trying to take control of the country – through the unions. This suggested deal was totally out of character; she told the man so.

If that was so, he replied, then her husband, by her own definition, was a traitor . . . and he had the proof.

'What proof?' Diana demanded incredulously.

He handed her a photograph. 'That's him – talking to a well-known Russian dealer. His percentage on fifty million pounds must have coloured his political views.'

Diana asked the man how *he* fitted. What part did he play? He explained that he had brought the two sides together: the seller and the buyer. He had the photograph taken as a form of insurance, just in case there was any problem over his cut. It was in Portugal that the deal was settled, where the labels were changed, and then the goods were sent . . . to the USSR. But the deal was never quite completed.

Diana handed the photograph back. She could see no threat. If it was Sydney it would be impossible to prove; it wasn't a very good likeness. 'You've got a lousy insurance agent, I'd say.'

The man insisted that Diana knew it was her husband. Diana made the obvious retort that if his story was true he would be in serious trouble himself; after all, he was still alive, Sydney wasn't.

The man smiled, a bitter smile. 'I have nothing to lose.'

Sensing Diana's predicament a few moments earlier, Charles had slipped out the front door in order to come back in a false entrance. He pressed the bell, then made a loud fuss of finding his keys and opening the door.

Diana and the man had little time to react. He stood there with the photograph in one hand as Charles came into the room.

'It's OK, Diana. I thought I'd left my keys ... Oh, did I arrive at an inopportune moment?'

'He was just leaving,' Diana said, with some relief at Charles's appearance.

Charles asked the man his name and was told it was Hanson. 'How do you do,' Charles rushed on. 'I'm Clark. Charles, not Sydney. Did you know my father?'

'Yes.'

'What a coincidence. So did I.'

Hanson gave Charles a black look and made ready to leave. He told Diana he'd be in touch, giving the photograph back to her.

'I don't think there's any need, do you?' Diana was cool, she felt in control.

Hanson made his way to the front door. Recovering the photograph from Diana, Charles followed him and returned it. Then he mimed picking up a bag by the door and giving it to him.

'Don't forget this. Looks like a money bag, empty too. Ah well, better luck elsewhere.'

He went on making inane pleasantries and goodbye noises, seemingly oblivious to the way Hanson was bristling. He slammed the door and chortled his way back to the sitting-room, feeling highly pleased with himself. That was the last she'd see of him, he assured Diana. She doubted it. With the clink of glasses as Charles poured them a celebratory drink, neither heard the slight noise of the photograph dropped back through the letter-box.

Diana found it a little later as she made her way to bed. She took it up with her and put it on her dressing-table. It *could* have been Sydney; if she had been told it was Sydney by somebody else she would probably have accepted that it was. But, looking at it very closely, she got the strong feeling it wasn't. She wondered how the other man, the supposed Russian, could be identified. She might as well start with Donald Sanders. They now seemed to be getting on better. He was certainly less obstructive than before – certainly less smug, not so condescending.

She held the photograph up in front of her so she could look over its edge at the painting of Sydney on the bedroom wall. No – it wasn't Sydney. In any case, she just couldn't imagine Sydney having *secretive* dealings with the Communists. It was one of the things he would really make speeches about; he was typical of those self-made men who 'saw reds under the beds'.

Donald Sanders wasn't very pleased. He had been nice enough when she telephoned to ask if he knew anything about Sydney being involved in a secret deal with the Russians. But her coming into his office to show him the photograph had gone too far: the whole thing was melodramatic, ridiculous.

'This damn biography,' he threw the photograph on to his desk, 'is serving no better purpose than to drive woodworm out of every corner. You'd be better occupied offering your services to Rentokil.'

Diana did feel a little foolish. 'You win. If he was genuine, he wouldn't have used that incredible nickname.'

Sanders raised an enquiring eyebrow; she hadn't mentioned it before.

'He called himself The Pineapple Man. Go ahead, be my guest and laugh. You really can now.'

But Sanders *didn't* laugh for a split second. Diana could see him react to the nickname, but he quickly covered it up by rising from his desk and asking for the lunch she had promised.

Diana wasn't so easily deterred. 'You know what a Pineapple Man is, don't you?'

Sanders dodged the question by suggesting Diana tell him her whole story from the beginning. As they proceeded through the outer office and into the lift she did tell him, starting with the telephone call. Sanders felt the whole thing was preposterous.

'Then perhaps you should meet him yourself,' Diana retorted.

'I do have a business to run, you know.'

'It might concern the business, mightn't it?' – Sanders shook his head at this – 'But perhaps it might worry you to find out exactly what it's all about?'

'Very well,' Sanders sighed, 'fix the time and place. I'll see him.'

'It's not as easy as that,' Diana replied. The lift doors opened and they walked through the reception area into the bright sunshine outside, Diana quickly finding her sunglasses and sliding them on.

As they stood waiting for the car to make its way through the heavy traffic, Diana explained how she had found a regular notation in Sydney's diary, two or three times a year, of a telegram sent to a box-number in Algeria – just saying 'Happy Birthday'. So she sent one to see what would happen – The Pineapple Man did.

Sanders seemed quite bewildered by the story. Diana felt sure he really didn't know what it was all about – but he *had* reacted to the nickname; she was certain of that.

They got into the car and gave the driver their destination.

There was an edge to Sanders's voice. 'Anyone involved in international trade knows the term, knows what a "Pineapple Man" means.'

'Then why didn't you admit it straight away?'

The book made him nervous, that was the reason. He had the feeling sometimes that if he uttered the Lord's Prayer it would end up in the book with a different meaning. But to be precise: a Pineapple Man was a fringe operator in the world of international trading – someone not quite to be trusted, someone who had perhaps become a little greedy, and was known for it.

'In other words, he's a marked man.'

'Because he cannot be trusted – that's the point,' Sanders looked directly at her as the car came to a halt. 'And I suppose that's why I may have seemed to skirt your enquiries.'

Tommy Meadows was polishing the mirror of the Rolls when the burly man – the one who had stood outside the house on the evening of Diana's birthday – was caught in the reflection. Tommy grinned in recognition, then turned and welcomed the man warmly. He motioned him into the car and they sat back on the comfortable rear seats.

'Right,' Tommy smiled at the man, 'spill the beans.'

'I was sent for.'

Tommy was amazed. 'But he's dead, surely you knew that.'

The man nodded, then gestured at the telephone attached to the seat beside him and told Tommy how he had got the usual telegram and had thought he'd better come. He had tried to phone through to the car, as expected, but had been told that the number was changed.

They had to, Tommy said; a lot of cranks were using it after the funeral.

The man asked after Diana: how she was getting on. Tommy said she was getting over it, then he looked shrewdly at the man and asked if he'd like to meet her, if that was why he had come over.

'I told you, Tommy, I got the cable.'

'But you didn't have to come.'

The man had seen Diana from a distance, Jane and Charles too. In fact, he had literally bumped into Jane. She had looked at him quite oddly, as if she wondered whether she knew him from somewhere.

Tommy laughed. There was a pause.

'So you've seen the whole family' – again the shrewd look – 'but it's not enough after all this time, is it?'

The man smiled at Tommy, then patted him affectionately on the knee. 'It'll have to be.'

213

Tommy insisted that it would be a good idea; the rats, packs of them, had been crawling out of the sewers since Sydney died.

'What she needs now is to find his real friends.'

It wasn't long before The Pineapple Man contacted Diana again. Sanders came over, as promised, and arrived at the house shortly before he was due. When the bell sounded he took up his position facing the hall door.

The man entered the room hesitantly – and froze when he saw Sanders. Diana introduced them, and Sanders suddenly moved forward, with his hand outstretched.

Startled by the quickness of the movement the man jumped back; he was obviously terrified. He turned to go. Sanders stopped him and demanded an explanation for the story he had given Lady Clark.

'I don't know anything. It's a lie. I haven't said anything.'

Sanders faced the man squarely and asked him if he was expected to believe that Lady Clark had made it all up. An inspiration struck him.

'Ah, I've got it. It's Leon! Leon's your problem, is that it?'

The name Leon had a powerful effect: perspiration broke out on the man's face and he turned pleadingly to Diana.

'I know nothing. I swear I know nothing. I just wanted money.'

The hare was trapped, Sanders moved in for the kill.

'Poaching on his territory, is it? Small arms? Leon won't like that. He's got his hit-men looking for you right now. You need money to just survive, don't you? Am I right?'

The man's mouth opened and shut. He stared at Sanders with a fixed look.

Satisfied that he had hit the target, Sanders turned away abruptly and looked out the window, as if he might see the said hit-men waiting in the street.

The Pineapple Man came to. 'You fascist bastard!' The

voice was filled with hate. He strode from the room. In the silence left behind they heard the slam of the front door.

Diana stared at Sanders with new respect. 'I had no idea you could be so terrifying.' She shuddered slightly. 'Who on earth's Leon?'

'I made an educated guess . . .' he replied.

Sanders, Diana could see, was elated in a quiet, controlled way – the way someone commiserates with you over your bad luck when they've just beaten you at tennis – you know they don't mean it at all, they're so absolutely delighted with their win. But this was a far harder world; it was probably a matter of life and death to that poor man. To Sanders it was a victory, another victory. It might be a good opportunity to get some real information from him. Most men could be relied on to be a little indiscreet when they were savouring a success. She rang for coffee.

Sanders described to her the world of the international traders, the ones on the fringes of things, bending the rules where necessary. They couldn't take risks. It was a risky business smuggling goods into Rhodesia, breaking the UN sanctions, arranging a massive bribe in order to win a contract. They had to be very careful; they had to trust each other – their word really was their bond. Once someone broke that trust, they were marked – they were Pineapple Men.

'That's a world Sydney was involved in?' Diana enquired.

'He survived it,' Sanders made a casual gesture of the hand.

'He survived in it, you mean?'

Sydney was a businessman, Sanders explained. He used what methods were necessary. They all did. Governments did too, especially the ones with the holier-than-thou attitude. Sanders got up to go.

'Forget it all, Diana. Go back to thinking of pineapples as something you eat.'

Diana came to the door with Sanders. She said, 'I feel sorry for that man.'

'Oh, you should,' Sanders grinned at her. 'If your man was in small arms, there is a man called Leon ... God help him if Leon finds him ...'

It had taken Tommy some persuasion to get Diana to come along. He'd managed to arouse her curiosity by telling her that the man he wanted her to meet had lived for Sydney. They had gone out for a ride in the car – obviously to a prearranged rendezvous Diana guessed as Tommy nodded in the direction of a man standing beside a postbox. Diana had an odd feeling looking at the man; there was something very familiar about him. She realised why when he turned sideways: his profile was remarkably like Sydney's; he was about the same age too.

When he noticed Tommy and the car he smiled warmly and walked over to join them. Tommy jumped out and opened the door.

'Lady Clark – Mr Kaplin,' Tommy was being deliberately pompous.

Diana took an instant liking to the man as she asked him to join her inside. 'Tommy tells me you can give me some interesting background information on Sydney. You know, I would guess' – glancing at Tommy smiling from the driver's seat – 'that I'm doing a book about Sydney.'

'Yes I do.' The voice was deep, slightly accented – so he wasn't English. On a sudden impulse Diana invited him to come home to have some lunch, Kaplin was pleasantly surprised, and agreed readily.

His story was extraordinary. He was Dutch he told her. He had spent part of the war years involved in an underground operation engaged in smuggling refugees, mainly Jewish, out of Holland. The Germans were given information about him and had gone to his house one night to arrest him, but he wasn't there – a warning had come

216

through in time. But the Germans had taken his wife and two sons into custody; they were later taken to an internment camp – he never saw them again.

He told this part of the story in a calm, matter-of-fact manner. He clearly must have come to terms with it years ago.

His situation in Holland was desperate; he had to avoid all his usual contacts in order to keep suspicion away from as many as possible. His one hope was to trace someone he hadn't seen for years – this old friend was involved in another underground railroad, one totally separate from his own. Kaplin had gone to a café where he thought he might find this man; he was sitting quietly in a corner when suddenly a man sat down at his table and pushed an English identity-disc across the table.

It was a simple case of mistaken identity. The man was an English soldier on the run who had been shown a picture of Sydney and told to contact him at the café – the disc was Sydney's own and proof that the English soldier came from friends.

'In those days, the resemblance was even stronger than now,' Kaplin laughed. The English soldier was Tommy Meadows's father. That had been the start of the lifelong connection between Tommy and Sydney.

Back in the café the two men had been eyeing each other with great uncertainty, when Sydney himself arrived. Tommy's father realised instantly what had happened, but before he could do anything a squad of SS men marched in. They went straight up to Sydney and ordered him to accompany them outside. The theory they formed later was that someone else had made the same identity mistake, but this time in reverse: they thought that Sydney might be the elusive Kaplin. It seemed funny afterwards – it certainly wasn't at the time.

Diana got up to pour some drinks.

Kaplin leapt to his feet: 'Please, allow me.' Diana nodded. 'Dry Martini with the ice out,' he stated.

'You know that?' Diana was surprised.

'You were much loved and talked about.'

Kaplin returned to his story. He and Tommy's father had waited nervously for more than an hour, Kaplin with the identity-disc still in his pocket. They had accepted each other's story; they really had no choice. Then Sydney reappeared in the café and came over with a cheery wave.

His German was perfect, of course, and his papers identifying him as a clerk with the transport people were authentic – as the SS discovered when they checked them. But they had gone through all his pockets, quite affably, as Sydney was good at making people laugh. He had said all the right things a good Nazi would. He insisted they went right ahead; they must be thorough – 'That's how we'll win the war.'

If the identity-disc had been found during that search ... it would have been a disaster. The lucky accident had been the saving of all three of them.

Kaplin pulled a small metal object out of his pocket. It was the same identity-disc. He said the purpose of his seeing Diana was to give it to her as a memento of Sydney.

Diana was deeply moved. She held the disc in her hand for some minutes, turning it over and over, as if the mere feel of it was some magic way of getting in touch again with her husband.

Kaplin then described how Sydney had arranged his escape from Holland. Eventually he got to England. He was instructed to go to the War Office with a coded message – he never discovered what it was – and once more the disc was used as a token of bona fides. He had kept it ever since.

Diana looked at the disc again, and then thrust it back at Kaplin. 'My husband gave it you to save your life – I think you should keep it.'

Kaplin took it back. 'It does hold a lot of memories.'

Diana asked why Kaplin hadn't been to see her before, especially as he and Sydney had kept in touch over the years. Kaplin explained that he had only just arrived in England, for the first time in several years. He was glad to meet her at last. They smiled at each other. Then Diana asked him if Sydney had ever taken payment for this people-smuggling he was apparently involved in during the war.

'Not that I know of,' Kaplin replied. 'Mind you, the diamonds were getting out of Amsterdam faster than the people.'

'Was Sydney involved in that?'

Kaplin eyed her curiously; he could see the drift of her questions. 'Sydney risked his neck to get me out, and *I* had nothing. I'm sorry if my arrival here has caused you to question his past.'

Diana made a gesture of apology; she had just been reminded that you don't question the integrity of the man you loved . . . you merely remember that love.

Kaplin went through the whole story again for Jane and Charles when they came in. They were amazed and delighted when shown the disc. Kaplin also pulled out an ancient-looking tooth brush; he explained that it had become almost a symbol to him. Sydney had needed to hide him for a week before Kaplin could go down the escape route. The toothbrush had meant he could clean his teeth. 'With all my experience of hiding people myself, I had never appreciated the importance of something like that. It meant I could walk past Germans without feeling I had been living in a hole for a week. That's important. If you feel it, you look it – then they get you.'

Kaplin told them how he had returned to Holland for a while after the war, but the memories were too painful so he had literally become a citizen of the world. But he had maintained his friendship with Sydney – for over thirty years.

Charles remarked that one thing puzzled him – the physical similarity. Knowing his father, he would have thought that he would have found some way of capitalising on it.

Kaplin started, then smiled. 'We had a few laughs with

women ... before he married Diana, of course.'

The atmosphere was warm and friendly, the four of them sitting relaxed and comfortable. The late-afternoon sunshine of a summer's day was enough to light the room still.

Then Ellen appeared at the door. There was someone to see Lady Clark, privately.

'Feel free to talk,' she smiled at Kaplin.

Jane urged him to continue, but Kaplin said it would be boring.

'Dad's love life boring?' Jane insisted. 'You're joking.'

Diana's visitor was a policeman, a detective-inspector. A man had been killed; her name and address was found on him. Could she help? The policeman held up a grubby passport, not a British one, maybe South American. The photograph wasn't very good – but it was The Pineapple Man.

Diana said she did recognise him. He had come round saying he was an old business acquaintance of her husband. She had told him Sir Sydney was dead and the man had left. That was all. How had he been killed?

It had happened in a crowded tube station, at rush hour. The killer would have been four stops away before anyone realised they were stumbling over a corpse. It looked like a professional job; the continental shiv had been left behind, deliberately no doubt.

'They always leave their card, it's a warning to others.' He was sorry to upset Lady Clark, his call was routine. They really had little chance of finding the murderer.

So Sanders's prediction had been fulfilled, frighteningly quickly. Nevertheless, the four of them had a very affable dinner and evening. Kaplin at last agreed to stay, and Tommy went over to his small hotel to collect his bags. As they were all about to go off to bed, Diana asked Kaplin to stay with her for a moment. She wanted to talk to him about something.

Diana told him the whole story: about Sydney and the supposed deal with the Russians. She showed him the photograph. Kaplin pointed out that it was hardly a good likeness. It could be anyone, it could be him. Diana said that Sanders always knew more than he let on; he had known The Pineapple Man and now that man was dead. Sydney had marked him, and he had been killed.

'I know I'm right, I can feel it ... Sydney left the order to kill him.' Diana was very upset. She turned towards the bookcase, her head bowed.

Kaplin instinctively stepped towards her and put a hand on her shoulder, she buried her head in his chest. After a long moment, he slowly lifted his arms and held her.

They stayed like that for a minute, then Kaplin heard the click of the door. He was quick enough to catch a glimpse of Jane disappearing. He gently moved away from the embrace and led Diana to a chair.

'Sometimes it's easier to talk to a stranger.'

Diana looked at him oddly. 'I wish you were a stranger.'

After that it didn't help the state of Diana's confused emotions to find Jane in her bedroom, looking at Sydney's portrait. It was the old slightly bitter, jealous Jane. The girl dropped a few obvious hints about Kaplin. 'I don't blame you,' she said. 'It's a second chance.'

Diana was worried. The physical similarity to Sydney was there, of course. But she and Jane had the same psychological need to find Sydney again. It was easy enough to transfer this to Kaplin. In a way, his visit had come too soon.

Her fears were realised again the next morning at breakfast. Finding Jane had started breakfast before her, Diana asked the girl if she had seen Mr Kaplin go out.

'You aren't keeping tabs on him already, are you?'

'I asked you a simple question,' Diana retorted.

'To which there's a simple answer. I haven't been up all night watching him.'

It was worse, later that morning, when Kaplin joined them in the living-room. He knocked and waited till Diana called out 'Come in'. He could sense there was an atmosphere straight away.

'You don't have to knock,' she said.

Jane broke in very sharply, 'Of course not. It's home from home.'

Kaplin apologised for intruding, but Jane now had the bit between her teeth. She went on to claim that it was she who was the real intruder, disrupting Diana's main purpose in life – digging out the gory details of her father's life and putting them into that damned biography.

She glared at Diana. 'She's had everything he could give her, but she won't let him go ... even now.'

Kaplin, the quiet, gentle man, suddenly flared out at Jane, calling her a spoiled, thankless child who thought only of herself.

Jane was stunned, deeply hurt – then her own anger burst out. 'Who the hell do you think you are!'

The two stared at each other, both of them wanting to apologise, but the moment had passed and Jane ran from the room.

The emotion of the scene made it easier for Kaplin to tell Diana what he thought she should know; he had been out that morning to see Donald Sanders, to warn him of his intentions.

Kaplin sat down opposite her and plunged straight in. He explained that he hadn't just been Sydney's friend; over the last ten years he had acted as Sydney's double from time to time. For the occasions when Sydney couldn't be in two places at once; or when he couldn't afford to be in a particular place at all. The routine had been simple: Sydney would telegraph him with a code-word; Kaplin would phone Tommy in the car to get the details. One of the jobs had been in Portugal – he was the man in the photograph, not Sydney. Sydney had no intention of doing that deal at all. Kaplin's job was to impersonate him in order to find out what was involved and who the people were. Once Sydney knew the background details he dropped the whole thing.

Diana asked why Sydney wanted to know these details. Kaplin didn't know – but Sanders might. He had asked him to call in that morning. He looked at his watch; in fact Sanders should be here any moment now.

Diana thought she understood: Kaplin had complete trust in Sydney; he would do anything he was asked to with complete loyalty, no questions asked. This seemed a common attribute in the people Sydney had gathered around him. She glanced down at her half-filled coffee-cup; there was no point in drinking it. She had let it go cold while she listened to Kaplin's story.

The door-bell rang, and soon they could hear Sanders's voice. It sounded as if he was talking to Jane. When Sanders came into the room, Kaplin got to his feet and told him he probably had the answers Diana wanted. Then he left the two of them alone.

At first Sanders hedged – as always. Then it came out that he was not so much worried about telling the truth as embarrassed by it. It was a part of Sydney he had found rather naïve and sentimental. Sydney had become, for want of a better phrase, a witch-hunter.

'You knew how Sydney felt about communists.'

Diana nodded. She knew. That's why she had found it so hard to believe The Pineapple Man's story.

Sanders told her that Sydney had conducted his own personal war against communism. It came out of a need to fight for capitalism, however misguided. In this case he had exposed the man in question as a trader for the communists. The man's credibility was now destroyed – he was a Pineapple Man.

Diana's mood was serious. 'So Sydney really did have that man killed in the end.'

Sanders explained that the man wasn't killed because he was a communist; he was killed by his own kind. 'He probably had it coming anyway.'

Diana was stung by Sanders's callousness. 'But Sydney dug him out and pointed the finger at him.'

'Only as a communist – not to be murdered,' Sanders insisted.

'And how many other "communists" did he find and label?'

'Then you tell me' – Sanders's voice was deliberate – 'how many people have labelled Sydney since he died? They've only come out now from their holes. Maybe Sydney was fighting a private war, but at least he did it face-to-face. You've got to give him something for that.'

The four of them spent the whole weekend together, just laughing and talking. Kaplin and Jane had obviously made it up privately; the girl's whole attitude had changed. She made almost too obvious a point of leaving Kaplin and Diana alone together from time to time – she'd knock on every door and wait rather too long before entering. It was quite clear that she was trying to push them together.

In one way Diana didn't mind this, but in another she resented it. She tried to analyse her feelings. Kaplin was comfortable to have around. His resemblance to Sydney was a help, particularly as his personality was so different; he didn't have that challenging humour, that dynamic energy. On Sunday night she found herself lying awake until the early hours of the morning. In the half-glow from the night-light in the hallway she could see the outline of Sydney's portrait on the wall. As she stared at it, she reflected that it wasn't Kaplin the man she was attracted to; she was actually reacting to her own need for comfort. That seemed to put it in perspective – you got awfully used to a favourite pair of old bedroom slippers, a particular bath-robe. She'd see in the morning ... and then she drifted off into sleep.

After breakfast, Diana asked Ellen for a second cup of coffee in the sitting-room. When she walked in, after collecting a file of notes from her bedroom, she noticed the tray had two cups on it. She stared at them for a second, puzzled – then Kaplin came in and wished her good-morning. Intuitively he felt something was about to happen, so he didn't say anything as he poured out the coffee.

'I don't know how to say what I want to say,' Diana smoothed a non-existent crease in her skirt. 'I wondered if you had any plans for the future'.

Kaplin looked at her, almost softly. 'Are you asking me to leave?'

Diana held his look and said, simply, 'Yes.'

They looked at each other for a long moment. The words were unsaid – but understood.

Diana continued, 'You've done so much.'

'Please. Don't say any more,' then Kaplin grinned at her. 'May I finish my coffee?'

Diana relaxed. 'I don't mean right now.'

Seconds later Kaplin finished his coffee in two fast swallows, stood up, bowed and said goodbye. He started to leave the room.

Diana hurried after him. 'Wait a minute. Please ...' As she caught up with him in the hall, she stopped when she saw his cases, already packed, standing by the door.

He shrugged apologetically. 'We don't need to talk about it, do we?' he said .

Tommy then burst through the door, seized the cases and announced that he'd be waiting in the car.

'Where are you going?' Diana asked.

'Somewhere,' he said. 'Starting again – for the third time. You know what they say.' He took her hand and kissed it. He turned to go.

'Happy Birthday!' Diana said.

Kaplin wondered for a minute, then laughed when he realised. 'I'm too old for birthdays now.'

Diana stood and watched him go. She was smiling. She felt at peace with herself.

14

The Pineapple Man wasn't the only creature to crawl out from under some rock. Jonathan Browning had been kept under observation for two days by another one. On the third day the man was joined by two others: one a big, hard-looking man; the other much smaller – he looked like some anonymous clerk. The three men rode in a white Ford Cortina; they followed Browning's battered Fiat as he made his way to the Cyprus High Commission. They waited patiently until he came out, got into his car and drove off towards Tottenham Court Road. The three men tailed him, two or three cars behind. This time Browning parked on a pair of yellow lines, and entered a Greek restaurant. About two hours later he came out with the girl he had arranged to meet for lunch. The three men got out of their own car and moved towards him.

Browning opened the passenger-door for the girl. He walked round to the driver's side. Just as he was about to insert the key in the lock, he felt two hands on his shoulders. He was turned round forcefully by one of them, and slammed against the car. Another man leant against the girl's door. There was nothing she could do but watch.

Browning's first thought was that it was a mugging. He protested that he had no money.

The clerkish man smiled. 'Do we look as if we need cash, Mr Browning?' he said mildly. 'We just want a word, that's all. And to give you a little encouragement.'

'Get this man off me,' Browning muttered. The man was very strong, and there was no way Browning could break the hold on his wrists. He tried jamming his knee in the man's crotch, but this move was easily evaded. The big man grinned, then butted his head hard into Browning's face. Browning could feel his lip split, and blood stream from his nose. The girl in the car screamed.

The little man looked almost bored. 'The word first. Sir Sydney Clark. Lay off that story. Or you'll get wasted.' He nodded at the terrified girl. 'One peep from you to the police, and your girl friend there might find herself with two mouths ... understand me?'

He reached out and tore Browning's keys from his fingers, then dropped them down a drain. 'Such a shame,' he said. 'You'll probably get a parking ticket, I shouldn't wonder. Now that encouragement I promised you ...'

The beating-up was quick, and very professional. The girl inside the car pressed her hand on the horn and held it there, hoping to attract someone's attention. As Browning slid down the side of the Fiat the men calmly, unhurriedly, walked back to their own car. The girl threw the door open and rushed round to where Browning lay. She gasped at what she saw, then looked up at the departing car, trying to memorise the registration number. The little man gave her a wave as it moved off.

The next morning Donald Sanders got a little 'encouragement' too. He looked with distaste at the elegant figure sitting opposite him. Tony Hambis was in his late thirties, very expensively dressed, well-coiffured. To Sanders it seemed there was too much gold on his fingers; his teeth were too perfect. The man smiled constantly, annoyingly.

Sanders explained that it simply wasn't possible for the Company to arrange for Hambis's men to be put on its ships as crew and then dropped at various African ports.

Hambis smiled. 'Don't talk rubbish, Mr Sanders. It is common practice.'

'We don't run mercenaries anywhere, Mr Hambis,' Sanders replied.

Hambis laughed, a little too long. He shifted his chair close to Sanders's desk and leaned on his elbows. Sanders could tell he'd eaten garlic at lunch. Hambis dropped his voice to a low, confidential tone and reminded him that Sydney Clark had made a very good business out of running people from one place to another. Mercenaries? Of course he had defended it all as necessary to stop the commie rot – but he'd still charged money for it. 'Personally, I don't give a damn who or where,' Hambis continued, 'as long as I make my few dollars. Now the usual routes into Southern Africa are blocked. You can help me with a way in and I intend to use it. You provide the transport.' He sat back in his chair and stared at Sanders. There was now no trace of his usual smile.

'If you don't, Clark's beginnings will be made common knowledge ... Your investors won't like it, you know. The institutions could start selling your shares and ...' He opened his hands, shrugged his shoulders. The smile had returned.

'I don't like blackmail,' Sanders said nervously.

'I don't either,' Hambis replied. 'No one does. So let's not bother with it, mmm?' He took out a gold cigarette-case, selected an Egyptian cigarette, and tapped it several times against the case.

'I don't like mercenaries,' Sanders said almost petulantly.

Hambis lit his cigarette, took a deep puff. He crossed his legs and glanced down at the elegant Gucci loafer on his foot, as if admiring it for a minute. 'I couldn't care less about your likes and dislikes.' Hambis pulled a newspaper out of his attaché-case; a paragraph was circled. He tossed it on the desk. 'Did you see this?'

Sanders glanced down at the item. The headline read: JOURNALIST BEATEN UP. It concerned Jonathan Browning. He read it once, then twice. He felt a twinge in his stomach. He knew what this man was capable of. Finally he pushed the paper aside, trying to make his voice sound casual. 'You did this?' The question was unnecessary.

Hambis looked pleased with himself. 'Mr Browning was,

what do you say, raking the muck. According to my sources, he was seen in the Greek Embassy, and in the Cyprus High Commission.'

Sanders surreptitiously wiped his sweaty palms on his trousers. 'We're not in Piraeus now, or in Marseilles, Mr Hambis.'

Hambis tapped his cigarette ash into the ashtray. He explained that it was just business. Browning could get in the way. And just for a book about his old friend, his father's old friend ... muck-raking.

'You don't want that, Mr Sanders, do you? I've done you a favour. Now I want one in return.'

'I don't think I can.'

Hambis looked unperturbed. 'I understand that Sydney's wife is working on some book too.' He spoke too casually for it to be anything but a threat.

Sanders was shocked. 'You can't touch her ...'

Hambis broadened his smile and got to his feet. 'Let's say forty-eight hours, Mr Sanders.' He gave a half-wave, half-salute, and left the room.

Diana learned about the attack on Jonathan Browning from Charles. The two of them were relaxing over cups of coffee after breakfast. Each was glancing through a newspaper: Diana *The Times*, Charles the *Daily Mail*. They had been discussing her book at the same time, Charles teasing her a little excessively about her 'nosing out the dirt'.

'I want the record straight, that's all, Charles. And I don't want to do it Jonathan Browning's way. Can you understand that?'

Charles grinned at her. 'You never did like competition, did you?'

'Browning is doing the book for what he can make out of it,' Diana snapped. 'The more scandal, the more people hurt, the better. I want an honest, factual ...'

Charles interrupted her. 'So *you're* not responsible for this? ... Arranging to put the rival out of the way?' He showed her his paper, pointing to an article about the attack on Browning. 'That'll keep him quiet for a while.'

Browning was sitting up in the hospital bed when Diana arrived. He was talking desultorily to the girl he had been with the day before. He was surprised to see Diana come to the side of the bed, holding up an enormous bunch of grapes.

'You made the dailies,' she smiled.

Browning groaned. 'Tea and sympathy I can do without.' Diana looked at the girl with interest. Browning introduced them. 'Lady Diana Clark, of that Ilk ... Lorna.'

'I won't stay long,' said Diana. 'You have some nasty friends, don't you?'

'No friends of mine.'

Diana asked him: 'Why do you think you were attacked, if it wasn't for money? Was it something you were working on?'

Browning raised an eyebrow. 'You do jump to conclusions, don't you?'

'I try to look before I jump.'

Lorna looked from one to the other. 'What on earth are you two talking about?'

Browning answered her, still looking steadily at Diana. 'Oh, everyone has a conspiracy theory nowadays. There's mileage in them.'

Diana said she'd better leave. She was glad to see he was almost out of bed ... it gave her a chance to catch up. She nodded goodbye to Lorna and left the ward quite convinced that Browning was lying in a hospital bed because of something to do with Sydney. She was certain he wasn't working on any other subject at the moment. The attack on him had to be some kind of warning-off.

Charles Clark's gambling itch was well known in the circles through which Hambis travelled – he felt it might possibly lead to another way of forcing Sanders to do what he wanted. He might be able to get some sort of hold on Charles. There were some Americans in town who always liked a high-stake game, and Charles was going to play them. So Hambis got himself invited also.

Charles brought two thousand pounds with him. He played with a certain flamboyance but he was a good player. Hambis played a tight marginal game, all the while keeping an eye on Charles. Charles won at first, then he lost two big pots – and he had held good hands too. His pile of money had decreased steadily ... then one of the biggest pots of the evening built up.

They were playing five-card stud. Charles had four spades showing, one an ace. He was coolly raising each time his turn came. One of the Americans looked at Charles's cards for a long time, then down at his own pair of kings. If Charles didn't have the flush, he could still have another ace in the hole. The American raised five hundred pounds; Charles calmly met the raise. It left him with about fifty pounds.

'I raise one thousand pounds. I'll have to drag – all right?'

'You can get the money?'

'Of course.'

The American looked at Charles's cards for a long time, then at Charles. He made his decision. 'I'll call you.' He put in a thousand pounds.

Charles's face went white. He tried to keep his voice calm. 'If you can call, you can beat me ...'

The American grinned, then flipped up his hole card. It was a three. He had only had the pair of kings showing.

'Jesus Christ,' Charles swore, 'I could have had aces. You never should have stayed in.'

'Look, kid. You play your game. I'll play mine ... now, you'd better get the money.'

'Well, at this time of night everything's shut.' Charles pulled out his chequebook and a pen.

'Hey fellow, I asked if you could get the money when

you dragged. I'm not taking paper. I fly home tomorrow.'

Charles laughed nervously. 'Where can I get the cash at this . . .'

Hambis interrupted. 'My friends, let's not fall out.' He turned to Charles. 'Sir, I'll accept your IOU.' He passed over a thousand pounds to the American. 'Is that all right?'

'Sure, sure . . . Come on, let's have the next hand.'

Charles indicated he was out, then asked Hambis if he could have a word with him. They went to one corner of the hotel suite. Charles wrote out the IOU.

'I'm grateful. You *will* be paid. A week or two would be convenient if you could wait.'

Hambis nodded in agreement.

'But I don't even know your name.'

'My name is Tony Hambis.' He nodded towards the winning player. 'That man's a professional, you know. He knew every card in your hand.'

Charles shrugged ruefully. 'Maybe you're right . . . but I still don't see why you should stump up for me.'

Hambis gave him a warm smile. 'Let's say it's in memory of some favours done a long time ago by a very nice man. But I warn you . . . beware of Greeks bearing gifts. Shall we go and find ourselves a drink?'

The charm was working. Charles agreed readily.

Late the next morning Hambis sat in his father's flat, staring moodily at the little cup of black, sweet coffee. The old man looked at him closely.

'Well, my son? You sit here in the afternoon. You drink coffee with your father . . . something is wrong.'

The younger man sighed. 'Sanders . . . he's creating a problem.'

The older man shook his head sadly. Sanders was not like Sydney Clark – if the latter saw a chance he would grab it.

Tony Hambis revealed a flash of anger. 'I gave him

forty-eight hours to consider. I showed him what happened to that journalist.'

His father looked at him sadly. 'I told you to leave that alone, Tonis.'

'You told me he was finding things, people ... things between you and me, and Clark.'

'I want nothing to do with that. I told you, this is not Piraeus.'

The son smiled. 'You sound like Sanders.' His father's attention seemed to be wandering then, so Tony Hambis sharply reminded him that he had been made a rich man by what he, his son, had done. And he would become even richer. Sanders would come to heel. There was another book being written, by the Clark widow. Pressure on her would be pressure on Sanders. 'He'll do as he's told. Believe me.'

Threats against women! The old man felt much saddened.

Diana thought that Jonathan Browning's vulnerable point might be through the girl. If he wouldn't tell her why he had been beaten up, Lorna might. She arranged for Tommy to follow the girl home and discover her address. Lorna was surprised to see Diana at the door, but invited her in. Diana could see that she was in the process of packing; apparently that was Browning's idea. She had been frightened by the attack on him; but before that there had been warning phone-calls – to his flat, and even to her flat as well, when he was there. For a moment, she confessed, Browning had entertained the wild idea that Diana might be behind it all.

'Do I look like the type who would have a man beaten up?' Diana asked.

'I don't know what the type is, do I?'

'I suppose not.'

Lorna made reference to the theory that Sydney actually bought his knighthood; that was what Browning was

currently looking into: all those charity benefactions ...
the East End clubs, boy's clubs, boxing clubs.

'It couldn't possibly have had anything to do with
simple generosity, I suppose?' Diana asked stiffly. 'In any
case, I hardly think your friend was beaten up over my
husband's charity work.'

Lorna was puzzled about something else. She informed
Diana that Greece was somehow involved. In fact Jonathan had planned to go there – then he had cancelled the
trip because the person he wanted to see had come to
London. That was when the threatening phone-calls
started. She jumped when she heard the flat door open,
then relaxed when Browning himself came into the room.
Still, both women were surprised to see him there.

'I thought you were meant to be ...' Lorna started.

Browning ignored her. 'The first thing I need is a very
large drink.' He was annoyed to see that Lorna hadn't
finished her packing, and he told her to get on with it. 'I
mean now.'

The girl left the room in a huff. Browning swung round
on Diana 'I'd like to see you tomorrow ... my pub. Two all
right?'

'Why?'

'Because this time, Diana, you're in well over your
head.' He took a large swallow of his drink. 'Oh sorry ...
cheers!'

Diana learned from Charles that there was actually a place
in the East End called the 'Sydney Clark Boxing Club',
but as far as he knew his father hadn't been near the place
for years. Diana found it all very hard to believe; she
remembered that Sydney had actually disliked boxing.

The club was there all right, in a rather seedy building.
The paint-spray people had been at work: the walls were
daubed with a variety of National Front slogans, and
answering ones from the Black Consciousness groups. Inside it didn't look so seedy: a big gym with a roped-off ring
in the centre. There seemed to be a lot of weight-training

equipment around; several boys were sweating through their exercises. In the ring two black boys were sparring, leather helmets on their heads, large protective belts guarding their crutches.

A bald man, about fifty but very fit-looking, was shouting instructions to each fighter. Diana waited for a minute. No one took any notice of her. Finally, she cleared her throat. 'Mr Sullivan?'

The man turned, 'Who wants him?'

'I'm Diana Clark ... you knew my husband I believe.'

Realisation dawned. Sullivan extended a massive hand. 'Oh sure. You mean Syd. He was a good fellow. I liked him.'

Diana smiled. 'So did I ...'

She told him that she was doing a sort of book on her husband. Oddly enough, there was a great deal she didn't know about him. This boxing club for instance. Sullivan explained that he had known Sydney for years, since the fifties. Sydney had always been straight with him. He had set up the club back in 1963.

'How much did he put in, do you remember?'

'Yeah – it was about fifty grand.' Seeing Diana's look of surprise, he explained that first there was the building to buy, then it had to be done up – all the equipment, showers and so on. It soon mounted up. The odd thing was that he had been so interested at first, put in all that money, set up a good committee too, came to all the meetings. Then, suddenly, he had stopped.

Diana told him some people were suggesting Sydney had virtually bought his knighthood. His behaviour over the club would be just the sort of thing to give them ammunition.

'If someone says that to me, he'll get a knuckle sandwich to bite on. He was a good man. He came from this area, he knew what these kids are up against. He remembered. I tell you, coming to a place like this helps keep them out of trouble. Let any man tell me he bought his knighthood and I'll flatten him ... I will.'

Diana felt a sense of relief, of comfort even.

Liz Walters was very curious about the visit of Tony Hambis. All the secretaries were talking about him; you'd have thought a film star had visited the office. She took some papers in for Donald to sign, and watched him for a moment as his pen scratched away.

'What was the Greek Romeo after?' she asked as she gathered the papers together. 'We aren't doing business with him, are we?'

'We might be forced to. He and his father did, well, some business with us some years ago, before you joined.'

Liz looked a little indignant. 'Who forces us to do business? What on earth do you mean? What sort of business did you do with this man?'

Sanders told her that Hambis Père et Fils moved people. In the fifties it was around the Middle East, Egypt, Iraq, Syria ... soldiers mostly, sometimes politicals. Those areas had become very sensitive to the Clark organisation; it wouldn't do for these things to come out.

'Tell him to go to hell.' Liz made it sound so simple.

He told her about the oblique threat to Diana, about what had happened to Browning.

'There's something Hambis is sensitive about ... something Browning was getting close to. Something Diana could get close to if she goes on with this damned book.' He suggested perhaps Liz could have a word with her. Diana didn't seem to listen to him much.

'She and I don't exactly see eye to eye either,' Liz pointed out.

'It might be worth a try. I'm pretty sure Hambis would lean on her if he felt it was the only way to get what he wants.'

Liz reluctantly agreed to make the effort. As it happened, she was due to see Diana the next night, about some of the papers Wilkins still needed in working out the final estate.

After Liz had explained the papers to Diana, they chatted over a drink. Liz asked how the book was going.

'Slowly,' Diana told her; Charles had almost persuaded her to give it up. Maybe she would ... 'I'll tell you something I've come up with, though. Did you know he was interested in boxing. Made large donations to a boxing club?'

Liz's face was expressionless. 'I didn't know.'

'True. I've been there, seen it. He paid up for a trust fund, and for the building. It was in March 1963, which I find very curious. The company books for that time show there was a little liquidity problem. I wonder where he picked up that much cash?' She looked hard at Liz; perhaps *she* didn't know – it was before her time after all.

Liz said she really had no idea, then she picked her words very carefully. 'Diana, Browning was a warning, you know that. And Donald is under great pressure, threats even.'

'Threats! Then he should go to the police.'

Liz pressed on. 'It would help if you laid off the book. For a while, at least.'

Diana finished her drink. 'Look, Sydney spends fifty thousand pounds he doesn't have. I want the answer – and threats from Donald won't stop me.'

'You've been warned.'

'Come on, Liz, don't be so melodramatic. You might as well dangle a Cartier bauble in front of a flower girl. Why, you're just guaranteeing I'll sit up and take notice.'

'You should leave it alone.'

Diana rose and fixed them both another drink without bothering to ask if Liz wanted one. She went on to talk about her marriage with Sydney, how little she knew about him. True, it was like that with most marriages. A man leaves in the morning, he comes back at night. How many wives know what's happened in between. The husband may be a forger, a rapist, a bigamist ... anything.

'I don't think that about Sydney, of course, but I do want to know why a man was beaten to pulp because of him. Now, I know Browning was planning to go to Athens, but he didn't because some Greek has come to London instead. I've discovered that Sydney and Donald were in Athens in 1963 – I think there's some connection with that mysterious fifty thousand pounds. Don't you?'

Liz remembered her own questions to Donald Sanders, about the man she had jokingly referred to as the Greek Romeo. She started to gather her things together to go. 'Diana, I feel I've failed. I don't suppose you'll listen, but I must tell you Donald sincerely believes you'll be in some danger if you go on with the book.'

'Does he?'

'Yes, he does. And you'd be well advised to pay attention to him.'

Diana was inclined to take the warning seriously, whatever she might say to Liz Walters or Donald Sanders. Tommy had continued his detective work to find out what he could about the Greek called Tony Hambis. The name had come up several times in conversations she had overheard at the office. After a few casual questions, Donald's secretary had told her Hambis was only recently arrived in London. It seemed a little too coincidental. Diana now felt sure he was Jonathan Browning's Greek. Tommy's little report didn't tell her much – though Hambis did go jogging every morning on Hampstead Heath. She would recognise him easily enough; he even looked elegant in a track-suit – it could have been made-to-measure. Then Tommy gave her a photograph.

'Good morning, Mr Hambis.'

He stopped, gave a charming smile. 'I'm sorry, I don't think I know . . .'

Diana stuck out her hand. 'Diana Clark. You know a friend of mine, I think.'

Hambis waited calmly.

'Jonathan Browning,' she watched him hesitate, then shake his head.

'No?' she said. 'Oh well ...'

Hambis looked at her for a long moment. 'I knew your husband, you know. I was very impressed with him. Would you like me to tell you about it?'

'Please do,' Diana replied.

Hambis remembered Sydney as a man who much enjoyed life, not like too many English. He had been a good friend to Hambis, and to his father – he had helped them. In those days his father had owned one leaky old boat; he was really only one step from being a peasant. Without his pushing his father would still be on that boat. But now ... he opened his arms, as if to encompass the world.

Diana asked him about Greece. 'Did you remain there when the colonels came to power?'

Hambis shrugged cynically. 'I don't bother my head about politics. They were there, the rulers. I was there to make money ... I did.'

'Browning was right,' Diana said involuntarily.

Hambis was sharp. 'I'm sorry. I told you, I don't know this one.' His eyes glinted. 'Did you know your son owes me money?'

My god, Diana thought, he's really just a gangster. 'Stepson, Mr Hambis. His debts are his own business.'

Hambis flashed his smile again. 'Naturally.'

'Did you do business with my husband?'

Hambis ignored the question. 'Come and meet my father.'

'Does he answer questions?'

'He enjoys beautiful women, almost as much as I do. I will call you ... this evening perhaps.' He lifted a hand and jogged off, Diana stood watching him go.

Browning didn't take very kindly to her news when she described her contact with Hambis at their scheduled meeting the next day.

'I'm telling you, be careful. You could end up in a dirty ditch somewhere. Just leave it alone.'

'Well, tell me something about Athens ... Piraeus.'

Browning sighed and took a deep swallow of his beer. 'Philipos Hambis was an old Piraeus hand. A trader. He owned a single flat-bottomed freighter ... then the son came into the business and suddenly the old boy retires. Tonis, the son, resurfaced in Marseilles. Stuffed with money.'

'And you think this is connected with some business he did with Sydney.'

Browning peered into his pint glass. 'You add up twos and make five, love.'

'Are you scared of him?'

'No,' Browning's eyes hardened. 'I'm just going to get him. That's all.'

'What about your famous objectivity,' Diana teased him.

Browning turned and spoke very seriously. 'Stay out, love. Let it ride this time. I'd hate to have to return your hospital visit.'

Sanders's secretary buzzed to say she had Mr Hambis on the line. Sanders pondered whether to take the call, then decided he'd better.

The Greek came straight to the point. 'Diana Clark has been on to me. I want her off my back.'

'I do not own Diana Clark.'

'Then warn her. And now I'll warn you. I want your decision very soon, and it must be favourable to me or you will regret your procrastination. Also the world will know what you and the noble Sir Sydney and my father did to make a very great deal of money in a very short space of time. Sydney won't damage – but she will, you will, your company will ...'

Hambis's next target was Charles Clark. He had been invited for a drink and came along unsuspectingly. Hambis suggested a little backgammon, good stakes to add a little excitement.

He played hard and ruthlessly. Charles was soon a loser.

'I'm delighted to have the money to play,' Hambis smiled, then his affability suddenly melted away. 'I would be grateful if you could let me have that loan back.'

Charles looked up in surprise. 'But, I thought you said . . .'

Hambis gestured to the backgammon board. 'Little boy, if you have the money to play, you have the money to pay me back.'

'I will pay you, I just need a little . . .'

'Now.'

'No.'

They stared at each other, then Hambis leant back and clasped his hands behind his head. 'Did you read about a journalist called Browning? Such a bad accident. He had some information, you see. Something which could foul up a deal I'm interested in. Now he's in the hospital. I must be frank. I have friends who can influence a situation.'

Charles looked at him disbelievingly. He felt he was sitting through an old Hollywood B picture. 'Look here, Hambis . . .'

The Greek held up an admonitory hand. 'Diana Clark has the same information, or will have soon. I want her to understand that it's a serious matter to ignore my advice – Donald Sanders's advice – that she goes quietly away and leaves business to businessmen.'

He was startled by a sudden hardness and maturity in Charles's voice.

'You may take this as an empty threat, you oily creep, but if Diana Clark is hurt, intimidated in any way, I'll find a way to break your back.'

Charles got up and quickly left the room. Hambis was half out of his chair. The grin had just started to come back, but there was a touch of nervousness in his bravado. The very real anger Charles had shown had surprised and disturbed him. Perhaps there was something of the old man in the boy after all. He snapped at his own father when he walked in and asked who had just left. And he told him to behave himself when they saw Diana Clark;

whatever he did he wasn't to talk too much. He was just to convince her that all he had ever done was to take her husband on a pleasure-trip around the Greek Islands. There was a very big fish to catch, and no one was going to get in the way.

'You think she will come,' the old man asked, 'after you have warned her off?'

'She is intrigued and she is inquisitive. I also think she is very angry. She will come certainly.'

His father stared at him. 'You harm a woman and you're no son to me.'

'Then don't make me. Steer her away. Understand me, Papa?'

Diana understood Hambis's message very well when she opened the door to a bruised and bleeding Charles. He wasn't as badly beaten up as Jonathan Browning had been; he was even able to make jokes. But he stopped her from calling the police, saying that wouldn't do any good.

'He wants to stop you writing your book.'

'What do you say, Charles?' Diana asked worriedly.

'I say if you do, I'll never take you out again.' He grinned at her.

At least she'd have one ally, she thought, as she made her way to see Donald Sanders the next morning. She minced no words in describing what had happened the night before. First Jonathan Browning, now Charles.

'I really don't know what we can do ...' Sanders started to say apologetically.

'I know what you can do, Donald. You can tell me all about it. You'd better, or I'll make so much trouble, you'll have to emigrate.' Her voice was calm.

Sanders had no doubt she meant every word. He spoke very quietly. 'He wants to use our ships ... putting in a fake crew, sailing into an African port.'

'Mercenaries?' Diana asked.

Sanders nodded. 'I said no. Now he threatens you, has

Charles beaten up. What the hell can I do?'

Diana looked at him sympathetically. 'I don't like mercenaries either.' Her voice sounded determined.

Sanders gave her a worried look. 'Diana, look I don't know what you're going to do. But just think a moment. If any of this gets out, our African subsidiaries wouldn't last five minutes.'

Diana gave a bitter smile. 'Oh, that's what it's about, is it?'

'It is a consideration.'

Diana turned towards the door. 'Goodbye, Donald. You'll hear from me shortly.'

When she got home Diana thought long and hard over a solitary pot of tea. A possible solution gradually formed in her mind, but she'd need Jonathan Browning's co-operation. And she'd get it too.

She deliberately let the two men, the father and son, wait for her that night at the restaurant Tony Hambis had suggested. She apologised for being late when she finally joined them.

'Greek time, my dear,' Tony Hambis was being very gracious. He introduced Diana to his father, and poured her a glass of retsina.

The old man enjoyed a pretty woman; he had a far more sincere charm than his son and he and Diana were soon getting on very well. She laughed at his stories, occasionally brushing his hand with her fingers.

The restaurant was full and jolly, the food and wine excellent. There was a happy atmosphere of bouzouki music and Greek dancing. The old man encouraged Diana to throw some plates on the floor to show her approval of the dancers.

'I'd rather dance,' she said challengingly, glancing at Tony Hambis. The younger man virtually sneered. 'You can dance this? Like a tourist perhaps?'

But he was wrong. Diana was very good indeed. It was Tony Hambis who was the flash merchant, much to his father's delight.

The old man clapped delightedly as they came back to the table. 'She dances well . . . for an English.'

Diana told him she had learned some years before, when she visited Crete several summers running. A small place called Matala.

'Ah, Matala. I know it well. Before the tourists it was something . . .'

'And Ipos,' Diana remembered, '. . . beautiful.'

They both reminisced about Paphos. The old man told her how he used to take his boat there many times. Now it was all hotels, restaurants . . . for the tourists. He sighed sadly.

Tony Hambis yawned. He was bored. He'd heard all this from his father far too many times.

Diana reached into her bag, and brought out a photograph. It was of the boat, the *Aphrodite*. Jonathan Browning had given it to her that afternoon. She pushed it across the table.

The old man clasped it, a look of delight on his face. 'My boat . . . the *Aphrodite*. Where did you get this? Here, your husband and I . . .'

Tony Hambis cut across his father, suspicion in his voice. 'Where did you get that?'

Diana turned to him and said sweetly, 'A friend gave it to me. You know him perhaps? Browning. Jonathan Browning.'

Hambis said nothing. He glared at Diana. She seemed to take no notice, she put her hand over the old man's hand still holding the photograph. 'You must keep it . . . please. A gift.' Diana kept her attention on the father, ignoring Tony's baleful glances. Finally she got the old man on to the dance floor.

He started to talk as they moved slowly and gracefully to the music. 'I liked your husband, Diana. He was a fine man.' He glanced over at his son. 'Tony tells me I must not speak out to you . . . he threatens you?'

Diana smiled at him encouragingly. He shook his head

sadly. 'I shamed my ship, you know. She was my first ship … my only ship. I shamed her.'

He led Diana into the small bar-area of the restaurant. There he told her of his days fighting against the Nazis in Macedonia. After the Nazis, the Civil War. Greek killing Greek. His wife was killed by a Greek bullet. When he came out of the mountains he vowed he'd never touch a gun ever again.

He told her of how he made a living trading in the Mediterranean. His eyes misted slightly. 'Ah, making land-fall along the red coasts of Crete in the early morning, lying in the harbour in Limassol with the peeling white and pink buildings under the evening light across the bay … but this was not enough for my son.'

Diana tried to ask him how he had met Sydney, what they did together. She knew Tony Hambis wouldn't leave them alone for much longer. She was right.

'Tired, old man?' The voice had an unpleasant edge to it. 'There's wine on the table. Drink it up, Papa. Drink it up. I'm sorry if he bored you, Diana.'

Diana protested that he hadn't at all. Tony Hambis led them both back to the table.

'Drink now, Papa,' he ordered. 'There's a car coming for you in a few minutes.'

Soon afterwards a waiter came to tell them the car had indeed arrived. The old man rose, took Diana's hand and kissed it. He patted her on the shoulder and looked at his son.

'Tonis, my son, remember what I told you.'

Diana watched him leave, slightly shaky, then turned to the younger man. 'I thought Greeks revered their parents.'

Tony Hambis snorted. 'Not this Greek.' There was bitterness in his voice as he told her what it was like living on a dirty, stinking ship – travelling the seas, scavenging a living. 'He talks … as if he missed it all. But he enjoys what we do now: the money, the good food. We eat the best, dress the best. We have the best.' He angrily tossed back his brandy, then he described the time that Sydney

Clark and Donald Sanders had come to them. They needed a boat. They said how they could make a lot of money. At first it was moving people, the displaced people from the war. Humanitarian that seemed. Fine. Then other people: into Lebanon, Syria, Iraq. Maybe they were soldiers, mercenaries. Who knows? Who cares? Tony didn't care. His father, he did – said he wanted nothing to do with war, with fighting. So he feels guilty, but at least he can feel guilty in comfort.

'Me, I believe, if you want something you fight for it. I wanted money. Sydney wanted money ... so we were mutually helpful. It went on to boxes. "Machine parts," Sydney said.' Hambis laughed.

'Guns?' Diana suggested.

Hambis laughed again. 'Who knows. I never opened the boxes. I took them from A to B, and got paid.'

'Why do you tell me this?' Diana asked; she couldn't resist the question.

Hambis tapped her hand several times. 'My dear, because no one will believe you. You cannot use it even if you wanted. There is no proof ... and you wouldn't use it, would you? Out of fear for his reputation.' He signalled for more brandy; he was relaxed, a confident man. He felt generous. 'I'm sorry about Charles, very sorry.' His speech was slightly slurred.

'My husband's son, not mine,' Diana murmured.

Tony Hambis waved an expansive hand. This chapter in the life of Sir Sydney Clark would never be written. No one wanted it to be written. So everyone was happy.

Diana took a sip of her own brandy. 'Well, it was all a long time ago.'

'No, not at all,' Hambis gloated.

'What do you mean?'

'Why do you think I'm here now? Talking to Sanders.'

'I don't know. Why don't you tell me, Tony?'

And he did ... in great detail.

As he heard the tape played back, his face was a stony

mask. Jonathan Browning held a smile of pure delight. They sat in Sanders's office as they listened to the last bits of the conversation – Diana asking Hambis what would happen if she told his government what she had been told that night.

Hambis had sounded quite gleeful. 'Without proof you would be wasting your time.'

For a moment, after Diana switched off, the only sound was the dying whisper of the tape.

Browning was the first. 'Rather embarrassing, Hambis, old boy.'

Hambis's face twisted into a terrible snarl as he looked at Diana. 'You bitch.'

Diana gave him one of her sweetest smiles. 'And the bitch will use it.'

'What about your husband's good name?' Hambis asked, half sneering, half hopeful.

'Oh, I didn't record all of it.'

Browning puffed gleefully at his large cigar, lit specially for the occasion. 'I think you've said enough, Hambis. We've copies lodged in solicitors' offices all over. So one of us gets damaged and you'd have no place to run to from the people you've doublecrossed. They'd take you apart piece by piece.' He opened the door. 'On your bike, laddie.'

Hambis hurried out. Sanders looked admiringly at Diana and Browning.

'I don't know what to say,' he murmured.

'That, Sanders, makes a change.' Browning took another puff of his cigar. 'I'd fumigate this office if I were you. Coming, Diana?' He gave Sanders a cheery wave as they left.

15

It had been one of those perfect country weekends. Diana was whistling to herself as she opened the house door. She felt marvellous, relaxed, refreshed. Ellen greeted her and took her weekend case. Liz Walters had rung to say she was coming round straight away in order to catch Diana as soon as she came in ... Miss Walters had sounded worried, Ellen reported.

The doorbell rang.

'That must be her now,' Diana said. 'Did she say what she wanted?'

'No, she didn't,' said Ellen as she went to answer the door.

Diana walked over to the table to look through her post. She spoke over her shoulder. 'Liz, some coffee?' Surprised to hear no answer she glanced towards the door. Liz was standing there motionless.

'You're not going to believe this, Diana. Donald's disappeared ...'

'Good Lord! What's happened?'

Liz gave an embarrassed laugh. 'Evaporated ... without trace.'

Diana was bewildered. 'How do you mean?'

There was an impatient edge to Liz's voice. 'Scarpered. Done a bunk. Pushed off ... It sounds crazy, I know. Tamsett phoned last night from Belfast ...'

'Just a minute, how do you know Donald's disappeared? Who's Tamsett?'

Liz came into the room and sat down on the arm of one of the chairs.

'I'm sorry. You don't know Tamsett, do you? He's chairman of the trust company they're investigating. Donald was supposed to be on the eight-thirty plane, but he didn't turn up.'

'Perhaps he just missed the plane.'

Liz opened her handbag to find a cigarette. 'Maybe ... but where is he now?'

'You're really worried, aren't you?'

'He didn't come into the office at all last week.'

Diana pointed out that that wasn't unusual – he was always shooting off here and there.

Liz took several nervous puffs of her cigarette. 'Well, he missed two board meetings, and a planning conference with Myles Thompson. His appointment book was stuffed full.'

'Did you contact him at all?'

Liz said she had, several times. He had just kept making excuses. Last night was the final straw – he was supposed to draw up a public statement with Tamsett, for the whole board to present to the Press that very morning. 'I can't tell you the chaos they're in as a result.'

'Have you tried to phone him this morning?'

Liz nodded. 'The Post Office say his phone's been off the hook since eleven o'clock yesterday.'

Sanders had in fact been there when Liz tried to ring through. He had been sitting in his flat sipping at a glass of whisky, staring into space, seemingly paying no attention to the Mozart record on the turntable.

The loud buzz sent down the receiver by the operator finally reached him. He looked at the telephone for a long while, then slowly rose to his feet and walked over to the desk in the corner. He ignored the buzz and sat down heavily in the desk chair.

He pulled open one drawer. Inside there was a jumble of army souvenirs: photographs, some training manuals, a Guards cap-badge. There was also an officer's web belt, a holster attached ... a revolver inside.

Sanders took it out. opened the breech – it was fully loaded. He walked over to his closet and pulled out a jacket, then a little hold-all. He opened this and dropped the revolver inside. He checked that he had his car keys ... and then left the flat.

The Mozart record was still playing, the phone buzzing.

Two boys playing outside looked up startled as Sanders pulled his car away with a shriek of the tyres.

Diana asked Liz what she had told Tamsett.

'I made something up – told him Donald had been ill. It sounded very lame.'

'Perhaps he *is* ill,' Diana suggested.

There was a note of desperation in Liz's voice. 'Then where is he?'

Diana wondered about contacting the hospitals, the police even. But they both felt uncertain about that course of action. Was there anybody else?

'There's Karen,' Liz said tentatively.

'I thought the reconciliation had failed.'

'Well yes, but they still see each other regularly, because of the boy ... You know she hates my guts, Diana.'

'So you want me to see her?'

'Would you? I really need to get back to the office ... to start making up stories. Do you think ... could you bear to call in at his flat?'

'But how would I get in?'

Liz was a bit evasive. 'You could try the porter. I've done that before. I must get straight back to the office, you see. Anyway, he was a friend of yours too, wasn't he?'

'Liz, really! Isn't that jumping to conclusions a bit quickly?'

'Of course it is. I'm sorry. It's just that ...' She jumped to her feet. 'You'll call me, at the office?'

Diana got up too. 'I'll go out with you. I might as well try and get into Donald's flat straight away.'

The porter was no problem. He knew Diana by name and

by sight. She told him the situation as far as she knew it. He quickly realised what Diana was worried about.

'Mr Sanders! He'd never do away with himself. Not him.' He offered to come up with Diana.

She thanked him, but no. 'I'll call you if I need you.'

As she opened the door she could hear the scraping sound of paper caught underneath. It was a telegram, addressed to Donald. She kept it in her hand as she entered the sitting-room. She looked around, then walked over to put the telephone-receiver back into place. She paused for a moment, half expecting it to ring immediately.

The room was quite bare – the shelves empty of books. The Sunday papers on the coffee-table looked unread. Full ashtrays and empty glasses were strewn around the room. She could hear some kind of electric noise, then realised the record-player was still on. She crossed to it and turned it off. Then she took a deep breath and quickly searched through the other rooms, there was no sign of Donald. She came back into the living-room. The only personal touch was a framed photograph on the mantelpiece. She picked it up.

The woman she recognised as Karen; the boy must be Peter. He looked about fifteen. Across the photograph was scrawled 'To Daddy with love' – it looked as if a four-year-old had written it. What a tragedy that was, she thought to herself. Diana replaced the photograph and purposely strode across the room to the telephone. She dialled a number and asked for Liz Walters – she explained there was no sign of Donald. 'Does he always live like this? Everything's all over the place ... There's a telegram ... Yes, I think you're right.'

She cradled the phone on her shoulder as she opened the envelope. 'It's from somebody called Frazer Carter. It says: GIVE DECISION URGENTEST. CONTACT IMMEDIATELY. Does that mean anything to you, Liz?'

'No, but whoever it is is pestering me also. What are you going to do now?'

'I think I'd better go down to see Karen, rather than

ring her ... By the way, how is Donald's son nowadays?'

Just then she caught sight of the empty revolver holster. Asking Liz to hang on, she crossed to the desk and picked up the holster. She quickly looked through all the drawers. There was no sign of a revolver. Had there ever been one?

She returned to the phone. 'Sorry, Liz, but I've just found something.' She told her about the holster. 'I don't know if it's important, but I think we've got to find him right away.'

It took Diana about an hour to reach the house. She saw the number right away. On a lawn outside, a boy was watering the flower-beds with a garden-hose – it was the same boy as in the photograph at Donald's flat. He watched as Diana climbed out of her car and approached him.

'Hello. You must be Peter. Do you know who I am?'

The boy grinned defensively. He didn't answer the question at first, but then, slowly and deliberately, with an equal stress on each word, said, 'I ... am ... Peter.'

He smiled proudly. He was a good-looking boy, his eyes alive, intelligent-looking. Liz had told her that he suffered from dysphasia: brain damage at birth. The boy was indeed intelligent; his handicap was verbal selection and communication.

Then Karen came out. She seemed only mildly surprised to see Diana and politely asked her in for some coffee.

While Diana waited in the living-room she tried to talk more with the boy. She picked up a wooden car sitting on the coffee-table.

'What a very nice car.'

'It ... is ... a ... red ... car.' There was that equal emphasis on the words again. But the boy's tone was firm, almost rebuking.

'He's not mad, you know, nor is it a toy.' Karen had come in with a tray of steaming coffee cups. 'Peter, take the red car and put it by the window.'

Diana felt guilty .'I'm sorry,' she said. She watched Peter take the car from her, then look around him with enormous concentration – as if he was trying to make out what a window was. He recognised it, and went to it. He looked back at his mother inquiringly.

'Good,' she said. 'Now sit here and have your coffee.' She looked defiantly at Diana. 'People often make the mistake of thinking dysphasics are insane. That couldn't be further from the truth. In fact, until you discover that, you can't get alongside them at all ... Are you mad?' she suddenly asked Peter, almost cruelly.

The boy shook his head angrily. 'I ... am ... not ... mad.'

Karen explained that the trouble was mainly verbal: sorting out the words, understanding them, pronouncing them. Then, without a pause, she asked Diana, 'To what may we attribute the honour?'

Diana was startled by the sudden change of subject. 'I beg your pardon?'

'This visit. I assume you didn't come here just to inquire after Donald's mad son.'

Diana explained she had come to ask where Donald was. Karen merely snorted; she wished she knew herself. He had been meant to come for Sunday lunch but had never turned up.

'Oh, it's happened before. His nerve fails, you see. Or snaps rather ... Bang, "Can't come today," he says.'

'He phones then?' enquired Diana. 'Did he do so yesterday?'

'He didn't, unless I've turned deaf.' Karen knew he had meant to fly to Belfast in the evening, but there was plenty of time between lunch and eight-thirty. 'What's eight-thirty?' she demanded of Peter.

'Half ... past . . .'

Diana cut across the boy. 'Have you heard he didn't go?'

Karen blazed at her. 'You must wait for him to finish. Go on,' she said to Peter, 'say it.'

Peter started again. 'Half ... past ... eight.'

'Good,' Karen grunted. 'So Donald didn't go to Belfast. Well, you know him. Always flitting everywhere ... Lord, how he flits.'

Diana felt the other woman was very close to hysteria. She wasn't sure how best to proceed. 'Do you know where he could be?' she asked gently.

'You mean he really has upped it? Well, I'll tell you one place he wouldn't be, given half the chance ... Here.' She ignored Diana's sympathetic glance and told Peter to look out the window for a green car. She was expecting someone, she explained to Diana.

'Would you like me to leave?'

'I shouldn't bother. This bloke knows Donald. He may even have some ideas ... He's really gone has he? Ha, I bet it's caused a panic.'

Diana smiled. 'So I gather.'

Karen gestured to the newspapers on the sofa beside her. 'I see somebody's waltzed off with two million from that building society of his.'

Diana knew nothing about that. 'Good Lord! Two million! How could they have ever done that?'

It was something to do with fictitious investors, Karen said, then looked up as a smiling Peter escorted someone into the room. 'I believe you know Jonathan Browning, don't you?'

Before she had a chance to say anything, Karen launched straight into explaining to him why Diana had come to see her.

Browning laughed delightedly. 'So Donald's done a bunk, has he?'

Diana looked at him apprehensively. 'I'm not sure you ought to know that.'

Browning reached over and patted Diana's hand. 'Don't worry, love. I'll take it as "off the record". OK? When did he go?' He saw Diana was still uncertain.

'Family friend, that's all,' he assured her again. He asked Peter to fetch the sherry bottle.

Diana looked sharply at Browning 'This is not for publication!'

Once again Karen turned on Diana furiously. 'You must learn to wait!' They all watched Peter think – then pick up an ashtray. Jonathan Browning's voice was very patient. 'Not the ashtray, mate. The bottle of sherry.' Peter looked around carefully, then pounced on the bottle and brought it triumphantly over to the coffee-table.

Karen signalled to Peter with her eyes. She started to explain to Diana that she could do terrible harm ...

But Diana misunderstood her. She thought she was referring to the dangers if Browning published something about Donald's disappearance.

'Oh that ...' Karen said in a bored voice.

' "Oh that" is your husband.'

Karen ignored her. She told Browning how she had just informed Diana that someone had pushed off with two million quid from that building society.

Diana was shocked. 'You're not possibly suggesting Donald's connected with that, in any way?'

Karen shook her head. She said, quite sincerely, that she didn't think he would be at all. 'He's probably hiding somewhere in shame.' Her laugh was nervous. Browning had been quietly thoughtful for a few moments.

'Diana,' he said carefully 'I'd like to suggest a deal. I'll help you find him, do the dirty work – as the family friend – provided you give me first crack at the story ... if there is a story ... when we find him.'

'Dirty work?' Diana questioned him, to give herself time to think.

'Hospitals, police, that sort of thing,' he explained. 'Have you tried them? Well, there you are then. Don't worry. I can be the soul of discretion. I've had plenty of experience.'

Diana believed she could trust him. 'Agreed,' she said.

'Good,' Browning rubbed his hands together and pushed himself to his feet. 'I'll dig into the finance dirt, you stick to the personal stuff.'

Diana took the telegram from her bag and offered it to him. 'Frazer Carter . . . mean anything?'

Browning answered promptly as he took it. 'World Development Bank. Middle East and African side.' He looked at the telegram. 'Well, well, well . . .'

Karen offered a suggestion: had Diana tried Donald's mother? When Diana said no she offered to give her the address.

'His sister Ruth lives there too. But be warned. Mother Sanders is the original Victorian battle-axe.'

Karen was, unfortunately, perfectly correct in her description. Donald's mother was certainly in her eighties. An upright figure, she stared at Diana imperiously with one eye. The other had a patch over it; it was weeping slightly, and every so often the old lady dabbed at it with the handkerchief held in her lap in one hand. The other hand clasped the knob of a cane; Diana thought it looked like some kind of wand of office.

She explained to Mrs Sanders and Donald's sister Ruth, who was sitting on the other side of the room, why she had come to see them.

Mrs Sanders was indignant. 'And you believe my son has stolen this money?'

Diana started to protest that nothing was further from her mind.

The old woman sniffed. 'If he had taken the money I could have forgiven him. But to have taken to his heels at the first sign of trouble – never.'

Diana said her theory, worry rather, was that Donald was ill.

'Yes, mother, he could be,' Ruth suggested timidly.

Mrs Sanders was inclined to doubt this. He had always been incompetent. His father always used to say, 'Give a job to Donald if you want to see it badly done.' She talked on through Ruth's protests and Diana's exclamation of surprise. Mrs Sanders meandered on about how he had gone to the best school, the best college at Cambridge;

how they had got him into the best regiment; how family connections had secured him a place in a merchant bank. '... and then he had to throw it away, to work with that man.'

Ruth was horrified. 'Mother, this is Lady Clark.'

'Your husband has a lot to answer for.'

Diana chose to ignore this and defend Donald. 'He is highly thought of in the City, Mrs Sanders.'

Mrs Sanders said she doubted that was any kind of recommendation.

'But Daddy was highly thought of in the City,' Ruth stammered.

The old lady's single eye stared at Diana unblinkingly. 'My husband, Lady Clark, shot himself when he found what he'd believed in was corrupted. Donald was ten years old at the time, but he never learnt that lesson.'

Diana was more than a little angry. 'Are you sure he hasn't, Mrs Sanders? It seems to me Donald has his fair share of integrity.'

The old woman was unconvinced. 'Is that what you call running away?'

Ruth patiently reminded her mother of how Donald had looked after the pair of them over the years, as well as his wife and that poor boy. Ever since he had been ten he had tried to be the man of the family, he had met his responsibilities, never complaining once ...

Diana looked around the room. It had a genteel shabbiness to it. But the women were well-dressed; at least they were in good clothes. There was an array of liqueur bottles on the sideboard. The shabbiness derived obviously from an unwillingness to let favourite things go, to change. Donald had certainly taken care of them well. But his childhood must have been really awful. She felt there were no clues for her here.

Jonathan Browning met Diana at Liz Walters's office later that night, well after six when the staff had all left. He had to report on the contact he had made with Frazer

257

Carter. It seemed Donald had been offered a big job by the World Development Bank – a very big job indeed. It would have meant him resigning all his directorships with the various Clark companies.

'It would have been goodbye to the cars, the houses, the boat, the flat, the friends, relations ... the loyalties, disloyalties – the enemies, lots of those I should think.'

Liz was pale. 'My God, I hope he was going to give us some warning.'

Browning was very chipper. 'Not much, not much at all.'

He explained it was a matter of going on to better things – apartments in New York, Paris and Athens, enormous salary, limousines, prestige. The power of the limitless financial resources of the WDB. The world at his doorstep, on its knees, cap in hand.

'Has he accepted the job?' Diana asked.

'I don't know – neither does Carter. Donald was supposed to phone him over the weekend.'

Diana asked Browning if he thought there was any reason for Donald not to accept.

Browning spread his arms to indicate the room, the building, all the Clark Holdings. He said all this could crumble if he did leave suddenly, without warning.

'Rubbish,' Liz said sharply.

Browning shrugged. He clearly didn't agree. 'He's been hanging on to the offer for the past five months.'

The two women looked at each other. They were both taken aback by this news, by the implications. There was a long pause while they all thought about it.

Browning broke the silence. 'Carter's very worried. He's done too much talking and got too few replies. His board is getting uppity and his enemies are sharpening their claws. He's quite desperate to find friend Donald.'

Diana told him about the possibility of the revolver.

'Well, well. What does that mean, I wonder?'

Liz looked at the other two tentatively. 'There is the

missing two million. If Donald did take it, he wouldn't risk Carter finding out.'

Browning hiked himself on to the desk. 'Correction: he wouldn't risk anybody finding out.'

The telephone rang. Liz Walters answered it and handed the receiver to Diana. 'It's his sister Ruth. She wants to talk to you.'

Diana spoke for just a few minutes, then hung up. She had been told there was a family cottage in the Lake District, with a telephone. Diana smoothed out the piece of paper on which she had scribbled the address and phone number. Liz instructed her to dial nine for an outside line.

They waited eagerly as Diana dialled the number. She looked up with a smile of triumph. Her call had been answered, then the connection immediately broken.

'He's there. I know he is,' she stated firmly.

Jonathan Browning stood up. 'Well, what are we waiting for? A drive through the night in the comfort of your Rolls won't be so bad.'

Diana drove for the first two hours, then Browning took over the wheel. They drove for some while without talking, Diana occasionally changing the cassette. There were twin speakers in the car so the music seemed to swell around them. Browning enjoyed the feel of driving the big car.

Suddenly Diana asked him about Karen: how long had he known her?

'Four or five months. I went to see her while I was researching the book.'

Diana turned the sound down. 'The boy seems to like you.'

'I like him. He doesn't waste words.' It was said kindly.

'Can't anything be done for him?'

'Well, intensive therapy helps. But it's a permanent thing . . . of course, Donald blames himself.'

259

'Of course,' Diana nodded sadly in agreement.

Browning glanced at her quickly. 'No. I mean he really does. He hit Karen once when she was carrying. That's why he can't bear to be with the boy.'

'I see ...'

'Do you know how long it's taken her to get Peter to that stage? All that "Put the red car on the blue book" ... eight years.'

They talked some more about Donald Sanders. Diana asked him if he knew that Sanders's father had committed suicide when he was ten.

'Karen told me.'

'Do you know why?'

Browning explained that the father had been a great follower of Hitler during the thirties. But when the news came out about the concentration camps he couldn't take it – so he shot himself.

'Donald never speaks of it,' Diana remarked.

'Well, no. He went to Hola himself.'

Diana was puzzled. 'Hola? What's that?'

Browning smiled enigmatically. 'You'd better ask him that yourself.'

It was nearly dawn when they reached their destination. They had followed Ruth's instructions and stopped the car on the hillside overlooking the cottage. Diana made a move to the hand-brake as if she meant to go on down.

Browning stopped her. 'Not now. Let him sleep.'

'He may not be sleeping.'

'Then a few hours won't make any difference.'

They drove back a few miles to a small hotel they had passed. Surprisingly, someone was moving about in the kitchen preparing early morning breakfasts and they were given two single rooms.

Diana found she couldn't sleep. After an hour she gave up trying and went downstairs to have some breakfast. It was delicious, and quite revived her. She glanced at her watch; if she left now she'd be at the cottage by eight. Surely that wouldn't be too early.

She left a note for Browning and headed back to the cottage they had seen a few hours before. It was a beautiful morning, and it was good to be alive. Poor Donald!

Diana peered through the cottage window, she could just see through into the small kitchen. Someone was moving around. Good. So he was up. She banged the knocker gently. It was a long time before Sanders came to the door.

'Oh ... you. What are you doing here?'

'Aren't you going to let me in?' She brushed past him as if he mightn't. The first thing she noticed was the revolver lying on a table. His appearance shocked her; he was usually always so neat and well-groomed – so smooth. But now – he clearly hadn't shaved for several days; his clothes looked as if he had slept in them. His face and eyes were nervy and strained.

'We were worried ... Liz and I.'

'She's not here with you?'

Diana shook her head, explaining she had come alone.

'How did you find me?' His manner was abrupt, suspicious.

Diana told him about Ruth.

'You went to see my mother?'

'Karen suggested it.'

He looked at her oddly. 'My God, you've been halfway round the world.'

'I told you we were worried ... Donald, what's going on?'

He walked to a chair and sat down heavily. He needed a few days' rest, that was all. Tamsett, Belfast – he seemed to only just remember, mention of them made no real impact. Diana tried to get him to talk, she felt that would be the best remedy – but it didn't work. Perhaps shock tactics?

'Donald, did you take that money?'

He made an angry gesture, as if brushing away an annoying fly. 'Of course not.'

'Then why are you hiding?'

He claimed he wasn't hiding at all, that he just needed the rest. He shrugged at Diana's mention of his diary full of appointments, of people waiting for him to make decisions. She could hardly recognise the rather arrogant man she knew, the smugness and self-satisfaction that could annoy her so much.

'Frazer Carter's been looking for you also.'

This time he was stung. 'Carter — how the hell do you know about that?'

Diana explained, and told him that Liz knew too. She wanted to know what he was going to do.

Sanders put one hand to his head. 'I wish I knew.'

Diana decided to take charge. First she made him shave — there was some soap and an old razor in the bathroom. She found some of his old clothes, clean and carefully packed away. They were from his Cambridge days, but they still fitted.

Diana complimented him on keeping his figure in spite of all those business lunches. He managed a small smile.

'Why Donald, I never realised how vain you were.' She pulled him by the arm. 'I see there's no food here, but I've just had the most delicious breakfast down the road.'

He protested that he wasn't hungry, but once the food was placed in front of him he started to eat with a good appetite. Diana excused herself for a minute. She was petrified Jonathan Browning might walk in. He was still in his room, shaving, when he was called to the house phone.

'He's here now. I've got him to eat, and he's beginning to talk.'

'I'm sure that's best,' Browning told her. 'Keep at it. I'll stay out of sight.'

After Sanders had finished eating they went down to the lake. He talked as they strolled along.

'My classics tutor at school was mad about the Stoics. For hour after hour he'd go on about Zeno and Cleanthes — life in accordance with nature. We all tried to live up to his idea of things. Pop was full of talk about hemlock

262

and the justifiable act, and about living bravely.' His laugh was bitter, his shoe scuffed at a stone and he bent down to pick it up. He threw it into the lake; it skimmed along the surface in three quick hops.

'I was never really tall,' he told Diana. 'Oh, not a dwarf, but from my earliest days it was drummed into me that height was a sign of aristocratic descent. For years I walked with my neck straining to make myself taller.' He stopped and looked at Diana. 'I wanted, you see ... I wanted to be an aristocrat, an aristocratic Stoic. Can you believe it?'

Diana took his arm. 'Your father's ... death couldn't have helped.'

'So you know about that?'

Diana nodded.

'Now he was ... immensely tall.' Again he sounded bitter.

They spent the whole day together, talking and talking still more. He improved greatly during all this. By the time they were sitting in front of an evening fire back at the cottage, sipping large drinks, Diana felt they had made tremendous progress. She stared into the flames for a moment, remembering Browning's comment about Hola.

'Donald, who – or what – was Hola?'

He smiled at her. 'You *have* been well briefed, haven't you? "No one can justify evil so eloquently as the Devil" – have you heard that?' He didn't wait for her to answer. 'Hola was one of our detention camps in Kenya.'

'What were you doing there?'

He sounded rueful. 'A glutton for punishment, you think? Or perhaps just an extended course in masochism. Good Stoics have to do these things, you know. I had myself sent out with an investigating team. Terrible things were being done there, terrible things. Men were being flogged to death, tortured, trampled to death.'

Diana was curious. 'By the British?'

She was told that it was a result of the Emergency, but

it created a great scandal. He remembered one European officer – he'd recognise him anywhere, even now. He was virtually killing a man right in front of him.

'I ordered him to stop. No regime can justify that sort of treatment.'

'Did you get it stopped?'

'Can you stop human nature with a simple word of command?'

'Donald, is that what you think it's all about?'

'I do now,' he replied.

Diana left Sanders in the cottage that night. She believed there was no longer any danger of him using the revolver. After she had told Jonathan Browning what was said, he agreed.

'Look, I think the best thing you can do is to keep talking to him. Don't worry, there's no story here for me. I'll get up at the crack of dawn tomorrow and head back to London by train.'

'Do you mind?'

'Mind? Missing the luxury of the Rolls ... and your company? Of course I mind.'

Diana and Donald Sanders had a long lunch the next day, enjoyed a good claret and then some vintage port. For a small Lake District hotel the place had an excellent cellar.

Donald mused about courage: '... real courage that is. It has nothing to do with behaviour under fire, or saving a man from drowning. It means summoning up the decision to take the next breath.'

Diana's brow wrinkled. 'Is that what the Stoics say?'

'No, it's what my father said.'

'But he opted out.'

Sanders played with his glass for a minute, then looked up at Diana.

'When he discovered that Hitler wasn't the god he wanted, he put a bullet in his brain.'

'But you haven't that sort of courage?'

Sanders shook his head, and emptied his brandy glass.

Later he returned to the same subject: Karen had courage, he said. All those years of patiently coaching Peter. But he agreed with Diana that since he was Karen's son she could hardly forsake him.

'Isn't that what you think I've done ... forsaken him?'

Diana delayed answering, then simply said, 'Yes.'

He smacked his hand on the table. 'You're absolutely bloody well right! It's what I tell myself all the time.'

He sat back wearily in his chair. He confessed to Diana that he had simply lost the courage to do his job. Not just the big things, the small everyday things as well. 'Shall I pop out and buy cigarettes now, or in ten minutes? Shall I phone Liz? Shall I write to Karen? Shall I go and see my mother?'

Diana tried to help by saying everybody felt like that sometime.

He shook his head. He had no answers anymore. No answers for Carter, for Liz, for Karen ... for anyone.

'It will come back.'

'No, no it won't. What may come will be an act, a lie.'

'Will you try? Stay away for a week or two, then come back. Talk to people, take some medical advice.'

He didn't answer for a long time.

'Diana,' he said at last, 'I'm very grateful for everything you've tried to do ... I'll see. I'm middle-aged, on my way out anyway. I've run once, I could again. I may stay here. I may move on.' He called for the bill, then suddenly clasped his hand to his jacket. 'Diana, I'm so sorry, I haven't got my credit cards, cheque-book.'

He looked so stricken Diana started to laugh. Donald hesitated – then joined in.

EPILOGUE

When I realised that I would have destroyed the marriage certificate, I understood for the first time that a book of exemplary scholarship was of minor importance to me – whatever I had professed, no matter what I had said about the duty of the biographer to the truth. I couldn't possibly be impartial about Sydney. Jane and Charles were his children; publication of the marriage certificate might harm them. It might lead to difficulties with their trust funds. There was no way I could let that happen.

But I would be destroying a vital piece of evidence, and ignoring it. I would be censoring my material.

Jonathan Browning would be doing the same of course. His book would be different, in any case. His training was as a financial journalist, so he'd probably have charts and graphs to prove his points. But he'd be censoring too – he had his opinion, so he looked for the evidence that proved that opinion. Unconsciously, therefore, he was censoring his material too.

In any case, I could see that I had used the book as a form of mental catharsis. I remembered someone saying once that the best thing to do when you were sad was to learn something. It could take a lifetime to learn astronomy, six lifetimes to learn literature.

Unconsciously, I had tried to follow that advice ... by learning about Sydney.

And learn I had – but so much was inconclusive, so little actually proved. As in Roshomon, people see the same event from completely different viewpoints. I remembered what someone had told me about an Oxford don giving a lesson on the rules of evidence. Suddenly there had been a loud interruption, a girl had run in screaming, some men had run after her. They grabbed her, her handbag, they dragged her away. From start to finish the 'happening' took fifteen seconds. The don had a list of prepared questions, some thirty. How many people were there, what colour was the girl's hair, how old was she, and so on? The students all had their answers, many were certain they had the right ones. The incident was re-staged, in slow motion, while the students corrected their answers ... few had even three-quarters of them correct.

Jonathan and I had often covered the same territory. He was a decent man – a fair one too. But he wanted a best-seller of a certain kind, and that meant he had to find scandal. He knew that was what the *Post* wanted; he believed that was what his readers would want.

Sydney was a genuinely generous man; I realised that because I had known him. He liked people and had often gone out of his way to help them. Not just charity either – there were so many examples. He had given a half-share of his best race-horse to the trainer when the horse was retired to stud, because the trainer was largely responsible for that horse being successful. I remembered one dinner party; the day before he had found out, quite by chance, that it was the birthday of the wife of one of his executives, newly promoted. He and his wife were coming to dinner for the first time. Sydney asked me to change the wines, each course was to have a wine of the year she was born in ... and that year was 1945, one of the best ever. With the main course he had served his last two bottles of 1945 Château Lafite – he had been saving them for his own birthday six months later.

Another time someone had been thrilled to find a miniature painting of his ancestral home in Sydney's study. As he left, Sydney presented him with the painting at the door, even though it broke up a set of six by the same painter which had taken him years to put together.

He liked people, he liked being able to use his money to please them – and this on the personal level, not on that of big public benefactions. They both had given him pleasure and satisfaction.

Now Jonathan Browning would claim Sydney was assuaging a guilty conscience ... and that was on a good day. On a bad day, he thought, Sydney had done his public charitable acts to buy his knighthood. But I knew this just wasn't so – Browning didn't know the man, I did. For that reason my book was necessary to set the balance straight. For one thing, Sydney didn't have a guilty conscience. He believed that the feeling of guilt was one of the most damaging, incapacitating of human emotions – that and worry about the future. The past was done, finished. A bucket of ashes, water under the bridge. Lessons could be learnt, of course, but that was all. It was no good thinking about what shouldn't have been done; it had been, and that was that. The moment couldn't be reversed. By the same token a person shouldn't worry about what may or may not happen.

Sydney was fond of quoting that there were two days in the week he kept absolutely free of worry or concern: 'One is yesterday ... the other is tomorrow.'

He lived for the present. I remember one occasion, after a good dinner somewhere, of course, and a bottle or two of fine wine, when he asked me how well I remembered *Alice Through the Looking Glass*.

'There was the character, do you recall, who said the rule is: Jam tomorrow, and jam yesterday ... but never jam today. And Alice protested that it sometimes had to be jam today. Well, I don't say sometimes – I say always.'

No, I was absolutely certain that Sydney didn't have a guilty conscience. Just as I was certain that he didn't do all that smuggling of people during the war as a profiteer. He must have taken terrible chances; he would have needed money or goods to barter with, to bribe people, to get false documents, and so on. Maybe it did lead to that starting capital he possessed at the end of the war, and why not? Sydney certainly believed in initiative rewarded.

If certain people whose lives he had saved were very rich, and they wanted to help him, why shouldn't they? No one had ever been able to show where that money came from. My own theory was that some of the people he helped to America did come from very wealthy families; certainly the girl he had married in Berlin did. Why couldn't some of them have given a brave young man some starting capital to help him get on his feet. They would have been shrewd men, they would have recognised his great ability ... it was probably very good business for them, an excellent investment. I know he helped people even when they had no money at all. Certainly Tom Vyner believed it, so did Kaplin. Then there was Tommy Meadows's own father.

Browning had evidence of Sydney breaking rules, and I was sure that he probably did so. He had done, to a degree, over setting up the trust funds. He was a bit of a cavalier, a bit of a pirate. He had a certain arrogance; if he thought petty rules made no sense he would ignore them. He believed the law to be an ass, that was true, but that didn't make him a bad person. He wasn't that.

Mary thought he had ignored the children. That was partly true too – but then it is partly true of any busy, successful man. Children are demanding; they take time. Our society is based on the premise that child-caring is the wife's job. It has to be sometimes. Sydney was strongly anti-communist, but there were some things he admired, some of the things Marx wrote, certainly. I knew he agreed with Marx that Victorian capitalist society was based on the domestic slavery of the wife. He gave the children what time he could, he took great delight in them, but he never felt they owed him anything. He loved them, but he respected their privacy, just as he expected them to respect his. He wanted them to be independent, to make their own choices, their own decisions. He wanted them to lead their own lives.

Any self-made man who gets knighted, or goes to the House of Lords, is wide open to the suspicion that they bought their honours. This was definitely going to be a tack of Browning's.

But it wasn't true of the man I knew. He enjoyed being Sir Sydney. I enjoyed being called Lady Clark. Why not? At least it's honest to admit it.

But Sydney didn't seek the approval of others; he just didn't need it ... and that's what buying an honour implies. While he adored people, he also learned from them, whether someone was a chef, a fisherman, a merchant banker, a professional sportsman. He learned from everyone. But he didn't need their applause – his own judgement was enough, his own opinion of himself and his actions was sufficient. Of course, he enjoyed any applause hugely ... but he didn't seek it.

Often he would have to make decisions that would make people unhappy, say things that would hurt them. But that would never affect him, it was just a fact of life. Sometimes people would disapprove, sometimes they would approve, sometimes it would be half and half. Many thought him flippant; they were snide about his frequent laughter ... 'Of course, he's not really English, is he?' But he wasn't flippant, or uncaring. He just found humour in any situation; he made people laugh. There's a story about a man in front of a firing-squad being offered a last cigarette. 'No thank you,' he says. 'Smoking damages your health.' ... It could have been Sydney.

People said he was frivolous at the wrong time – but that, to Sydney, was just a matter of convention. For him there was really no such thing as the right time, in the right place.

I understood the obstructions placed in my way by the people around him. Mary Clark was inevitably jealous of my position as her successor. Liz Walters resented me too; both she and Donald Sanders were very worried about what my book would say. They feared the damage it could cause their reputations, to the position of the Clark companies. It was their whole life; they were like a priest and a nun taking lifelong vows to the Church.

Sydney had believed in getting the best people around him. He usually did. But Liz and Donald were frightened people – they didn't have his courage, his lack of fear of failure. Without Sydney they were a ship without a rudder. Perhaps that was Sydney's greatest mistake: he should have better prepared for what would happen to the empire he had built up, after he had gone. Jonathan Browning claimed Donald Sanders would not take that job with the World Development Bank because of what could happen to Clark Holdings.

Liz had denied it, but I remembered the look in her eyes: she wondered too, she was no more confident than Browning maintained Sanders was. If Sydney were still alive, he would agree. He was so strong, so energetic. His leaving left too large a gap – those closest to him were too flawed to carry on in the same way.

I wondered how people would react to the books when they came out. They would see that Sydney had enjoyed himself; he was hedonistic. But then they knew that anyhow. They would see he bent, if not broke, the rules. But other people always benefited too. He was never greedy, never a miser ... even Jonathan Browning's book would have to show that. He had given millions away – but perhaps his greatest gift was the example of his own life. He had lived his life to the full, he had fulfilled himself. He had had such a wonderful joy of life.

NON-FICTION

- [ ] JAMES HUNT: AGAINST ALL ODDS — 80p
- [ ] BLACK SATURDAY — Alexander McKee — 80p
- [ ] STAR-FILE ANNUAL — Dafydd Rees — £1·50
- [ ] THE HAMLYN BOOK OF CROSSWORDS 1 — 60p
- [ ] THE HAMLYN BOOK OF CROSSWORDS 2 — 60p
- [ ] THE HAMLYN FAMILY GAMES BOOK — Gyles Brandreth — 75p
- [ ] MIXER & BLENDER COOKBOOK — Myra Street — 80p
- [ ] MARGUERITE PATTEN'S FAMILY COOKBOOK — 95p

All these books are available at your local bookshop or newsagent, or can be ordered direct from the publisher. Just tick the titles you want and fill in the form below.

NAME...

ADDRESS...

....

Write to Hamlyn Paperbacks Cash Sales, PO Box 11, Falmouth, Cornwall TR10 9EN.

Please enclose remittance to the value of the cover price plus:

UK: 22p for the first book plus 10p per copy for each additional book ordered to a maximum charge of 92p.

BFPO and EIRE: 22p for the first book plus 10p per copy for the next 6 books, thereafter 4p per book.

OVERSEAS: 30p for the first book and 10p for each additional book.

Whilst every effort is made to keep prices low it is sometimes necessary to increase cover prices and also postage and packing rates at short notice. Hamlyn Paperbacks reserve the right to show new retail prices on covers which may differ from those previously advertised in the text or elsewhere.